Catherine: A Story by William Makepeace Thackeray

The great author of Vanity Fair and The Luck Of Barry Lyndon was born in India in 1811.

At age 5 his father died and his mother sent him back to England. His education was of the best but he himself seemed unable to apply his talents to a rigorous work ethic.

However, once he harnessed his talents the works flowed in novels, articles, short stories, sketches and lectures.

Sadly, his personal life was rather more difficult. After a few years of marriage his wife began to suffer from depression and over the years became detached from reality. Thackeray himself suffered from ill health later in his life and the one pursuit that kept him moving forward was that of writing. In his life time, he was placed second only to Dickens. High praise indeed.

Index of Contents

ADVERTISEMENT

The story of "Catherine," which appeared in Fraser's Magazine in 1839-40, was written by Mr. Thackeray, under the name of Ikey Solomons, Jun., to counteract the injurious influence of some popular fictions of that day, which made heroes of highwaymen and burglars, and created a false sympathy for the vicious and criminal.

With this purpose, the author chose for the subject of his story a woman named Catherine Hayes, who was burned at Tyburn, in 1726, for the deliberate murder of her husband, under very revolting circumstances. Mr. Thackeray's aim obviously was to describe the career of this wretched woman and her associates with such fidelity to truth as to exhibit the danger and folly of investing such persons with heroic and romantic qualities.

CHAPTER I

INTRODUCING TO THE READER THE CHIEF PERSONAGES OF THIS NARRATIVE

At that famous period of history, when the seventeenth century (after a deal of quarrelling, king-killing, reforming, republicanising, restoring, re-restoring, play-writing, sermon-writing, Oliver-Cromwellising, Stuartising, and Orangising, to be sure) had sunk into its grave, giving place to the lusty eighteenth; when Mr. Isaac Newton was a tutor of Trinity, and Mr. Joseph Addison Commissioner of Appeals; when the presiding genius that watched over the destinies of the French nation had played out all the best cards in his hand, and his adversaries began to pour in their trumps; when there were two kings in Spain employed perpetually in running away from one another; when there was a queen in England, with such rogues for Ministers as have never been seen, no, not in our own day; and a General, of whom it may be severely argued, whether he was the meanest miser or the greatest hero in the world; when Mrs. Masham had not yet put Madam Marlborough's nose out of joint; when people had their ears cut off for writing very meek political pamphlets; and very large full-bottomed wigs were just beginning to be worn with powder; and the face of Louis the Great, as his was handed in to him behind the bed-curtains, was, when issuing thence, observed to look longer, older, and more dismal daily....

About the year One thousand seven hundred and five, that is, in the glorious reign of Queen Anne, there existed certain characters, and befell a series of adventures, which, since they are strictly in accordance with the present fashionable style and taste; since they have been already partly described in the "Newgate Calendar;" since they are (as shall be seen anon) agreeably low, delightfully disgusting, and at the same time eminently pleasing and pathetic, may properly be set down here.

And though it may be said, with some considerable show of reason, that agreeably low and delightfully disgusting characters have already been treated, both copiously and ably, by some eminent writers of the present (and, indeed, of future) ages; though to tread in the footsteps of the immortal FAGIN requires a genius of inordinate stride, and to go a-robbing after the late though deathless TURPIN, the renowned JACK SHEPPARD, or the embryo DUVAL, may be impossible, and not an infringement, but a wasteful indication of ill-will towards the eighth commandment; though it may, on the one hand, be asserted that only vain coxcombs would dare to write on subjects already described by men really and deservedly eminent; on the other hand, that these subjects have been described so fully, that nothing more can be said about them; on the third hand (allowing, for the sake of argument, three hands to one figure of speech), that the public has heard so much of them, as to be quite tired of rogues, thieves, cutthroats, and Newgate altogether;—though all these objections may be urged, and each is excellent, yet we intend to take a few more pages from the "Old Bailey Calendar," to bless the public with one more draught from the Stone Jug:[*]—yet awhile to listen, hurdle-mounted, and riding down the Oxford

Road, to the bland conversation of Jack Ketch, and to hang with him round the neck of his patient, at the end of our and his history. We give the reader fair notice, that we shall tickle him with a few such scenes of villainy, throat-cutting, and bodily suffering in general, as are not to be found, no, not in—; never mind comparisons, for such are odious.

* This, as your Ladyship is aware, is the polite name for Her Majesty's Prison of Newgate.

In the year 1705, then, whether it was that the Queen of England did feel seriously alarmed at the notion that a French prince should occupy the Spanish throne; or whether she was tenderly attached to the Emperor of Germany; or whether she was obliged to fight out the quarrel of William of Orange, who made us pay and fight for his Dutch provinces; or whether poor old Louis Quatorze did really frighten her; or whether Sarah Jennings and her husband wanted to make a fight, knowing how much they should gain by it;—whatever the reason was, it was evident that the war was to continue, and there was almost as much soldiering and recruiting, parading, pike and gun-exercising, flag-flying, drum-beating, powder-blazing, and military enthusiasm, as we can all remember in the year 1801, what time the Corsican upstart menaced our shores. A recruiting-party and captain of Cutts's regiment (which had been so mangled at Blenheim the year before) were now in Warwickshire; and having their depot at Warwick, the captain and his attendant, the corporal, were used to travel through the country, seeking for heroes to fill up the gaps in Cutts's corps,—and for adventures to pass away the weary time of a country life.

Our Captain Plume and Sergeant Kite (it was at this time, by the way, that those famous recruiting-officers were playing their pranks in Shrewsbury) were occupied very much in the same manner with Farquhar's heroes. They roamed from Warwick to Stratford, and from Stratford to Birmingham, persuading the swains of Warwickshire to leave the plough for the Pike, and despatching, from time to time, small detachments of recruits to extend Marlborough's lines, and to act as food for the hungry cannon at Ramillies and Malplaquet.

Of those two gentlemen who are about to act a very important part in our history, one only was probably a native of Britain,—we say probably, because the individual in question was himself quite uncertain, and, it must be added, entirely indifferent about his birthplace; but speaking the English language, and having been during the course of his life pretty generally engaged in the British service, he had a tolerably fair claim to the majestic title of Briton. His name was Peter Brock, otherwise Corporal Brock, of Lord Cutts's regiment of dragoons; he was of age about fifty-seven (even that point has never been ascertained); in height about five feet six inches; in weight, nearly thirteen stone; with a chest that the celebrated Leitch himself might envy; an arm that was like an opera-dancer's leg; a stomach so elastic that it would accommodate itself to any given or stolen quantity of food; a great aptitude for strong liquors; a considerable skill in singing chansons de table of not the most delicate kind; he was a lover of jokes, of which he made many, and passably bad; when pleased, simply coarse, boisterous, and jovial; when angry, a perfect demon: bullying, cursing, storming, fighting, as is sometimes the wont with gentlemen of his cloth and education.

Mr. Brock was strictly, what the Marquis of Rodil styled himself in a proclamation to his soldiers after running away, a hijo de la guerra—a child of war. Not seven cities, but one or two regiments, might contend for the honour of giving him birth; for his mother, whose name he took, had acted as camp-follower to a Royalist regiment; had then obeyed the Parliamentarians; died in Scotland when Monk was commanding in that country; and the first appearance of Mr. Brock in a public capacity displayed him as a fifer in the General's own regiment of Coldstreamers, when they marched from Scotland to London, and from a republic at once into a monarchy. Since that period, Brock had been always with the army, he had had, too, some promotion, for he spake of having a command at the battle of the Boyne; though probably (as he never mentioned the fact) upon the losing side. The very year before this narrative commences, he had been one of Mordaunt's forlorn hope at Schellenberg, for which service he was promised a pair of colours; he lost them, however, and was almost shot (but fate did not ordain that his career should close in that way) for drunkenness and insubordination immediately after the battle; but having in some measure reinstated himself by a display of much gallantry at Blenheim, it was found advisable to send him to England for the purposes of recruiting, and remove him altogether from the regiment where his gallantry only rendered the example of his riot more dangerous.

Mr. Brock's commander was a slim young gentleman of twenty-six, about whom there was likewise a history, if one would take the trouble to inquire. He was a Bavarian by birth (his mother being an English lady), and enjoyed along with a dozen other brothers the title of count: eleven of these, of course, were penniless; one or two were priests, one a monk, six or seven in various military services, and the elder at home at Schloss Galgenstein breeding horses, hunting wild boars, swindling tenants, living in a great house with small means; obliged to be sordid at home all the year, to be splendid for a month at the capital, as is the way with many other noblemen. Our young count, Count Gustavus Adolphus Maximilian von Galgenstein, had been in the service of the French as page to a nobleman; then of His Majesty's gardes du corps; then a lieutenant and captain in the Bavarian service; and when, after the battle of Blenheim, two regiments of Germans came over to the winning side, Gustavus Adolphus Maximilian found himself among them; and at the epoch when this story commences, had enjoyed English pay for a year or more. It is unnecessary to say how he exchanged into his present regiment; how it appeared that, before her marriage, handsome John Churchill had known the young gentleman's mother, when they were both penniless hangers-on at Charles the Second's court;—it is, we say, quite useless to repeat all the scandal of which we are perfectly masters, and to trace step by step the events of his history. Here, however, was Gustavus Adolphus, in a small inn, in a small village of Warwickshire, on an autumn evening in the year 1705; and at the very moment when this history begins, he and Mr. Brock, his corporal and friend, were seated at a round table before the kitchen-fire while a small groom of the establishment was leading up and down on the village green, before the inn door, two black, glossy, long-tailed, barrel-bellied, thick-flanked, arch-necked, Roman-nosed Flanders horses, which were the property of the two gentlemen now taking their ease at the "Bugle Inn." The two gentlemen were seated at their ease at the inn table, drinking mountain-wine; and if the reader fancies from the sketch which we have given of their lives, or from his own blindness and belief in the perfectibility of human nature, that the sun of that autumn evening shone upon any two men in county or city, at desk or harvest, at Court or at Newgate, drunk or sober, who were greater rascals than Count Gustavus Galgenstein and Corporal Peter Brock, he is egregiously mistaken, and his knowledge of human nature is not worth a fig. If they had not been two prominent scoundrels, what earthly business should we have in detailing their histories? What would the public care for them? Who would meddle with dull virtue, humdrum sentiment, or stupid innocence, when vice, agreeable vice, is the only thing which the readers of romances care to hear?

The little horse-boy, who was leading the two black Flanders horses up and down the green, might have put them in the stable for any good that the horses got by the gentle exercise which they were now taking in the cool evening air, as their owners had not ridden very far or very hard, and there was not a hair turned of their sleek shining coats; but the lad had been especially ordered so to walk the horses about until he received further commands from the gentlemen reposing in the "Bugle" kitchen; and the idlers of the village seemed so pleased with the beasts, and their smart saddles and shining bridles, that it would have been a pity to deprive them of the pleasure of contemplating such an innocent spectacle.

Over the Count's horse was thrown a fine red cloth, richly embroidered in yellow worsted, a very large count's coronet and a cipher at the four corners of the covering; and under this might be seen a pair of gorgeous silver stirrups, and above it, a couple of silver-mounted pistols reposing in bearskin holsters; the bit was silver too, and the horse's head was decorated with many smart ribbons. Of the Corporal's steed, suffice it to say, that the ornaments were in brass, as bright, though not perhaps so valuable, as those which decorated the Captain's animal. The boys, who had been at play on the green, first paused and entered into conversation with the horse-boy; then the village matrons followed; and afterwards, sauntering by ones and twos, came the village maidens, who love soldiers as flies love treacle; presently the males began to arrive, and lo! the parson of the parish, taking his evening walk with Mrs. Dobbs, and the four children his offspring, at length joined himself to his flock.

To this audience the little ostler explained that the animals belonged to two gentlemen now reposing at the "Bugle:" one young with gold hair, the other old with grizzled locks; both in red coats; both in jack-boots; putting the house into a bustle, and calling for the best. He then discoursed to some of his own companions regarding the merits of the horses; and the parson, a learned man, explained to the villagers, that one of the travellers must be a count, or at least had a count's horsecloth; pronounced that the stirrups were of real silver, and checked the impetuosity of his son, William Nassau Dobbs, who was for mounting the animals, and who expressed a longing to fire off one of the pistols in the holsters.

As this family discussion was taking place, the gentlemen whose appearance had created so much attention came to the door of the inn, and the elder and stouter was seen to smile at his companion; after which he strolled leisurely over the green, and seemed to examine with much benevolent satisfaction the assemblage of villagers who were staring at him and the quadrupeds.

Mr. Brock, when he saw the parson's band and cassock, took off his beaver reverently, and saluted the divine: "I hope your reverence won't baulk the little fellow," said he; "I think I heard him calling out for a ride, and whether he should like my horse, or his Lordship's horse, I am sure it is all one. Don't be afraid, sir! the horses are not tired; we have only come seventy mile to-day, and Prince Eugene once rode a matter of fifty-two leagues (a hundred and fifty miles), sir, upon that horse, between sunrise and sunset."

"Gracious powers! on which horse?" said Doctor Dobbs, very solemnly.

"On THIS, sir,—on mine, Corporal Brock of Cutts's black gelding, 'William of Nassau.' The Prince, sir, gave it me after Blenheim fight, for I had my own legs carried away by a cannon-ball, just as I cut down two of Sauerkrauter's regiment, who had made the Prince prisoner."

"Your own legs, sir!" said the Doctor. "Gracious goodness! this is more and more astonishing!"

"No, no, not my own legs, my horse's I mean, sir; and the Prince gave me 'William of Nassau' that very day."

To this no direct reply was made; but the Doctor looked at Mrs. Dobbs, and Mrs. Dobbs and the rest of the children at her eldest son, who grinned and said, "Isn't it wonderful?" The Corporal to this answered nothing, but, resuming his account, pointed to the other horse and said, "THAT horse, sir—good as mine is—that horse, with the silver stirrups, is his Excellency's horse, Captain Count Maximilian Gustavus Adolphus von Galgenstein, captain of horse and of the Holy Roman Empire" (he lifted here his hat with much gravity, and all the crowd, even to the parson, did likewise). "We call him 'George of Denmark,' sir, in compliment to Her Majesty's husband: he is Blenheim too, sir; Marshal Tallard rode him on that day, and you know how HE was taken prisoner by the Count."

"George of Denmark, Marshal Tallard, William of Nassau! this is strange indeed, most wonderful! Why, sir, little are you aware that there are before you, AT THIS MOMENT, two other living beings who bear these venerated names! My boys, stand forward! Look here, sir: these children have been respectively named after our late sovereign and the husband of our present Queen."

"And very good names too, sir; ay, and very noble little fellows too; and I propose that, with your reverence and your ladyship's leave, William Nassau here shall ride on George of Denmark, and George of Denmark shall ride on William of Nassau."

When this speech of the Corporal's was made, the whole crowd set up a loyal hurrah; and, with much gravity, the two little boys were lifted up into the saddles; and the Corporal leading one, entrusted the other to the horse-boy, and so together marched stately up and down the green.

The popularity which Mr. Brock gained by this manoeuvre was very great; but with regard to the names of the horses and children, which coincided so extraordinarily, it is but fair to state, that the christening of the quadrupeds had only taken place about two minutes before the dragoon's appearance on the green. For if the fact must be confessed, he, while seated near the inn window, had kept a pretty wistful eye upon all going on without; and the horses marching thus to and fro for the wonderment of the village, were only placards or advertisements for the riders.

There was, besides the boy now occupied with the horses, and the landlord and landlady of the "Bugle Inn," another person connected with that establishment—a very smart, handsome, vain, giggling servant-girl, about the age of sixteen, who went by the familiar name of Cat, and attended upon the gentlemen in the parlour, while the landlady was employed in cooking their supper in the kitchen. This young person had been educated in the village poor-house, and having been pronounced by Doctor Dobbs and the schoolmaster the idlest, dirtiest, and most passionate little minx with whom either had ever had to do, she was, after receiving a very small portion of literary instruction (indeed it must be stated that the young lady did not know her letters), bound apprentice at the age of nine years to Mrs. Score, her relative, and landlady of the "Bugle Inn."

If Miss Cat, or Catherine Hall, was a slattern and a minx, Mrs. Score was a far superior shrew; and for the seven years of her apprenticeship the girl was completely at her mistress's mercy. Yet though wondrously stingy, jealous, and violent, while her maid was idle and extravagant, and her husband seemed to abet the girl, Mrs. Score put up with the wench's airs, idleness, and caprices, without ever wishing to dismiss her from the "Bugle." The fact is, that Miss Catherine was a great beauty, and for about two years, since her fame had begun to spread, the custom of the inn had also increased vastly. When there was a debate whether the farmers, on their way from market, would take t'other pot, Catherine, by appearing with it, would straightway cause the liquor to be swallowed and paid for; and when the traveller who proposed riding that night and sleeping at Coventry or Birmingham, was asked by Miss Catherine whether he would like a fire in his bedroom, he generally was induced to occupy it, although he might before have vowed to Mrs. Score that he would not for a thousand guineas be absent from home that night. The girl had, too, half-a-dozen lovers in the village; and these were bound in honour to spend their pence at the alehouse she inhabited. O woman, lovely woman! what strong resolves canst thou twist round thy little finger! what gunpowder passions canst thou kindle with a single sparkle of thine eye! what lies and fribble nonsense canst thou make us listen to, as they were gospel truth or splendid wit! above all what bad liquor canst thou make us swallow when thou puttest a kiss within the cup—and we are content to call the poison wine!

The mountain-wine at the "Bugle" was, in fact, execrable; but Mrs. Cat, who served it to the two soldiers, made it so agreeable to them, that they found it a passable, even a pleasant task, to swallow the contents of a second bottle. The miracle had been wrought instantaneously on her appearance: for whereas at that very moment the Count was employed in cursing the wine, the landlady, the wine-grower, and the English nation generally, when the young woman entered and (choosing so to interpret the oaths) said, "Coming, your honour; I think your honour called"—Gustavus Adolphus whistled, stared at her very hard, and seeming quite dumb-stricken by her appearance, contented himself by swallowing a whole glass of mountain by way of reply.

Mr. Brock was, however, by no means so confounded as his captain: he was thirty years older than the latter, and in the course of fifty years of military life had learned to look on the most dangerous enemy, or the most beautiful woman, with the like daring, devil-may-care determination to conquer.

"My dear Mary," then said that gentleman, "his honour is a lord; as good as a lord, that is; for all he allows such humble fellows as I am to drink with him."

Catherine dropped a low curtsey, and said, "Well, I don't know if you are joking a poor country girl, as all you soldier gentlemen do; but his honour LOOKS like a lord: though I never see one, to be sure."

"Then," said the Captain, gathering courage, "how do you know I look like one, pretty Mary?"

"Pretty Catherine: I mean Catherine, if you please, sir."

Here Mr. Brock burst into a roar of laughter, and shouting with many oaths that she was right at first, invited her to give him what he called a buss.

Pretty Catherine turned away from him at this request, and muttered something about "Keep your distance, low fellow! buss indeed; poor country girl," etc. etc., placing herself, as if for protection, on the side of the Captain. That gentleman looked also very angry; but whether at the sight of innocence so outraged, or the insolence of the Corporal for daring to help himself first, we cannot say. "Hark ye, Mr. Brock," he cried very fiercely, "I will suffer no such liberties in my presence: remember, it is only my condescension which permits you to share my bottle in this way; take care I don't give you instead a taste of my cane." So saying, he, in a protecting manner, placed one hand round Mrs. Catherine's waist, holding the other clenched very near to the Corporal's nose.

Mrs. Catherine, for HER share of this action of the Count's, dropped another curtsey and said, "Thank you, my Lord." But Galgenstein's threat did not appear to make any impression on Mr. Brock, as indeed there was no reason that it should; for the Corporal, at a combat of fisticuffs, could have pounded his commander into a jelly in ten minutes; so he contented himself by saying, "Well, noble Captain, there's no harm done; it IS an honour for poor old Peter Brock to be at table with you, and I AM sorry, sure enough."

"In truth, Peter, I believe thou art; thou hast good reason, eh, Peter? But never fear, man; had I struck thee, I never would have hurt thee."

"I KNOW you would not," replied Brock, laying his hand on his heart with much gravity; and so peace was made, and healths were drunk. Miss Catherine condescended to put her lips to the Captain's glass; who swore that the wine was thus converted into nectar; and although the girl had not previously heard of that liquor, she received the compliment as a compliment, and smiled and simpered in return.

The poor thing had never before seen anybody so handsome, or so finely dressed as the Count; and, in the simplicity of her coquetry, allowed her satisfaction to be quite visible. Nothing could be more clumsy than the gentleman's mode of complimenting her; but for this, perhaps, his speeches were more effective than others more delicate would have been; and though she said to each, "Oh, now, my Lord," and "La, Captain, how can you flatter one so?" and "Your honour's laughing at me," and made such polite speeches as are used on these occasions, it was manifest from the flutter and blush, and the grin of satisfaction which lighted up the buxom features of the little country beauty, that the Count's first operations had been highly successful. When following up his attack, he produced from his neck a small locket (which had been given him by a Dutch lady at the Brill), and begged Miss Catherine to wear it for his sake, and chucked her under the chin and called her his little rosebud, it was pretty clear how things would go: anybody who could see the expression of Mr. Brock's countenance at this event might judge of the progress of the irresistible High-Dutch conqueror.

Being of a very vain communicative turn, our fair barmaid gave her two companions, not only a pretty long account of herself, but of many other persons in the village, whom she could perceive from the window opposite to which she stood. "Yes, your honour," said she—"my Lord, I mean; sixteen last March, though there's a many girl in the village that at my age is quite chits. There's Polly Randall now, that red-haired girl along with Thomas Curtis: she's seventeen if she's a day, though he is the very first sweetheart she has had. Well, as I am saying, I was bred up here in the village—father and mother died very young, and I was left a poor orphan—well, bless us! if Thomas haven't kissed her!—to the care of Mrs. Score, my aunt, who has been a mother to me—a stepmother, you know;—and I've been to Stratford fair, and to Warwick many a time; and there's two people who have offered to marry me, and ever so many who want to, and I won't have none—only a gentleman, as I've always said; not a poor clodpole, like Tom there with the red waistcoat (he was one that asked me), nor a drunken fellow like Sam Blacksmith yonder, him whose wife has got the black eye, but a real gentleman, like—"

"Like whom, my dear?" said the Captain, encouraged.

"La, sir, how can you? Why, like our squire, Sir John, who rides in such a mortal fine gold coach; or, at least, like the parson, Doctor Dobbs—that's he, in the black gown, walking with Madam Dobbs in red."

"And are those his children?"

"Yes: two girls and two boys; and only think, he calls one William Nassau, and one George Denmark—isn't it odd?" And from the parson, Mrs. Catherine went on to speak of several humble personages of the village community, who, as they are not necessary to our story, need not be described at full length. It was when, from the window, Corporal Brock saw the altercation between the worthy divine and his son, respecting the latter's ride, that he judged it a fitting time to step out on the green, and to bestow on the two horses those famous historical names which we have just heard applied to them.

Mr. Brock's diplomacy was, as we have stated, quite successful; for, when the parson's boys had ridden and retired along with their mamma and papa, other young gentlemen of humbler rank in the village were placed upon "George of Denmark" and "William of Nassau;" the Corporal joking and laughing with all the grown-up people. The women, in spite of Mr. Brock's age, his red nose, and a certain squint of his eye, vowed the Corporal was a jewel of a man; and among the men his popularity was equally great.

"How much dost thee get, Thomas Clodpole?" said Mr. Brock to a countryman (he was the man whom Mrs. Catherine had described as her suitor), who had laughed loudest at some of his jokes: "how much dost thee get for a week's work, now?"

Mr. Clodpole, whose name was really Bullock, stated that his wages amounted to "three shillings and a puddn."

"Three shillings and a puddn!—monstrous!—and for this you toil like a galley-slave, as I have seen them in Turkey and America,—ay, gentlemen, and in the country of Prester John! You shiver out of bed on icy winter mornings, to break the ice for Ball and Dapple to drink."

"Yes, indeed," said the person addressed, who seemed astounded at the extent of the Corporal's information.

"Or you clean pigsty, and take dung down to meadow; or you act watchdog and tend sheep; or you sweep a scythe over a great field of grass; and when the sun has scorched the eyes out of your head, and sweated the flesh off your bones, and well-nigh fried the soul out of your body, you go home, to what?—three shillings a week and a puddn! Do you get pudding every day?"

"No; only Sundays."

"Do you get money enough?"

"No, sure."

"Do you get beer enough?"

"Oh no, NEVER!" said Mr. Bullock quite resolutely.

"Worthy Clodpole, give us thy hand: it shall have beer enough this day, or my name's not Corporal Brock. Here's the money, boy! there are twenty pieces in this purse: and how do you think I got 'em? and how do you think I shall get others when these are gone?—by serving Her Sacred Majesty, to be sure: long life to her, and down with the French King!"

Bullock, a few of the men, and two or three of the boys, piped out an hurrah, in compliment to this speech of the Corporal's: but it was remarked that the greater part of the crowd drew back—the women whispering ominously to them and looking at the Corporal.

"I see, ladies, what it is," said he. "You are frightened, and think I am a crimp come to steal your sweethearts away. What! call Peter Brock a double-dealer? I tell you what, boys, Jack Churchill himself has shaken this hand, and drunk a pot with me: do you think he'd shake hands with a rogue? Here's Tummas Clodpole has never had beer enough, and here am I will stand treat to him and any other gentleman: am I good enough company for him? I have money, look you, and like to spend it: what should I be doing dirty actions for—hay, Tummas?"

A satisfactory reply to this query was not, of course, expected by the Corporal nor uttered by Mr. Bullock; and the end of the dispute was, that he and three or four of the rustic bystanders were quite convinced of the good intentions of their new friend, and accompanied him back to the "Bugle," to regale upon the promised beer. Among the Corporal's guests was one young fellow whose dress would show that he was somewhat better to do in the world than Clodpole and the rest of the sunburnt ragged troop, who were marching towards the alehouse. This man was the only one of his hearers who, perhaps, was sceptical as to the truth of his stories; but as soon as Bullock accepted the invitation to drink, John Hayes, the carpenter (for such was his name and profession), said, "Well, Thomas, if thou goest, I will go too."

"I know thee wilt," said Thomas: "thou'lt goo anywhere Catty Hall is, provided thou canst goo for nothing."

"Nay, I have a penny to spend as good as the Corporal here."

"A penny to KEEP, you mean: for all your love for the lass at the 'Bugle,' did thee ever spend a shilling in the house? Thee wouldn't go now, but that I am going too, and the Captain here stands treat."

"Come, come, gentlemen, no quarrelling," said Mr. Brock. "If this pretty fellow will join us, amen say I: there's lots of liquor, and plenty of money to pay the score. Comrade Tummas, give us thy arm. Mr. Hayes, you're a hearty cock, I make no doubt, and all such are welcome. Come along, my gentleman farmers, Mr. Brock shall have the honour to pay for you all." And with this, Corporal Brock, accompanied by Messrs. Hayes, Bullock, Blacksmith, Baker's-boy, Butcher, and one or two others, adjourned to the inn; the horses being, at the same time, conducted to the stable.

Although we have, in this quiet way, and without any flourishing of trumpets, or beginning of chapters, introduced Mr. Hayes to the public; and although, at first sight, a sneaking carpenter's boy may seem hardly worthy of the notice of an intelligent reader, who looks for a good cut-throat or highwayman for a hero, or a pickpocket at the very least: this gentleman's words and actions should be carefully studied by the public, as he is destined to appear before them under very polite and curious circumstances during the course of this history. The speech of the rustic Juvenal, Mr. Clodpole, had seemed to infer that Hayes was at once careful of his money and a warm admirer of Mrs. Catherine of the "Bugle:" and both the charges were perfectly true. Hayes's father was reported to be a man of some substance; and young John, who was performing his apprenticeship in the village, did not fail to talk very big of his pretensions to fortune—of his entering, at the close of his indentures, into partnership with his father—and of the comfortable farm and house over which Mrs. John Hayes, whoever she might be, would one day preside. Thus, next to the barber and butcher, and above even his own master, Mr. Hayes took rank in the village: and it must not be concealed that his representation of wealth had made some impression upon Mrs. Hall toward whom the young gentleman had cast the eyes of affection. If he had been tolerably well-looking, and not pale, rickety, and feeble as he was; if even he had been ugly, but withal a man of spirit, it is probable the girl's kindness for him would have been much more decided. But he was a poor weak creature, not to compare with honest Thomas Bullock, by at least nine inches; and so notoriously timid, selfish, and stingy, that there was a kind of shame in receiving his addresses openly; and what encouragement Mrs. Catherine gave him could only be in secret.

But no mortal is wise at all times: and the fact was, that Hayes, who cared for himself intensely, had set his heart upon winning Catherine; and loved her with a desperate greedy eagerness and desire of possession, which makes passions for women often so fierce and unreasonable among very cold and selfish men. His parents (whose frugality he had inherited) had tried in vain to wean him from this passion, and had made many fruitless attempts to engage him with women who possessed money and desired husbands; but Hayes was, for a wonder, quite proof against their attractions; and, though quite ready to acknowledge the absurdity of his love for a penniless alehouse servant-girl, nevertheless persisted in it doggedly. "I know I'm a fool," said he; "and what's more, the girl does not care for me; but marry her I must, or I think I shall just die: and marry her I will." For very much to the credit of Miss Catherine's modesty, she had declared that marriage was with her a sine qua non, and had dismissed, with the loudest scorn and indignation, all propositions of a less proper nature.

Poor Thomas Bullock was another of her admirers, and had offered to marry her; but three shillings a week and a puddn was not to the girl's taste, and Thomas had been scornfully rejected. Hayes had also made her a direct proposal. Catherine did not say no: she was too prudent: but she was young and could wait; she did not care for Mr. Hayes yet enough to marry him—(it did not seem, indeed, in the young woman's nature to care for anybody)—and she gave her adorer flatteringly to understand that, if nobody better appeared in the course of a few years, she might be induced to become Mrs. Hayes. It was a dismal prospect for the poor fellow to live upon the hope of being one day Mrs. Catherine's pis-aller.

In the meantime she considered herself free as the wind, and permitted herself all the innocent gaieties which that "chartered libertine," a coquette, can take. She flirted with all the bachelors, widowers, and married men, in a manner which did extraordinary credit to her years: and let not the reader fancy such pastimes unnatural at her early age. The ladies—Heaven bless them!—are, as a general rule, coquettes from babyhood upwards. Little SHE'S of three years old play little airs and graces upon small heroes of five; simpering misses of nine make attacks upon young gentlemen of twelve; and at sixteen, a well-grown girl, under encouraging circumstances—say, she is pretty, in a family of ugly elder sisters, or an only child and heiress, or a humble wench at a country inn, like our fair Catherine—is at the very pink and prime of her coquetry: they will jilt you at that age with an ease and arch infantine simplicity that never can be surpassed in maturer years.

Miss Catherine, then, was a franche coquette, and Mr. John Hayes was miserable. His life was passed in a storm of mean passions and bitter jealousies, and desperate attacks upon the indifference-rock of Mrs. Catherine's heart, which not all his tempest of love could beat down. O cruel cruel pangs of love unrequited! Mean rogues feel them as well as great heroes. Lives there the man in Europe who has not felt them many times?—who has not knelt, and fawned, and supplicated, and wept, and cursed, and raved, all in vain; and passed long wakeful nights with ghosts of dead hopes for company; shadows of buried remembrances that glide out of their graves of nights, and whisper, "We are dead now, but we WERE once; and we made you happy, and we come now to mock you:—despair, O lover, despair, and die"?—O cruel pangs!—dismal nights!—Now a sly demon creeps under your nightcap, and drops into your ear those soft hope-breathing sweet words, uttered on the well-remembered evening: there, in the drawer of your dressing-table (along with the razors, and Macassar oil), lies the dead flower that Lady Amelia Wilhelmina wore in her bosom on the night of a certain ball—the corpse of a glorious hope that seemed once as if it would live for ever, so strong was it, so full of joy and sunshine: there, in your writing-desk, among a crowd of unpaid bills, is the dirty scrap of paper, thimble-sealed, which came in company with a pair of muffetees of her knitting (she was a butcher's daughter, and did all she could, poor thing!), begging "you would ware them at collidge, and think of her who"—married a public-house three weeks afterwards, and cares for you no more now than she does for the pot-boy. But why multiply instances, or seek to depict the agony of poor mean-spirited John Hayes? No mistake can be greater than that of fancying such great emotions of love are only felt by virtuous or exalted men: depend upon it, Love, like Death, plays havoc among the pauperum tabernas, and sports with rich and poor, wicked and virtuous, alike. I have often fancied, for instance, on seeing the haggard pale young old-clothesman, who wakes the echoes of our street with his nasal cry of "Clo'!"—I have often, I said, fancied that, besides the load of exuvial coats and breeches under which he staggers, there is another weight on him—an atrior cura at his tail—and while his unshorn lips and nose together are performing that mocking, boisterous, Jack-indifferent cry of "Clo', clo'!" who knows what woeful utterances are crying from the heart within? There he is, chaffering with the footman at No. 7 about an old dressing-gown: you think his whole soul is bent only on the contest about the garment. Psha! there is, perhaps, some faithless girl in Holywell Street who fills up his heart; and that desultory Jew-boy is a peripatetic hell! Take another instance:—take the man in the beef-shop in Saint Martin's Court. There he is, to all appearances quite calm: before the same round of beef—from morning till sundown—for hundreds of years very likely. Perhaps when the shutters are closed, and all the world tired and silent, there is HE silent, but untired—cutting, cutting, cutting. You enter, you get your meat to your liking, you depart; and, quite unmoved, on, on he goes, reaping ceaselessly the Great Harvest of Beef. You would fancy that if Passion ever failed to conquer, it had in vain assailed the calm bosom of THAT MAN. I doubt it, and would give much to know his history.

Who knows what furious Aetna-flames are raging underneath the surface of that calm flesh-mountain—who can tell me that that calmness itself is not DESPAIR?

The reader, if he does not now understand why it was that Mr. Hayes agreed to drink the Corporal's proffered beer, had better just read the foregoing remarks over again, and if he does not understand THEN, why, small praise to his brains. Hayes could not bear that Mr. Bullock should have a chance of seeing, and perhaps making love to Mrs. Catherine in his absence; and though the young woman never diminished her coquetries, but, on the contrary, rather increased them in his presence, it was still a kind of dismal satisfaction to be miserable in her company.

On this occasion, the disconsolate lover could be wretched to his heart's content; for Catherine had not a word or a look for him, but bestowed all her smiles upon the handsome stranger who owned the black horse. As for poor Tummas Bullock, his passion was never violent; and he was content in the present instance to sigh and drink beer. He sighed and drank, sighed and drank, and drank again, until he had swallowed so much of the Corporal's liquor, as to be induced to accept a guinea from his purse also; and found himself, on returning to reason and sobriety, a soldier of Queen Anne's.

But oh! fancy the agonies of Mr. Hayes when, seated with the Corporal's friends at one end of the kitchen, he saw the Captain at the place of honour, and the smiles which the fair maid bestowed upon him; when, as she lightly whisked past him with the Captain's supper, she, pointing to the locket that once reposed on the breast of the Dutch lady at the Brill, looked archly on Hayes and said, "See, John, what his Lordship has given me;" and when John's face became green and purple with rage and jealousy, Mrs. Catherine laughed ten times louder, and cried "Coming, my Lord," in a voice of shrill triumph, that bored through the soul of Mr. John Hayes and left him gasping for breath.

On Catherine's other lover, Mr. Thomas, this coquetry had no effect: he, and two comrades of his, had by this time quite fallen under the spell of the Corporal; and hope, glory, strong beer, Prince Eugene, pair of colours, more strong beer, her blessed Majesty, plenty more strong beer, and such subjects, martial and bacchic, whirled through their dizzy brains at a railroad pace.

And now, if there had been a couple of experienced reporters present at the "Bugle Inn," they might have taken down a conversation on love and war—the two themes discussed by the two parties occupying the kitchen—which, as the parts were sung together, duetwise, formed together some very curious harmonies. Thus, while the Captain was whispering the softest nothings, the Corporal was shouting the fiercest combats of the war; and, like the gentleman at Penelope's table, on it exiguo pinxit praelia tota bero. For example:

CAPTAIN. What do you say to a silver trimming, pretty Catherine? Don't you think a scarlet riding-cloak, handsomely laced, would become you wonderfully well?—and a grey hat with a blue feather—and a pretty nag to ride on—and all the soldiers to present arms as you pass, and say, "There goes the Captain's lady"? What do you think of a side-box at Lincoln's Inn playhouse, or of standing up to a minuet with my Lord Marquis at—?

CORPORAL. The ball, sir, ran right up his elbow, and was found the next day by Surgeon Splinter of ours,—where do you think, sir?—upon my honour as a gentleman it came out of the nape of his—

CAPTAIN. Necklace—and a sweet pair of diamond earrings, mayhap—and a little shower of patches, which ornament a lady's face wondrously—and a leetle rouge—though, egad! such peach-cheeks as yours don't want it;—fie! Mrs. Catherine, I should think the birds must come and peck at them as if they were fruit—

CORPORAL. Over the wall; and three-and-twenty of our fellows jumped after me. By the Pope of Rome, friend Tummas, that was a day!—Had you seen how the Mounseers looked when four-and-twenty rampaging he-devils, sword and pistol, cut and thrust, pell-mell came tumbling into the redoubt! Why, sir, we left in three minutes as many artillerymen's heads as there were cannon-balls. It was, "Ah sacre!" "Damn you, take that!" "O mon Dieu!" "Run him through!" "Ventrebleu!" and it WAS ventrebleu with him, I warrant you; for bleu, in the French language, means "through;" and ventre—why, you see, ventre means—

CAPTAIN. Waists, which are worn now excessive long; and for the hoops, if you COULD but see them—stap my vitals, my dear, but there was a lady at Warwick's Assembly (she came in one of my Lord's coaches) who had a hoop as big as a tent: you might have dined under it comfortably;—ha! ha! 'pon my faith, now—

CORPORAL. And there we found the Duke of Marlborough seated along with Marshal Tallard, who was endeavouring to drown his sorrow over a cup of Johannisberger wine; and a good drink too, my lads, only not to compare to Warwick beer. "Who was the man who has done this?" said our noble General. I stepped up. "How many heads was it," says he, "that you cut off?" "Nineteen," says I, "besides wounding several." When he heard it (Mr. Hayes, you don't drink) I'm blest if he didn't burst into tears! "Noble noble fellow," says he. "Marshal, you must excuse me if I am pleased to hear of the destruction of your countrymen. Noble noble fellow!—here's a hundred guineas for you." Which sum he placed in my hand. "Nay," says the Marshal "the man has done his duty:" and, pulling out a magnificent gold diamond-hilted snuff-box, he gave me—

MR. BULLOCK. What, a goold snuff-box? Wauns, but thee WAST in luck, Corporal!

CORPORAL. No, not the snuff-box, but—A PINCH OF SNUFF,—ha! ha!—run me through the body if he didn't. Could you but have seen the smile on Jack Churchill's grave face at this piece of generosity! So, beckoning Colonel Cadogan up to him, he pinched his Ear and whispered—

CAPTAIN. "May I have the honour to dance a minuet with your Ladyship?" The whole room was in titters at Jack's blunder; for, as you know very well, poor Lady Susan HAS A WOODEN LEG. Ha! ha! fancy a minuet and a wooden leg, hey, my dear?—

MRS. CATHERINE. Giggle—giggle—giggle: he! he! he! Oh, Captain, you rogue, you—

SECOND TABLE. Haw! haw! haw! Well you be a foony mon, Sergeant, zure enoff.

This little specimen of the conversation must be sufficient. It will show pretty clearly that EACH of the two military commanders was conducting his operations with perfect success. Three of the detachment of five attacked by the Corporal surrendered to him: Mr. Bullock, namely, who gave in at a very early stage of the evening, and ignominiously laid down his arms under the table, after standing not more than a dozen volleys of beer; Mr. Blacksmith's boy, and a labourer whose name we have not been able to learn. Mr. Butcher himself was on the point of yielding, when he was rescued by the furious charge of a detachment that marched to his relief: his wife namely, who, with two squalling children, rushed into the "Bugle," boxed Butcher's ears, and kept up such a tremendous fire of oaths and screams upon the Corporal, that he was obliged to retreat. Fixing then her claws into Mr. Butcher's hair, she proceeded to drag him out of the premises; and thus Mr. Brock was overcome. His attack upon John Hayes was a still greater failure; for that young man seemed to be invincible by drink, if not by love: and at the end of the drinking-bout was a great deal more cool than the Corporal himself; to whom he wished a very polite good-evening, as calmly he took his hat to depart. He turned to look at Catherine, to be sure, and then he was not quite so calm: but Catherine did not give any reply to his good-night. She was seated at the Captain's table playing at cribbage with him; and though Count Gustavus Maximilian lost every game, he won more than he lost,—sly fellow!—and Mrs. Catherine was no match for him.

It is to be presumed that Hayes gave some information to Mrs. Score, the landlady: for, on leaving the kitchen, he was seen to linger for a moment in the bar; and very soon after Mrs. Catherine was called away from her attendance on the Count, who, when he asked for a sack and toast, was furnished with those articles by the landlady herself: and, during the half-hour in which he was employed in consuming this drink, Monsieur de Galgenstein looked very much disturbed and out of humour, and cast his eyes to the door perpetually; but no Catherine came. At last, very sulkily, he desired to be shown to bed, and walked as well as he could (for, to say truth, the noble Count was by this time somewhat unsteady on his legs) to his chamber. It was Mrs. Score who showed him to it, and closed the curtains, and pointed triumphantly to the whiteness of the sheets.

"It's a very comfortable room," said she, "though not the best in the house; which belong of right to your Lordship's worship; but our best room has two beds, and Mr. Corporal is in that, locked and double-locked, with his three tipsy recruits. But your honour will find this here bed comfortable and well-aired; I've slept in it myself this eighteen years."

"What, my good woman, you are going to sit up, eh? It's cruel hard on you, madam."

"Sit up, my Lord? bless you, no! I shall have half of our Cat's bed; as I always do when there's company." And with this Mrs. Score curtseyed and retired.

Very early the next morning the active landlady and her bustling attendant had prepared the ale and bacon for the Corporal and his three converts, and had set a nice white cloth for the Captain's breakfast. The young blacksmith did not eat with much satisfaction; but Mr. Bullock and his friend betrayed no sign of discontent, except such as may be consequent upon an evening's carouse. They walked very contentedly to be registered before Doctor Dobbs, who was also justice of the peace, and went in search of their slender bundles, and took leave of their few acquaintances without much regret: for the gentlemen had been bred in the workhouse, and had not, therefore, a large circle of friends.

It wanted only an hour of noon, and the noble Count had not descended. The men were waiting for him, and spent much of the Queen's money (earned by the sale of their bodies overnight) while thus expecting him. Perhaps Mrs. Catherine expected him too, for she had offered many times to run up—with my Lord's boots—with the hot water—to show Mr. Brock the way; who sometimes condescended to officiate as barber. But on all these occasions Mrs. Score had prevented her; not scolding, but with much gentleness and smiling. At last, more gentle and smiling than ever, she came downstairs and said, "Catherine darling, his honour the Count is mighty hungry this morning, and vows he could pick the wing of a fowl. Run down, child, to Farmer Brigg's and get one: pluck it before you bring it, you know, and we will make his Lordship a pretty breakfast."

Catherine took up her basket, and away she went by the back-yard, through the stables. There she heard the little horse-boy whistling and hissing after the manner of horseboys; and there she learned that Mrs. Score had been inventing an ingenious story to have her out of the way. The ostler said he was just going to lead the two horses round to the door. The Corporal had been, and they were about to start on the instant for Stratford.

The fact was that Count Gustavus Adolphus, far from wishing to pick the wing of a fowl, had risen with a horror and loathing for everything in the shape of food, and for any liquor stronger than small beer. Of this he had drunk a cup, and said he should ride immediately to Stratford; and when, on ordering his horses, he had asked politely of the landlady "why the devil SHE always came up, and why she did not send the girl," Mrs. Score informed the Count that her Catherine was gone out for a walk along with the young man to whom she was to be married, and would not be visible that day. On hearing this the Captain ordered his horses that moment, and abused the wine, the bed, the house, the landlady, and everything connected with the "Bugle Inn."

Out the horses came: the little boys of the village gathered round; the recruits, with bunches of ribands in their beavers, appeared presently; Corporal Brock came swaggering out, and, slapping the pleased blacksmith on the back, bade him mount his horse; while the boys hurrah'd. Then the Captain came out, gloomy and majestic; to him Mr. Brock made a military salute, which clumsily, and with much grinning, the recruits imitated. "I shall walk on with these brave fellows, your honour, and meet you at Stratford," said the Corporal. "Good," said the Captain, as he mounted. The landlady curtseyed; the children hurrah'd more; the little horse-boy, who held the bridle with one hand and the stirrup with the other, and expected a crown-piece from such a noble gentleman, got only a kick and a curse, as Count von Galgenstein shouted, "Damn you all, get out of the way!" and galloped off; and John Hayes, who had been sneaking about the inn all the morning, felt a weight off his heart when he saw the Captain ride off alone.

O foolish Mrs. Score! O dolt of a John Hayes! If the landlady had allowed the Captain and the maid to have their way, and meet but for a minute before recruits, sergeant, and all, it is probable that no harm would have been done, and that this history would never have been written.

When Count von Galgenstein had ridden half a mile on the Stratford road, looking as black and dismal as Napoleon galloping from the romantic village of Waterloo, he espied, a few score yards onwards, at the turn of the road, a certain object which caused him to check his horse suddenly, brought a tingling red into his cheeks, and made his heart to go thump—thump! against his side. A young lass was sauntering slowly along the footpath, with a basket swinging from one hand, and a bunch of hedge-flowers in the other. She stopped once or twice to add a fresh one to her nosegay, and might have seen him, the Captain thought; but no, she never looked directly towards him, and still walked on. Sweet innocent! she was singing as if none were near; her voice went soaring up to the clear sky, and the Captain put his horse on the grass, that the sound of the hoofs might not disturb the music.

"When the kine had given a pailful,
And the sheep came bleating home,
Poll, who knew it would be healthful,
Went a-walking out with Tom.
Hand in hand, sir, on the land, sir,
As they walked to and fro,
Tom made jolly love to Polly,
But was answered no, no, no."

The Captain had put his horse on the grass, that the sound of his hoofs might not disturb the music; and now he pushed its head on to the bank, where straightway "George of Denmark" began chewing of such a salad as grew there. And now the Captain slid off stealthily; and smiling comically, and hitching up his great jack-boots, and moving forward with a jerking tiptoe step, he, just as she was trilling the last o-o-o of the last no in the above poem of Tom D'Urfey, came up to her, and touching her lightly on the waist, said,

"My dear, your very humble servant."

Mrs. Catherine (you know you have found her out long ago!) gave a scream and a start, and would have turned pale if she could. As it was, she only shook all over, and said,

"Oh, sir, how you DID frighten me!"

"Frighten you, my rosebud! why, run me through, I'd die rather than frighten you. Gad, child, tell me now, am I so VERY frightful?"

"Oh no, your honour, I didn't mean that; only I wasn't thinking to meet you here, or that you would ride so early at all: for, if you please, sir, I was going to fetch a chicken for your Lordship's breakfast, as my mistress said you would like one; and I thought, instead of going to Farmer Brigg's, down Birmingham way, as she told me, I'd go to Farmer Bird's, where the chickens is better, sir,—my Lord, I mean."

"Said I'd like a chicken for breakfast, the old cat! why, I told her I would not eat a morsel to save me—I was so dru—I mean I ate such a good supper last night—and I bade her to send me a pot of small beer, and to tell you to bring it; and the wretch said you were gone out with your sweetheart—"

"What! John Hayes, the creature? Oh, what a naughty story-telling woman!"

"—You had walked out with your sweetheart, and I was not to see you any more; and I was mad with rage, and ready to kill myself; I was, my dear."

"Oh, sir! pray, PRAY don't."

"For your sake, my sweet angel?"

"Yes, for my sake, if such a poor girl as me can persuade noble gentlemen."

"Well, then, for YOUR sake, I won't; no, I'll live; but why live? Hell and fury, if I do live I'm miserable without you; I am,—you know I am,—you adorable, beautiful, cruel, wicked Catherine!"

Catherine's reply to this was "La, bless me! I do believe your horse is running away." And so he was! for having finished his meal in the hedge, he first looked towards his master and paused, as it were, irresolutely; then, by a sudden impulse, flinging up his tail and his hind legs, he scampered down the road.

Mrs. Hall ran lightly after the horse, and the Captain after Mrs. Hall; and the horse ran quicker and quicker every moment, and might have led them a long chase,—when lo! debouching from a twist in the road, came the detachment of cavalry and infantry under Mr. Brock. The moment he was out of sight of the village, that gentleman had desired the blacksmith to dismount, and had himself jumped into the saddle, maintaining the subordination of his army by drawing a pistol and swearing that he would blow out the brains of any person who attempted to run. When the Captain's horse came near the detachment he paused, and suffered himself to be caught by Tummas Bullock, who held him until the owner and Mrs. Catherine came up.

Mr. Bullock looked comically grave when he saw the pair; but the Corporal graciously saluted Mrs. Catherine, and said it was a fine day for walking.

"La, sir, and so it is," said she, panting in a very pretty and distressing way, "but not for RUNNING. I do protest—ha!—and vow that I really can scarcely stand. I'm so tired of running after that naughty naughty horse!"

"How do, Cattern?" said Thomas. "Zee, I be going a zouldiering because thee wouldn't have me." And here Mr. Bullock grinned. Mrs. Catherine made no sort of reply, but protested once more she should die of running. If the truth were told, she was somewhat vexed at the arrival of the Corporal's detachment, and had had very serious thoughts of finding herself quite tired just as he came in sight.

A sudden thought brought a smile of bright satisfaction in the Captain's eyes. He mounted the horse which Tummas still held. "TIRED, Mrs Catherine," said he, "and for my sake? By heavens! you shan't walk a step farther. No, you shall ride back with a guard of honour! Back to the village, gentlemen!—rightabout face! Show those fellows, Corporal, how to rightabout face. Now, my dear, mount behind me on Snowball; he's easy as a sedan. Put your dear little foot on the toe of my boot. There now,—up!—jump! hurrah!"

"THAT'S not the way, Captain," shouted out Thomas, still holding on to the rein as the horse began to move. "Thee woan't goo with him, will thee, Catty?"

But Mrs. Catherine, though she turned away her head, never let go her hold round the Captain's waist; and he, swearing a dreadful oath at Thomas, struck him across the face and hands with his riding whip. The poor fellow, who at the first cut still held on to the rein, dropped it at the second, and as the pair galloped off, sat down on the roadside and fairly began to weep.

"MARCH, you dog!" shouted out the Corporal a minute after. And so he did: and when next he saw Mrs. Catherine she WAS the Captain's lady sure enough, and wore a grey hat, with a blue feather, and red riding-coat trimmed with silverlace. But Thomas was then on a bare-backed horse, which Corporal Brock was flanking round a ring, and he was so occupied looking between his horse's ears that he had no time to cry then, and at length got the better of his attachment.

This being a good opportunity for closing Chapter I, we ought, perhaps, to make some apologies to the public for introducing them to characters that are so utterly worthless; as we confess all our heroes, with the exception of Mr. Bullock, to be. In this we have consulted nature and history, rather than the prevailing taste and the general manner of authors. The amusing novel of "Ernest Maltravers," for instance, opens with a seduction; but then it is performed by people of the strictest virtue on both sides: and there is so much religion and philosophy in the heart of the seducer, so much tender innocence in the soul of the seduced, that—bless the little dears!—their very peccadilloes make one interested in them; and their naughtiness becomes quite sacred, so deliciously is it described. Now, if we ARE to be interested by rascally actions, let us have them with plain faces, and let them be performed, not by virtuous philosophers, but by rascals. Another clever class of novelists adopt the contrary system, and create interest by making their rascals perform virtuous actions. Against these popular plans we here solemnly appeal. We say, let your rogues in novels act like rogues, and your honest men like honest men; don't let us have any juggling and thimble-rigging with virtue and vice, so that, at the end of three volumes, the bewildered reader shall not know which is which; don't let us find ourselves kindling at the generous qualities of thieves, and sympathising with the rascalities of noble hearts. For our own part, we know what the public likes, and have chosen rogues for our characters, and have taken a story from the "Newgate Calendar," which we hope to follow out to edification. Among the rogues, at least, we will have nothing that shall be mistaken for virtues. And if the British public (after calling for three or four editions) shall give up, not only our rascals, but the rascals of all other authors, we shall be content:—we shall apply to Government for a pension, and think that our duty is done.

CHAPTER II

IN WHICH ARE DEPICTED THE PLEASURES OF A SENTIMENTAL ATTACHMENT

It will not be necessary, for the purpose of this history, to follow out very closely all the adventures which occurred to Mrs. Catherine from the period when she quitted the "Bugle" and became the Captain's lady; for although it would be just as easy to show as not, that the young woman, by following the man of her heart, had only yielded to an innocent impulse, and by remaining with him for a certain period, had proved the depth and strength of her affection for him,—although we might make very tender and eloquent apologies for the error of both parties, the reader might possibly be disgusted at such descriptions and such arguments: which, besides, are already done to his hand in the novel of "Ernest Maltravers" before mentioned.

From the gentleman's manner towards Mrs. Catherine, and from his brilliant and immediate success, the reader will doubtless have concluded, in the first place, that Gustavus Adolphus had not a very violent affection for Mrs. Cat; in the second place, that he was a professional lady-killer, and therefore likely at some period to resume his profession; thirdly, and to conclude, that a connection so begun, must, in the nature of things, be likely to end speedily.

And so, to do the Count justice, it would, if he had been allowed to follow his own inclination entirely; for (as many young gentlemen will, and yet no praise to them) in about a week he began to be indifferent, in a month to be weary, in two months to be angry, in three to proceed to blows and curses; and, in short, to repent most bitterly the hour when he had ever been induced to present Mrs. Catherine the toe of his boot, for the purpose of lifting her on to his horse.

"Egad!" said he to the Corporal one day, when confiding his griefs to Mr. Brock, "I wish my toe had been cut off before ever it served as a ladder to this little vixen."

"Or perhaps your honour would wish to kick her downstairs with it?" delicately suggested Mr. Brock.

"Kick her! why, the wench would hold so fast by the banisters that I COULD not kick her down, Mr. Brock. To tell you a bit of a secret, I HAVE tried as much—not to kick her—no, no, not kick her, certainly: that's ungentlemanly—but to INDUCE her to go back to that cursed pot-house where we fell in with her. I have given her many hints—"

"Oh, yes, I saw your honour give her one yesterday—with a mug of beer. By the laws, as the ale run all down her face, and she clutched a knife to run at you, I don't think I ever saw such a she-devil! That woman will do for your honour some day, if you provoke her."

"Do for ME? No, hang it, Mr. Brock, never! She loves every hair of my head, sir: she worships me, Corporal. Egad, yes! she worships me; and would much sooner apply a knife to her own weasand than scratch my little finger!"

"I think she does," said Mr. Brock.

"I'm sure of it," said the Captain. "Women, look you, are like dogs, they like to be ill-treated: they like it, sir; I know they do. I never had anything to do with a woman in my life but I ill-treated her, and she liked me the better."

"Mrs. Hall ought to be VERY fond of you then, sure enough!" said Mr. Corporal.

"Very fond;—ha, ha! Corporal, you wag you—and so she IS very fond. Yesterday, after the knife-and-beer scene—no wonder I threw the liquor in her face: it was so dev'lish flat that no gentleman could drink it: and I told her never to draw it till dinner-time—"

"Oh, it was enough to put an angel in a fury!" said Brock.

"Well, yesterday, after the knife business, when you had got the carver out of her hand, off she flings to her bedroom, will not eat a bit of dinner forsooth, and remains locked up for a couple of hours. At two o'clock afternoon (I was over a tankard), out comes the little she-devil, her face pale, her eyes bleared, and the tip of her nose as red as fire with sniffling and weeping. Making for my hand, 'Max,' says she, 'will you forgive me?' 'What!' says I. 'Forgive a murderess?' says I. 'No, curse me, never!' 'Your cruelty will kill me,' sobbed she. 'Cruelty be hanged!' says I; 'didn't you draw that beer an hour before dinner?' She could say nothing to THIS, you know, and I swore that every time she did so, I would fling it into her face again. Whereupon back she flounced to her chamber, where she wept and stormed until night-time."

"When you forgave her?"

"I DID forgive her, that's positive. You see I had supped at the 'Rose' along with Tom Trippet and half-a-dozen pretty fellows; and I had eased a great fat-headed Warwickshire landjunker—what d'ye call him?—squire, of forty pieces; and I'm dev'lish good-humoured when I've won, and so Cat and I made it up: but I've taught her never to bring me stale beer again—ha, ha!"

This conversation will explain, a great deal better than any description of ours, however eloquent, the state of things as between Count Maximilian and Mrs. Catherine, and the feelings which they entertained for each other. The woman loved him, that was the fact. And, as we have shown in the previous chapter how John Hayes, a mean-spirited fellow as ever breathed, in respect of all other passions a pigmy, was in the passion of love a giant, and followed Mrs. Catherine with a furious longing which might seem at the first to be foreign to his nature; in the like manner, and playing at cross-purposes, Mrs. Hall had become smitten of the Captain; and, as he said truly, only liked him the better for the brutality which she received at his hands. For it is my opinion, madam, that love is a bodily infirmity, from which humankind can no more escape than from small-pox; and which attacks every one of us, from the first duke in the Peerage down to Jack Ketch inclusive: which has no respect for rank, virtue, or roguery in man, but sets each in his turn in a fever; which breaks out the deuce knows how or why, and, raging its appointed time, fills each individual of the one sex with a blind fury and longing for some one of the other (who may be pure, gentle, blue-eyed, beautiful, and good; or vile, shrewish, squinting, hunchbacked, and hideous, according to circumstances and luck); which dies away, perhaps, in the natural course, if left to have its way, but which contradiction causes to rage more furiously than ever. Is not history, from the Trojan war upwards and downwards, full of instances of such strange inexplicable passions? Was not Helen, by the most moderate calculation, ninety years of age when she went off with His Royal Highness Prince Paris of Troy? Was not Madame La Valliere ill-made, blear-eyed, tallow-complexioned, scraggy, and with hair like tow? Was not Wilkes the ugliest, charmingest, most successful man in the world? Such instances might be carried out so as to fill a volume; but cui bono? Love is fate, and not will; its origin not to be explained, its progress irresistible: and the best proof of this may be had at Bow Street any day, where if you ask any officer of the establishment how they take most thieves, he will tell you at the houses of the women. They must see the dear creatures though they hang for it; they will love, though they have their necks in the halter. And with regard to the other position, that ill-usage on the part of the man does not destroy the affection of the woman, have we not numberless police-reports, showing how, when a bystander would beat a husband for beating his wife, man and wife fall together on the interloper and punish him for his meddling?

These points, then, being settled to the satisfaction of all parties, the reader will not be disposed to question the assertion that Mrs. Hall had a real affection for the gallant Count, and grew, as Mr. Brock was pleased to say, like a beefsteak, more tender as she was thumped. Poor thing, poor thing! his flashy airs and smart looks had overcome her in a single hour; and no more is wanted to plunge into love over head and ears; no more is wanted to make a first love with—and a woman's first love lasts FOR EVER (a man's twenty-fourth or twenty-fifth is perhaps the best): you can't kill it, do what you will; it takes root, and lives and even grows, never mind what the soil may be in which it is planted, or the bitter weather it must bear—often as one has seen a wallflower grow—out of a stone.

In the first weeks of their union, the Count had at least been liberal to her: she had a horse and fine clothes, and received abroad some of those flattering attentions which she held at such high price. He had, however, some ill-luck at play, or had been forced to pay some bills, or had some other satisfactory reason for being poor, and his establishment was very speedily diminished. He argued that, as Mrs. Catherine had been accustomed to wait on others all her life, she might now wait upon herself and him; and when the incident of the beer arose, she had been for some time employed as the Count's housekeeper, with unlimited superintendence over his comfort, his cellar, his linen, and such matters as bachelors are delighted to make over to active female hands. To do the poor wretch justice, she actually kept the man's menage in the best order; nor was there any point of extravagance with which she could be charged, except a little extravagance of dress displayed on the very few occasions when he condescended to walk abroad with her, and extravagance of language and passion in the frequent quarrels they had together. Perhaps in such a connection as subsisted between this precious couple, these faults are inevitable on the part of the woman. She must be silly and vain, and will pretty surely therefore be fond of dress; and she must, disguise it as she will, be perpetually miserable and brooding over her fall, which will cause her to be violent and quarrelsome.

Such, at least, was Mrs. Hall; and very early did the poor vain misguided wretch begin to reap what she had sown.

For a man, remorse under these circumstances is perhaps uncommon. No stigma affixes on HIM for betraying a woman; no bitter pangs of mortified vanity; no insulting looks of superiority from his neighbour, and no sentence of contemptuous banishment is read against him; these all fall on the tempted, and not on the tempter, who is permitted to go free. The chief thing that a man learns after having successfully practised on a woman is to despise the poor wretch whom he has won. The game, in fact, and the glory, such as it is, is all his, and the punishment alone falls upon her. Consider this, ladies, when charming young gentlemen come to woo you with soft speeches. You have nothing to win, except wretchedness, and scorn, and desertion. Consider this, and be thankful to your Solomons for telling it.

It came to pass, then, that the Count had come to have a perfect contempt and indifference for Mrs. Hall;—how should he not for a young person who had given herself up to him so easily?—and would have been quite glad of any opportunity of parting with her. But there was a certain lingering shame about the man, which prevented him from saying at once and abruptly, "Go!" and the poor thing did not choose to take such hints as fell out in the course of their conversation and quarrels. And so they kept on together, he treating her with simple insult, and she hanging on desperately, by whatever feeble twig she could find, to the rock beyond which all was naught, or death, to her.

Well, after the night with Tom Trippet and the pretty fellows at the "Rose," to which we have heard the Count allude in the conversation just recorded, Fortune smiled on him a good deal; for the Warwickshire squire, who had lost forty pieces on that occasion, insisted on having his revenge the night after; when, strange to say, a hundred and fifty more found their way into the pouch of his Excellency the Count. Such a sum as this quite set the young nobleman afloat again, and brought back a pleasing equanimity to his mind, which had been a good deal disturbed in the former difficult circumstances; and in this, for a little and to a certain extent, poor Cat had the happiness to share. He did not alter the style of his establishment, which consisted, as before, of herself and a small person who acted as scourer, kitchen-wench, and scullion; Mrs. Catherine always putting her hand to the principal pieces of the dinner; but he treated his mistress with tolerable good-humour; or, to speak more correctly, with such bearable brutality as might be expected from a man like him to a woman in her condition. Besides, a certain event was about to take place, which not unusually occurs in circumstances of this nature, and Mrs. Catherine was expecting soon to lie in.

The Captain, distrusting naturally the strength of his own paternal feelings, had kindly endeavoured to provide a parent for the coming infant; and to this end had opened a negotiation with our friend Mr. Thomas Bullock, declaring that Mrs. Cat should have a fortune of twenty guineas, and reminding Tummas of his ancient flame for her: but Mr. Tummas, when this proposition was made to him, declined it, with many oaths, and vowed that he was perfectly satisfied with his present bachelor condition. In this dilemma, Mr. Brock stepped forward, who declared himself very ready to accept Mrs. Catherine and her fortune: and might possibly have become the possessor of both, had not Mrs. Cat, the moment she heard of the proposed arrangement, with fire in her eyes, and rage—oh, how bitter!—in her heart, prevented the success of the measure by proceeding incontinently to the first justice of the peace, and there swearing before his worship who was the father of the coming child.

This proceeding, which she had expected would cause not a little indignation on the part of her lord and master, was received by him, strangely enough, with considerable good-humour: he swore that the wench had served him a good trick, and was rather amused at the anger, the outbreak of fierce rage and contumely, and the wretched wretched tears of heartsick desperation, which followed her announcement of this step to him. For Mr. Brock, she repelled his offer with scorn and loathing, and treated the notion of a union with Mr. Bullock with yet fiercer contempt. Marry him indeed! a workhouse pauper carrying a brown-bess! She would have died sooner, she said, or robbed on the highway. And so, to do her justice, she would: for the little minx was one of the vainest creatures in existence, and vanity (as I presume everybody knows) becomes THE principle in certain women's hearts—their moral spectacles, their conscience, their meat and drink, their only rule of right and wrong.

As for Mr. Tummas, he, as we have seen, was quite unfriendly to the proposition as she could be; and the Corporal, with a good deal of comical gravity, vowed that, as he could not be satisfied in his dearest wishes, he would take to drinking for a consolation: which he straightway did.

"Come, Tummas," said he to Mr. Bullock "since we CAN'T have the girl of our hearts, why, hang it, Tummas, let's drink her health!" To which Bullock had no objection. And so strongly did the disappointment weigh upon honest Corporal Brock, that even when, after unheard-of quantities of beer, he could scarcely utter a word, he was seen absolutely to weep, and, in accents almost unintelligible, to curse his confounded ill-luck at being deprived, not of a wife, but of a child: he wanted one so, he said, to comfort him in his old age.

The time of Mrs. Catherine's couche drew near, arrived, and was gone through safely. She presented to the world a chopping boy, who might use, if he liked, the Galgenstein arms with a bar-sinister; and in her new cares and duties had not so many opportunities as usual of quarrelling with the Count: who, perhaps, respected her situation, or, at least, was so properly aware of the necessity of quiet to her, that he absented himself from home morning, noon, and night.

The Captain had, it must be confessed, turned these continued absences to a considerable worldly profit, for he played incessantly; and, since his first victory over the Warwickshire Squire, Fortune had been so favourable to him, that he had at various intervals amassed a sum of nearly a thousand pounds, which he used to bring home as he won; and which he deposited in a strong iron chest, cunningly screwed down by himself under his own bed. This Mrs. Catherine regularly made, and the treasure underneath it could be no secret to her. However, the noble Count kept the key, and bound her by many solemn oaths (that he discharged at her himself) not to reveal to any other person the existence of the chest and its contents.

But it is not in a woman's nature to keep such secrets; and the Captain, who left her for days and days, did not reflect that she would seek for confidants elsewhere. For want of a female companion, she was compelled to bestow her sympathies upon Mr. Brock; who, as the Count's corporal, was much in his lodgings, and who did manage to survive the disappointment which he had experienced by Mrs. Catherine's refusal of him.

About two months after the infant's birth, the Captain, who was annoyed by its squalling, put it abroad to nurse, and dismissed its attendant. Mrs. Catherine now resumed her household duties, and was, as before, at once mistress and servant of the establishment. As such, she had the keys of the beer, and was pretty sure of the attentions of the Corporal; who became, as we have said, in the Count's absence, his lady's chief friend and companion. After the manner of ladies, she very speedily confided to him all her domestic secrets; the causes of her former discontent; the Count's ill-treatment of her; the wicked names he called her; the prices that all her gowns had cost her; how he beat her; how much money he won and lost at play; how she had once pawned a coat for him; how he had four new ones, laced, and paid for; what was the best way of cleaning and keeping gold-lace, of making cherry-brandy, pickling salmon, etc., etc. Her confidences upon all these subjects used to follow each other in rapid succession; and Mr. Brock became, ere long, quite as well acquainted with the Captain's history for the last year as the Count himself:—for he was careless, and forgot things; women never do. They chronicle all the lover's small actions, his words, his headaches, the dresses he has worn, the things he has liked for dinner on certain days;—all which circumstances commonly are expunged from the male brain immediately after they have occurred, but remain fixed with the female.

To Brock, then, and to Brock only (for she knew no other soul), Mrs. Cat breathed, in strictest confidence, the history of the Count's winnings, and his way of disposing of them; how he kept his money screwed down in an iron chest in their room; and a very lucky fellow did Brock consider his officer for having such a large sum. He and Cat looked at the chest: it was small, but mighty strong, sure enough, and would defy picklocks and thieves. Well, if any man deserved money, the Captain did ("though he might buy me a few yards of that lace I love so," interrupted Cat),—if any man deserved money, he did, for he spent it like a prince, and his hand was always in his pocket.

It must now be stated that Monsieur de Galgenstein had, during Cat's seclusion, cast his eyes upon a young lady of good fortune, who frequented the Assembly at Birmingham, and who was not a little smitten by his title and person. The "four new coats, laced, and paid for," as Cat said, had been purchased, most probably, by his Excellency for the purpose of dazzling the heiress; and he and the coats had succeeded so far as to win from the young woman an actual profession of love, and a promise of marriage provided Pa would consent. This was obtained,—for Pa was a tradesman; and I suppose every one of my readers has remarked how great an effect a title has on the lower classes. Yes, thank Heaven! there is about a freeborn Briton a cringing baseness, and lickspittle awe of rank, which does not exist under any tyranny in Europe, and is only to be found here and in America.

All these negotiations had been going on quite unknown to Cat; and, as the Captain had determined, before two months were out, to fling that young woman on the pave, he was kind to her in the meanwhile: people always are when they are swindling you, or meditating an injury against you.

The poor girl had much too high an opinion of her own charms to suspect that the Count could be unfaithful to them, and had no notion of the plot that was formed against her. But Mr. Brock had: for he had seen many times a gilt coach with a pair of fat white horses ambling in the neighbourhood of the town, and the Captain on his black steed caracolling majestically by its side; and he had remarked a fat, pudgy, pale-haired woman treading heavily down the stairs of the Assembly, leaning on the Captain's arm: all these Mr. Brock had seen, not without reflection. Indeed, the Count one day, in great good-humour, had slapped him on the shoulder and told him that he was about speedily to purchase a regiment; when, by his great gods, Mr. Brock should have a pair of colours. Perhaps this promise occasioned his silence to Mrs. Catherine hitherto; perhaps he never would have peached at all; and perhaps, therefore, this history would never have been written, but for a small circumstance which occurred at this period.

"What can you want with that drunken old Corporal always about your quarters?" said Mr. Trippet to the Count one day, as they sat over their wine, in the midst of a merry company, at the Captain's rooms.

"What!" said he. "Old Brock? The old thief has been more useful to me than many a better man. He is as brave in a row as a lion, as cunning in intrigue as a fox; he can nose a dun at an inconceivable distance, and scent out a pretty woman be she behind ever so many stone walls. If a gentleman wants a good rascal now, I can recommend him. I am going to reform, you know, and must turn him out of my service."

"And pretty Mrs. Cat?"

"Oh, curse pretty Mrs. Cat! she may go too."

"And the brat?"

"Why, you have parishes, and what not, here in England. Egad! if a gentleman were called upon to keep all his children, there would be no living: no, stap my vitals! Croesus couldn't stand it."

"No, indeed," said Mr. Trippet: "you are right; and when a gentleman marries, he is bound in honour to give up such low connections as are useful when he is a bachelor."

"Of course; and give them up I will, when the sweet Mrs. Dripping is mine. As for the girl, you can have her, Tom Trippet, if you take a fancy to her; and as for the Corporal, he may be handed over to my successor in Cutts's:—for I will have a regiment to myself, that's poz; and to take with me such a swindling, pimping, thieving, brandy-faced rascal as this Brock will never do. Egad! he's a disgrace to the service. As it is, I've often a mind to have the superannuated vagabond drummed out of the corps."

Although this resume of Mr. Brock's character and accomplishments was very just, it came perhaps with an ill grace from Count Gustavus Adolphus Maximilian, who had profited by all his qualities, and who certainly would never have given this opinion of them had he known that the door of his dining-parlour was open, and that the gallant Corporal, who was in the passage, could hear every syllable that fell from the lips of his commanding officer. We shall not say, after the fashion of the story-books, that Mr. Brock listened with a flashing eye and a distended nostril; that his chest heaved tumultuously, and that his hand fell down mechanically to his side, where it played with the brass handle of his sword. Mr. Kean would have gone through most of these bodily exercises had he been acting the part of a villain enraged and disappointed like Corporal Brock; but that gentleman walked away without any gestures of any kind, and as gently as possible. "He'll turn me out of the regiment, will he?" says he, quite piano; and then added (con molta espressione), "I'll do for him."

And it is to be remarked how generally, in cases of this nature, gentlemen stick to their word.

CHAPTER III

IN WHICH A NARCOTIC IS ADMINISTERED, AND A GREAT DEAL OF GENTEEL SOCIETY DEPICTED

When the Corporal, who had retreated to the street-door immediately on hearing the above conversation, returned to the Captain's lodgings and paid his respects to Mrs. Catherine, he found that lady in high good-humour. The Count had been with her, she said, along with a friend of his, Mr. Trippet; had promised her twelve yards of the lace she coveted so much; had vowed that the child should have as much more for a cloak; and had not left her until he had sat with her for an hour, or more, over a bowl of punch, which he made on purpose for her. Mr. Trippet stayed too. "A mighty pleasant man," said she; "only not very wise, and seemingly a good deal in liquor."

"A good deal indeed!" said the Corporal. "He was so tipsy just now that he could hardly stand. He and his honour were talking to Nan Fantail in the market-place; and she pulled Trippet's wig off, for wanting to kiss her."

"The nasty fellow!" said Mrs. Cat, "to demean himself with such low people as Nan Fantail, indeed! Why, upon my conscience now, Corporal, it was but an hour ago that Mr. Trippet swore he never saw such a pair of eyes as mine, and would like to cut the Captain's throat for the love of me. Nan Fantail, indeed!"

"Nan's an honest girl, Madam Catherine, and was a great favourite of the Captain's before someone else came in his way. No one can say a word against her—not a word."

"And pray, Corporal, who ever did?" said Mrs. Cat, rather offended. "A nasty, ugly slut! I wonder what the men can see in her?"

"She has got a smart way with her, sure enough; it's what amuses the men, and—"

"And what? You don't mean to say that my Max is fond of her NOW?" said Mrs. Catherine, looking very fierce.

"Oh, no; not at all: not of HER;—that is—"

"Not of HER!" screamed she. "Of whom, then?"

"Oh, psha! nonsense! Of you, my dear, to be sure; who else should he care for? And, besides, what business is it of mine?" And herewith the Corporal began whistling, as if he would have no more of the conversation. But Mrs. Cat was not to be satisfied,—not she,—and carried on her cross-questions.

"Why, look you," said the Corporal, after parrying many of these,—"Why, look you, I'm an old fool, Catherine, and I must blab. That man has been the best friend I ever had, and so I was quiet; but I can't keep it in any longer,—no, hang me if I can! It's my belief he's acting like a rascal by you: he deceives you, Catherine; he's a scoundrel, Mrs. Hall, that's the truth on't."

Catherine prayed him to tell all he knew; and he resumed.

"He wants you off his hands; he's sick of you, and so brought here that fool Tom Trippet, who has taken a fancy to you. He has not the courage to turn you out of doors like a man; though indoors he can treat you like a beast. But I'll tell you what he'll do. In a month he will go to Coventry, or pretend to go there, on recruiting business. No such thing, Mrs. Hall; he's going on MARRIAGE business; and he'll leave you without a farthing, to starve or to rot, for him. It's all arranged, I tell you: in a month, you are to be starved into becoming Tom Trippet's mistress; and his honour is to marry rich Miss Dripping, the twenty-thousand-pounder from London; and to purchase a regiment;—and to get old Brock drummed out of Cutts's too," said the Corporal, under his breath. But he might have spoken out, if he chose; for the poor young woman had sunk on the ground in a real honest fit.

"I thought I should give it her," said Mr. Brock as he procured a glass of water; and, lifting her on to a sofa, sprinkled the same over her. "Hang it! how pretty she is."

When Mrs. Catherine came to herself again, Brock's tone with her was kind, and almost feeling. Nor did the poor wench herself indulge in any subsequent shiverings and hysterics, such as usually follow the fainting-fits of persons of higher degree. She pressed him for further explanations, which he gave, and to which she listened with a great deal of calmness; nor did many tears, sobs, sighs, or exclamations of sorrow or anger escape from her: only when the Corporal was taking his leave, and said to her point-blank,—"Well, Mrs. Catherine, and what do you intend to do?" she did not reply a word; but gave a look which made him exclaim, on leaving the room,—

"By heavens! the woman means murder! I would not be the Holofernes to lie by the side of such a Judith as that—not I!" And he went his way, immersed in deep thought. When the Captain returned at night, she did not speak to him; and when he swore at her for being sulky, she only said she had a headache, and was dreadfully ill; with which excuse Gustavus Adolphus seemed satisfied, and left her to herself.

He saw her the next morning for a moment: he was going a-shooting.

Catherine had no friend, as is usual in tragedies and romances,—no mysterious sorceress of her acquaintance to whom she could apply for poison,—so she went simply to the apothecaries, pretending at each that she had a dreadful toothache, and procuring from them as much laudanum as she thought would suit her purpose.

When she went home again she seemed almost gay. Mr. Brock complimented her upon the alteration in her appearance; and she was enabled to receive the Captain at his return from shooting in such a manner as made him remark that she had got rid of her sulks of the morning, and might sup with them, if she chose to keep her good-humour. The supper was got ready, and the gentlemen had the punch-bowl when the cloth was cleared,—Mrs. Catherine, with her delicate hands, preparing the liquor.

It is useless to describe the conversation that took place, or to reckon the number of bowls that were emptied; or to tell how Mr. Trippet, who was one of the guests, and declined to play at cards when some of the others began, chose to remain by Mrs. Catherine's side, and make violent love to her. All this might be told, and the account, however faithful, would not be very pleasing. No, indeed! And here, though we are only in the third chapter of this history, we feel almost sick of the characters that appear in it, and the adventures which they are called upon to go through. But how can we help ourselves? The public will hear of nothing but rogues; and the only way in which poor authors, who must live, can act honestly by the public and themselves, is to paint such thieves as they are: not, dandy, poetical, rose-water thieves; but real downright scoundrels, leading scoundrelly lives, drunken, profligate, dissolute, low; as scoundrels will be. They don't quote Plato, like Eugene Aram; or live like gentlemen, and sing the pleasantest ballads in the world, like jolly Dick Turpin; or prate eternally about "to kalon,"[*] like that precious canting Maltravers, whom we all of us have read about and pitied; or die whitewashed saints, like poor "Biss Dadsy" in "Oliver Twist." No, my dear madam, you and your daughters have no right to admire and sympathise with any such persons, fictitious or real: you ought to be made cordially to detest, scorn, loathe, abhor, and abominate all people of this kidney. Men of genius like those whose works we have above alluded to, have no business to make these characters interesting or agreeable; to be feeding your morbid fancies, or indulging their own, with such monstrous food. For our parts, young ladies, we beg you to bottle up your tears, and not waste a single drop of them on any one of the heroes or heroines in this history: they are all rascals, every soul of them, and behave "as sich." Keep your sympathy for those who deserve it: don't carry it, for preference, to the Old Bailey, and grow maudlin over the company assembled there.

* Anglicised version of the author's original Greek text.

Just, then, have the kindness to fancy that the conversation which took place over the bowls of punch which Mrs. Catherine prepared, was such as might be expected to take place where the host was a dissolute, dare-devil, libertine captain of dragoons, the guests for the most part of the same class, and the hostess a young woman originally from a country alehouse, and for the present mistress to the entertainer of the society. They talked, and they drank, and they grew tipsy; and very little worth hearing occurred during the course of the whole evening. Mr. Brock officiated, half as the servant, half as the companion of the society. Mr. Thomas Trippet made violent love to Mrs. Catherine, while her lord and master was playing at dice with the other gentlemen: and on this night, strange to say, the Captain's fortune seemed to desert him. The Warwickshire Squire, from whom he had won so much, had an amazing run of good luck. The Captain called perpetually for more drink, and higher stakes, and lost almost every throw. Three hundred, four hundred, six hundred—all his winnings of the previous months were swallowed up in the course of a few hours. The Corporal looked on; and, to do him justice, seemed very grave as, sum by sum, the Squire scored down the Count's losses on the paper before him.

Most of the company had taken their hats and staggered off. The Squire and Mr. Trippet were the only two that remained, the latter still lingering by Mrs. Catherine's sofa and table; and as she, as we have stated, had been employed all the evening in mixing the liquor for the gamesters, he was at the headquarters of love and drink, and had swallowed so much of each as hardly to be able to speak.

The dice went rattling on; the candles were burning dim, with great long wicks. Mr. Trippet could hardly see the Captain, and thought, as far as his muzzy reason would let him, that the Captain could not see him: so he rose from his chair as well as he could, and fell down on Mrs. Catherine's sofa. His eyes were fixed, his face was pale, his jaw hung down; and he flung out his arms and said, in a maudlin voice, "Oh, you byoo-oo-oo-tifile Cathrine, I must have a kick-kick-iss."

"Beast!" said Mrs. Catherine, and pushed him away. The drunken wretch fell off the sofa, and on to the floor, where he stayed; and, after snorting out some unintelligible sounds, went to sleep.

The dice went rattling on; the candles were burning dim, with great long wicks.

"Seven's the main," cried the Count. "Four. Three to two against the caster."

"Ponies," said the Warwickshire Squire.

Rattle, rattle, rattle, rattle, clatter, NINE. Clap, clap, clap, clap, ELEVEN. Clutter, clutter, clutter, clutter: "Seven it is," says the Warwickshire Squire. "That makes eight hundred, Count."

"One throw for two hundred," said the Count. "But stop! Cat, give us some more punch."

Mrs. Cat came forward; she looked a little pale, and her hand trembled somewhat. "Here is the punch, Max," said she. It was steaming hot, in a large glass. "Don't drink it all," said she; "leave me some."

"How dark it is!" said the Count, eyeing it.

"It's the brandy," said Cat.

"Well, here goes! Squire, curse you! here's your health, and bad luck to you!" and he gulped off more than half the liquor at a draught. But presently he put down the glass and cried, "What infernal poison is this, Cat?"

"Poison!" said she. "It's no poison. Give me the glass." And she pledged Max, and drank a little of it. "'Tis good punch, Max, and of my brewing; I don't think you will ever get any better." And she went back to the sofa again, and sat down, and looked at the players.

Mr. Brock looked at her white face and fixed eyes with a grim kind of curiosity. The Count sputtered, and cursed the horrid taste of the punch still; but he presently took the box, and made his threatened throw.

As before, the Squire beat him; and having booked his winnings, rose from table as well as he might and besought to lead him downstairs; which Mr. Brock did.

Liquor had evidently stupefied the Count: he sat with his head between his hands, muttering wildly about ill-luck, seven's the main, bad punch, and so on. The street-door banged to; and the steps of Brock and the Squire were heard, until they could be heard no more.

"Max," said she; but he did not answer. "Max," said she again, laying her hand on his shoulder.

"Curse you," said that gentleman, "keep off, and don't be laying your paws upon me. Go to bed, you jade, or to —, for what I care; and give me first some more punch—a gallon more punch, do you hear?"

The gentleman, by the curses at the commencement of this little speech, and the request contained at the end of it, showed that his losses vexed him, and that he was anxious to forget them temporarily.

"Oh, Max!" whimpered Mrs. Cat, "you—don't—want any more punch?"

"Don't! Shan't I be drunk in my own house, you cursed whimpering jade, you? Get out!" and with this the Captain proceeded to administer a blow upon Mrs. Catherine's cheek.

Contrary to her custom, she did not avenge it, or seek to do so, as on the many former occasions when disputes of this nature had arisen between the Count and her; but now Mrs. Catherine fell on her knees and, clasping her hands and looking pitifully in the Count's face, cried, "Oh, Count, forgive me, forgive me!"

"Forgive you! What for? Because I slapped your face? Ha, ha! I'll forgive you again, if you don't mind."

"Oh, no, no, no!" said she, wringing her hands. "It isn't that. Max, dear Max, will you forgive me? It isn't the blow—I don't mind that; it's—"

"It's what, you—maudlin fool?"

"IT'S THE PUNCH!"

The Count, who was more than half seas over, here assumed an air of much tipsy gravity. "The punch! No, I never will forgive you that last glass of punch. Of all the foul, beastly drinks I ever tasted, that was the worst. No, I never will forgive you that punch."

"Oh, it isn't that, it isn't that!" said she.

"I tell you it is that,—you! That punch, I say that punch was no better than paw—aw-oison." And here the Count's head sank back, and he fell to snore.

"IT WAS POISON!" said she.

"WHAT!" screamed he, waking up at once, and spurning her away from him. "What, you infernal murderess, have you killed me?"

"Oh, Max!—don't kill me, Max! It was laudanum—indeed it was. You were going to be married, and I was furious, and I went and got—"

"Hold your tongue, you fiend," roared out the Count; and with more presence of mind than politeness, he flung the remainder of the liquor (and, indeed, the glass with it) at the head of Mrs. Catherine. But the poisoned chalice missed its mark, and fell right on the nose of Mr. Tom Trippet, who was left asleep and unobserved under the table.

Bleeding, staggering, swearing, indeed a ghastly sight, up sprang Mr. Trippet, and drew his rapier. "Come on," says he; "never say die! What's the row? I'm ready for a dozen of you." And he made many blind and furious passes about the room.

"Curse you, we'll die together!" shouted the Count, as he too pulled out his toledo, and sprang at Mrs. Catherine.

"Help! murder! thieves!" shrieked she. "Save me, Mr. Trippet, save me!" and she placed that gentleman between herself and the Count, and then made for the door of the bedroom, and gained it, and bolted it.

"Out of the way, Trippet," roared the Count—"out of the way, you drunken beast! I'll murder her, I will—I'll have the devil's life." And here he gave a swinging cut at Mr. Trippet's sword: it sent the weapon whirling clean out of his hand, and through a window into the street.

"Take my life, then," said Mr. Trippet: "I'm drunk, but I'm a man, and, damme! will never say die."

"I don't want your life, you stupid fool. Hark you, Trippet, wake and be sober, if you can. That woman has heard of my marriage with Miss Dripping."

"Twenty thousand pound," ejaculated Trippet.

"She has been jealous, I tell you, and POISONED us. She has put laudanum into the punch."

"What, in MY punch?" said Trippet, growing quite sober and losing his courage. "O Lord! O Lord!"

"Don't stand howling there, but run for a doctor; 'tis our only chance." And away ran Mr. Trippet, as if the deuce were at his heels.

The Count had forgotten his murderous intentions regarding his mistress, or had deferred them at least, under the consciousness of his own pressing danger. And it must be said, in the praise of a man who had fought for and against Marlborough and Tallard, that his courage in this trying and novel predicament never for a moment deserted him, but that he showed the greatest daring, as well as ingenuity, in meeting and averting the danger. He flew to the sideboard, where were the relics of a supper, and seizing the mustard and salt pots, and a bottle of oil, he emptied them all into a jug, into which he further poured a vast quantity of hot water. This pleasing mixture he then, without a moment's hesitation, placed to his lips, and swallowed as much of it as nature would allow him. But when he had imbibed about a quart, the anticipated effect was produced, and he was enabled, by the power of this ingenious extemporaneous emetic, to get rid of much of the poison which Mrs. Catherine had administered to him.

He was employed in these efforts when the doctor entered, along with Mr. Brock and Mr. Trippet; who was not a little pleased to hear that the poisoned punch had not in all probability been given to him. He was recommended to take some of the Count's mixture, as a precautionary measure; but this he refused, and retired home, leaving the Count under charge of the physician and his faithful corporal.

It is not necessary to say what further remedies were employed by them to restore the Captain to health; but after some time the doctor, pronouncing that the danger was, he hoped, averted, recommended that his patient should be put to bed, and that somebody should sit by him; which Brock promised to do.

"That she-devil will murder me, if you don't," gasped the poor Count. "You must turn her out of the bedroom; or break open the door, if she refuses to let you in."

And this step was found to be necessary; for, after shouting many times, and in vain, Mr. Brock found a small iron bar (indeed, he had the instrument for many days in his pocket), and forced the lock. The room was empty, the window was open: the pretty barmaid of the "Bugle" had fled.

"The chest," said the Count—"is the chest safe?"

The Corporal flew to the bed, under which it was screwed, and looked, and said, "It IS safe, thank Heaven!" The window was closed. The Captain, who was too weak to stand without help, was undressed and put to bed. The Corporal sat down by his side; slumber stole over the eyes of the patient; and his wakeful nurse marked with satisfaction the progress of the beneficent restorer of health.

When the Captain awoke, as he did some time afterwards, he found, very much to his surprise, that a gag had been placed in his mouth, and that the Corporal was in the act of wheeling his bed to another part of the room. He attempted to move, and gave utterance to such unintelligible sounds as could issue through a silk handkerchief.

"If your honour stirs or cries out in the least, I will cut your honour's throat," said the Corporal.

And then, having recourse to his iron bar (the reader will now see why he was provided with such an implement, for he had been meditating this coup for some days), he proceeded first to attempt to burst the lock of the little iron chest in which the Count kept his treasure, and, failing in this, to unscrew it from the ground; which operation he performed satisfactorily.

"You see, Count," said he, calmly, "when rogues fall out there's the deuce to pay. You'll have me drummed out of the regiment, will you? I'm going to leave it of my own accord, look you, and to live like a gentleman for the rest of my days. Schlafen Sie wohl, noble Captain: bon repos. The Squire will be with you pretty early in the morning, to ask for the money you owe him."

With these sarcastic observations Mr. Brock departed; not by the window, as Mrs. Catherine had done, but by the door, quietly, and so into the street. And when, the next morning, the doctor came to visit his patient, he brought with him a story how, at the dead of night, Mr. Brock had roused the ostler at the stables where the Captain's horses were kept—had told him that Mrs. Catherine had poisoned the Count, and had run off with a thousand pounds; and how he and all lovers of justice ought to scour the country in pursuit of the criminal. For this end Mr. Brock mounted the Count's best horse—that very animal on which he had carried away Mrs. Catherine: and thus, on a single night, Count Maximilian had lost his mistress, his money, his horse, his corporal, and was very near losing his life.

CHAPTER IV

IN WHICH MRS. CATHERINE BECOMES AN HONEST WOMAN AGAIN

In this woeful plight, moneyless, wifeless, horseless, corporalless, with a gag in his mouth and a rope round his body, are we compelled to leave the gallant Galgenstein, until his friends and the progress of this history shall deliver him from his durance. Mr. Brock's adventures on the Captain's horse must likewise be pretermitted; for it is our business to follow Mrs. Catherine through the window by which she made her escape, and among the various chances that befell her.

She had one cause to congratulate herself,—that she had not her baby at her back; for the infant was safely housed under the care of a nurse, to whom the Captain was answerable. Beyond this her prospects were but dismal: no home to fly to, but a few shillings in her pocket, and a whole heap of injuries and dark revengeful thoughts in her bosom: it was a sad task to her to look either backwards or forwards. Whither was she to fly? How to live? What good chance was to befriend her? There was an angel watching over the steps of Mrs. Cat—not a good one, I think, but one of those from that unnameable place, who have their many subjects here on earth, and often are pleased to extricate them from worse perplexities.

Mrs. Cat, now, had not committed murder, but as bad as murder; and as she felt not the smallest repentance in her heart—as she had, in the course of her life and connection with the Captain, performed and gloried in a number of wicked coquetries, idlenesses, vanities, lies, fits of anger, slanders, foul abuses, and what not—she was fairly bound over to this dark angel whom we have alluded to; and he dealt with her, and aided her, as one of his own children.

I do not mean to say that, in this strait, he appeared to her in the likeness of a gentleman in black, and made her sign her name in blood to a document conveying over to him her soul, in exchange for certain conditions to be performed by him. Such diabolical bargains have always appeared to me unworthy of the astute personage who is supposed to be one of the parties to them; and who would scarcely be fool enough to pay dearly for that which he can have in a few years for nothing. It is not, then, to be supposed that a demon of darkness appeared to Mrs. Cat, and led her into a flaming chariot harnessed by dragons, and careering through air at the rate of a thousand leagues a minute. No such thing; the vehicle that was sent to aid her was one of a much more vulgar description.

The "Liverpool carryvan," then, which in the year 1706 used to perform the journey between London and that place in ten days, left Birmingham about an hour after Mrs. Catherine had quitted that town; and as she sat weeping on a hillside, and plunged in bitter meditation, the lumbering, jingling vehicle overtook her. The coachman was marching by the side of his horses, and encouraging them to maintain their pace of two miles an hour; the passengers had some of them left the vehicle, in order to walk up the hill; and the carriage had arrived at the top of it, and, meditating a brisk trot down the declivity, waited there until the lagging passengers should arrive: when Jehu, casting a good-natured glance upon Mrs. Catherine, asked the pretty maid whence she was come, and whether she would like a ride in his carriage. To the latter of which questions Mrs. Catherine replied truly yes; to the former, her answer was that she had come from Stratford; whereas, as we very well know, she had lately quitted Birmingham.

"Hast thee seen a woman pass this way, on a black horse, with a large bag of goold over the saddle?" said Jehu, preparing to mount upon the roof of his coach.

"No, indeed," said Mrs. Cat.

"Nor a trooper on another horse after her—no? Well, there be a mortal row down Birmingham way about sich a one. She have killed, they say, nine gentlemen at supper, and have strangled a German prince in bed. She have robbed him of twenty thousand guineas, and have rode away on a black horse."

"That can't be I," said Mrs. Cat, naively, "for I have but three shillings and a groat."

"No, it can't be thee, truly, for where's your bag of goold? and, besides, thee hast got too pretty a face to do such wicked things as to kill nine gentlemen and strangle a German prince."

"Law, coachman," said Mrs. Cat, blushing archly— "Law, coachman, DO you think so?" The girl would have been pleased with a compliment even on her way to be hanged; and the parley ended by Mrs. Catherine stepping into the carriage, where there was room for eight people at least, and where two or three individuals had already taken their places. For these Mrs. Catherine had in the first place to make a story, which she did; and a very glib one for a person of her years and education. Being asked whither she was bound, and how she came to be alone of a morning sitting by a road-side, she invented a neat history suitable to the occasion, which elicited much interest from her fellow-passengers: one in particular, a young man, who had caught a glimpse of her face under her hood, was very tender in his attentions to her.

But whether it was that she had been too much fatigued by the occurrences of the past day and sleepless night, or whether the little laudanum which she had drunk a few hours previously now began to act upon her, certain it is that Mrs. Cat now suddenly grew sick, feverish, and extraordinarily sleepy; and in this state she continued for many hours, to the pity of all her fellow-travellers. At length the "carryvan" reached the inn, where horses and passengers were accustomed to rest for a few hours, and to dine; and Mrs. Catherine was somewhat awakened by the stir of the passengers, and the friendly voice of the inn-servant welcoming them to dinner. The gentleman who had been smitten by her beauty now urged her very politely to descend; which, taking the protection of his arm, she accordingly did.

He made some very gallant speeches to her as she stepped out; and she must have been very much occupied by them, or wrapt up in her own thoughts, or stupefied by sleep, fever, and opium, for she did not take any heed of the place into which she was going: which, had she done, she would probably have preferred remaining in the coach, dinnerless and ill. Indeed, the inn into which she was about to make her entrance was no other than the "Bugle," from which she set forth at the commencement of this history; and which then, as now, was kept by her relative, the thrifty Mrs. Score. That good landlady, seeing a lady, in a smart hood and cloak, leaning, as if faint, upon the arm of a gentleman of good appearance, concluded them to be man and wife, and folks of quality too; and with much discrimination, as well as sympathy, led them through the public kitchen to her own private parlour, or bar, where she handed the lady an armchair, and asked what she would like to drink. By this time, and indeed at the very moment she heard her aunt's voice, Mrs. Catherine was aware of her situation; and when her companion retired, and the landlady, with much officiousness, insisted on removing her hood, she was quite prepared for the screech of surprise which Mrs. Score gave on dropping it, exclaiming, "Why, law bless us, it's our Catherine!"

"I'm very ill, and tired, aunt," said Cat; "and would give the world for a few hours' sleep."

"A few hours and welcome, my love, and a sack-posset too. You do look sadly tired and poorly, sure enough. Ah, Cat, Cat! you great ladies are sad rakes, I do believe. I wager now, that with all your balls, and carriages, and fine clothes, you are neither so happy nor so well as when you lived with your poor old aunt, who used to love you so." And with these gentle words, and an embrace or two, which Mrs. Catherine wondered at, and permitted, she was conducted to that very bed which the Count had occupied a year previously, and undressed, and laid in it, and affectionately tucked up by her aunt, who marvelled at the fineness of her clothes, as she removed them piece by piece; and when she saw that in Mrs. Catherine's pocket there was only the sum of three and fourpence, said, archly, "There was no need of money, for the Captain took care of that."

Mrs. Cat did not undeceive her; and deceived Mrs. Score certainly was,—for she imagined the well-dressed gentleman who led Cat from the carriage was no other than the Count; and, as she had heard, from time to time, exaggerated reports of the splendour of the establishment which he kept up, she was induced to look upon her niece with the very highest respect, and to treat her as if she were a fine lady. "And so she IS a fine lady," Mrs. Score had said months ago, when some of these flattering stories reached her, and she had overcome her first fury at Catherine's elopement. "The girl was very cruel to leave me; but we must recollect that she is as good as married to a nobleman, and must all forget and forgive, you know."

This speech had been made to Doctor Dobbs, who was in the habit of taking a pipe and a tankard at the "Bugle," and it had been roundly reprobated by the worthy divine; who told Mrs. Score, that the crime of Catherine was only the more heinous, if it had been committed from interested motives; and protested that, were she a princess, he would never speak to her again. Mrs. Score thought and pronounced the Doctor's opinion to be very bigoted; indeed, she was one of those persons who have a marvellous respect for prosperity, and a corresponding scorn for ill-fortune. When, therefore, she returned to the public room, she went graciously to the gentleman who had led Mrs. Catherine from the carriage, and with a knowing curtsey welcomed him to the "Bugle;" told him that his lady would not come to dinner, but bade her say, with her best love to his Lordship, that the ride had fatigued her, and that she would lie in bed for an hour or two.

This speech was received with much wonder by his Lordship; who was, indeed, no other than a Liverpool tailor going to London to learn fashions; but he only smiled, and did not undeceive the landlady, who herself went off, smilingly, to bustle about dinner.

The two or three hours allotted to that meal by the liberal coachmasters of those days passed away, and Mr. Coachman, declaring that his horses were now rested enough, and that they had twelve miles to ride, put the steeds to, and summoned the passengers. Mrs. Score, who had seen with much satisfaction that her niece was really ill, and her fever more violent, and hoped to have her for many days an inmate in her house, now came forward, and casting upon the Liverpool tailor a look of profound but respectful melancholy, said, "My Lord (for I recollect your Lordship quite well), the lady upstairs is so ill, that it would be a sin to move her: had I not better tell coachman to take down your Lordship's trunks, and the lady's, and make you a bed in the next room?"

Very much to her surprise, this proposition was received with a roar of laughter. "Madam," said the person addressed, "I'm not a lord, but a tailor and draper; and as for that young woman, before to-day I never set eyes on her."

"WHAT!" screamed out Mrs. Score. "Are not you the Count? Do you mean to say that you a'n't Cat's—? DO you mean to say that you didn't order her bed, and that you won't pay this here little bill?" And with this she produced a document, by which the Count's lady was made her debtor in a sum of half-a-guinea.

These passionate words excited more and more laughter. "Pay it, my Lord," said the coachman; "and then come along, for time presses." "Our respects to her Ladyship," said one passenger. "Tell her my

Lord can't wait," said another; and with much merriment one and all quitted the hotel, entered the coach, and rattled off.

Dumb—pale with terror and rage—bill in hand, Mrs. Score had followed the company; but when the coach disappeared, her senses returned. Back she flew into the inn, overturning the ostler, not deigning to answer Doctor Dobbs (who, from behind soft tobacco-fumes, mildly asked the reason of her disturbance), and, bounding upstairs like a fury, she rushed into the room where Catherine lay.

"Well, madam!" said she, in her highest key, "do you mean that you have come into this here house to swindle me? Do you dare for to come with your airs here, and call yourself a nobleman's lady, and sleep in the best bed, when you're no better nor a common tramper? I'll thank you, ma'am, to get out, ma'am. I'll have no sick paupers in this house, ma'am. You know your way to the workhouse, ma'am, and there I'll trouble you for to go." And here Mrs. Score proceeded quickly to pull off the bedclothes; and poor Cat arose, shivering with fright and fever.

She had no spirit to answer, as she would have done the day before, when an oath from any human being would have brought half-a-dozen from her in return; or a knife, or a plate, or a leg of mutton, if such had been to her hand. She had no spirit left for such repartees; but in reply to the above words of Mrs. Score, and a great many more of the same kind—which are not necessary for our history, but which that lady uttered with inconceivable shrillness and volubility, the poor wench could say little,—only sob and shiver, and gather up the clothes again, crying, "Oh, aunt, don't speak unkind to me! I'm very unhappy, and very ill!"

"Ill, you strumpet! ill, be hanged! Ill is as ill does; and if you are ill, it's only what you merit. Get out! dress yourself—tramp! Get to the workhouse, and don't come to cheat me any more! Dress yourself—do you hear? Satin petticoat forsooth, and lace to her smock!"

Poor, wretched, chattering, burning, shivering Catherine huddled on her clothes as well she might: she seemed hardly to know or see what she was doing, and did not reply a single word to the many that the landlady let fall. Cat tottered down the narrow stairs, and through the kitchen, and to the door; which she caught hold of, and paused awhile, and looked into Mrs. Score's face, as for one more chance. "Get out, you nasty trull!" said that lady, sternly, with arms akimbo; and poor Catherine, with a most piteous scream and outgush of tears, let go of the door-post and staggered away into the road.

"Why, no—yes—no—it is poor Catherine Hall, as I live!" said somebody, starting up, shoving aside Mrs. Score very rudely, and running into the road, wig off and pipe in hand. It was honest Doctor Dobbs; and the result of his interview with Mrs. Cat was, that he gave up for ever smoking his pipe at the "Bugle;" and that she lay sick of a fever for some weeks in his house.

Over this part of Mrs. Cat's history we shall be as brief as possible; for, to tell the truth, nothing immoral occurred during her whole stay at the good Doctor's house; and we are not going to insult the reader by offering him silly pictures of piety, cheerfulness, good sense, and simplicity; which are milk-and-water virtues after all, and have no relish with them like a good strong vice, highly peppered. Well, to be short: Doctor Dobbs, though a profound theologian, was a very simple gentleman; and before Mrs. Cat had been a month in the house, he had learned to look upon her as one of the most injured and repentant characters in the world; and had, with Mrs. Dobbs, resolved many plans for the future welfare of the young Magdalen. "She was but sixteen, my love, recollect," said the Doctor; "she was carried off, not by her own wish either. The Count swore he would marry her; and, though she did not leave him until that monster tried to poison her, yet think what a fine Christian spirit the poor girl has shown! she forgives him as heartily—more heartily, I am sure, than I do Mrs. Score for turning her adrift in that wicked way." The reader will perceive some difference in the Doctor's statement and ours, which we assure him is the true one; but the fact is, the honest rector had had his tale from Mrs. Cat, and it was not in his nature to doubt, if she had told him a history ten times more wonderful.

The reverend gentleman and his wife then laid their heads together; and, recollecting something of John Hayes's former attachment to Mrs. Cat, thought that it might be advantageously renewed, should Hayes be still constant. Having very adroitly sounded Catherine (so adroitly, indeed, as to ask her "whether she would like to marry John Hayes?"), that young woman had replied, "No. She had loved John Hayes—he had been her early, only love; but she was fallen now, and not good enough for him." And this made the Dobbs family admire her more and more, and cast about for means to bring the marriage to pass.

Hayes was away from the village when Mrs. Cat had arrived there; but he did not fail to hear of her illness, and how her aunt had deserted her, and the good Doctor taken her in. The worthy Doctor himself met Mr. Hayes on the green; and, telling him that some repairs were wanting in his kitchen begged him to step in and examine them. Hayes first said no, plump, and then no, gently; and then pished, and then psha'd; and then, trembling very much, went in: and there sat Mrs. Catherine, trembling very much too.

What passed between them? If your Ladyship is anxious to know, think of that morning when Sir John himself popped the question. Could there be anything more stupid than the conversation which took place? Such stuff is not worth repeating: no, not when uttered by people in the very genteelest of company; as for the amorous dialogue of a carpenter and an ex-barmaid, it is worse still. Suffice it to say, that Mr. Hayes, who had had a year to recover from his passion, and had, to all appearances, quelled it, was over head and ears again the very moment he saw Mrs. Cat, and had all his work to do again.

Whether the Doctor knew what was going on, I can't say; but this matter is certain, that every evening Hayes was now in the rectory kitchen, or else walking abroad with Mrs. Catherine: and whether she ran away with him, or he with her, I shall not make it my business to inquire; but certainly at the end of three months (which must be crowded up into this one little sentence), another elopement took place in the village. "I should have prevented it, certainly," said Doctor Dobbs—whereat his wife smiled; "but the young people kept the matter a secret from me." And so he would, had he known it; but though Mrs. Dobbs had made several attempts to acquaint him with the precise hour and method of the intended elopement, he peremptorily ordered her to hold her tongue. The fact is, that the matter had been discussed by the rector's lady many times. "Young Hayes," would she say "has a pretty little fortune and trade of his own; he is an only son, and may marry as he likes; and, though not specially handsome, generous, or amiable, has an undeniable love for Cat (who, you know, must not be particular), and the sooner she marries him, I think, the better. They can't be married at our church you know, and—" "Well," said the Doctor, "if they are married elsewhere, I can't help it, and know nothing about it, look you." And upon this hint the elopement took place: which, indeed, was peaceably performed early one Sunday morning about a month after; Mrs. Hall getting behind Mr. Hayes on a pillion, and all the children of the parsonage giggling behind the window-blinds to see the pair go off.

During this month Mr. Hayes had caused the banns to be published at the town of Worcester; judging rightly that in a great town they would cause no such remark as in a solitary village, and thither he conducted his lady. O ill-starred John Hayes! whither do the dark Fates lead you? O foolish Doctor

Dobbs, to forget that young people ought to honour their parents, and to yield to silly Mrs. Dobbs's ardent propensity for making matches!

The London Gazette of the 1st April, 1706, contains a proclamation by the Queen for putting into execution an Act of Parliament for the encouragement and increase of seamen, and for the better and speedier manning of Her Majesty's fleet, which authorises all justices to issue warrants to constables, petty constables, headboroughs, and tything-men, to enter and, if need be, to break open the doors of any houses where they shall believe deserting seamen to be; and for the further increase and encouragement of the navy, to take able-bodied landsmen when seamen fail. This Act, which occupies four columns of the Gazette, and another of similar length and meaning for pressing men into the army, need not be quoted at length here; but caused a mighty stir throughout the kingdom at the time when it was in force.

As one has seen or heard, after the march of a great army, a number of rogues and loose characters bring up the rear; in like manner, at the tail of a great measure of State, follow many roguish personal interests, which are protected by the main body. The great measure of Reform, for instance, carried along with it much private jobbing and swindling—as could be shown were we not inclined to deal mildly with the Whigs; and this Enlistment Act, which, in order to maintain the British glories in Flanders, dealt most cruelly with the British people in England (it is not the first time that a man has been pinched at home to make a fine appearance abroad), created a great company of rascals and informers throughout the land, who lived upon it; or upon extortion from those who were subject to it, or not being subject to it were frightened into the belief that they were.

When Mr. Hayes and his lady had gone through the marriage ceremony at Worcester, the former, concluding that at such a place lodging and food might be procured at a cheaper rate, looked about carefully for the meanest public-house in the town, where he might deposit his bride.

In the kitchen of this inn, a party of men were drinking; and, as Mrs. Hayes declined, with a proper sense of her superiority, to eat in company with such low fellows, the landlady showed her and her husband to an inner apartment, where they might be served in private.

The kitchen party seemed, indeed, not such as a lady would choose to join. There was one huge lanky fellow, that looked like a soldier, and had a halberd; another was habited in a sailor's costume, with a fascinating patch over one eye; and a third, who seemed the leader of the gang, was a stout man in a sailor's frock and a horseman's jack-boots, whom one might fancy, if he were anything, to be a horse-marine.

Of one of these worthies, Mrs. Hayes thought she knew the figure and voice; and she found her conjectures were true, when, all of sudden, three people, without "With your leave," or "By your leave," burst into the room, into which she and her spouse had retired. At their head was no other than her old friend, Mr. Peter Brock; he had his sword drawn, and his finger to his lips, enjoining silence, as it were, to Mrs. Catherine. He with the patch on his eye seized incontinently on Mr. Hayes; the tall man with the halberd kept the door; two or three heroes supported the one-eyed man; who, with a loud voice, exclaimed, "Down with your arms—no resistance! you are my prisoner, in the Queen's name!"

And here, at this lock, we shall leave the whole company until the next chapter; which may possibly explain what they were.

CHAPTER V

CONTAINS MR. BROCK'S AUTOBIOGRAPHY, AND OTHER MATTERS

"You don't sure believe these men?" said Mrs. Hayes, as soon as the first alarm caused by the irruption of Mr. Brock and his companions had subsided. "These are no magistrate's men: it is but a trick to rob you of your money, John."

"I will never give up a farthing of it!" screamed Hayes.

"Yonder fellow," continued Mrs. Catherine, "I know, for all his drawn sword and fierce looks; his name is—"

"Wood, madam, at your service!" said Mr. Brock. "I am follower to Mr. Justice Gobble, of this town: a'n't I, Tim?" said Mr. Brock to the tall halberdman who was keeping the door.

"Yes indeed," said Tim, archly; "we're all followers of his honour Justice Gobble."

"Certainly!" said the one-eyed man.

"Of course!" cried the man in the nightcap.

"I suppose, madam, you're satisfied NOW?" continued Mr. Brock, alias Wood. "You can't deny the testimony of gentlemen like these; and our commission is to apprehend all able-bodied male persons who can give no good account of themselves, and enrol them in the service of Her Majesty. Look at this Mr. Hayes" (who stood trembling in his shoes). "Can there be a bolder, properer, straighter gentleman? We'll have him for a grenadier before the day's over!"

"Take heart, John—don't be frightened. Psha! I tell you I know the man" cried out Mrs. Hayes: "he is only here to extort money."

"Oh, for that matter, I DO think I recollect the lady. Let me see; where was it? At Birmingham, I think,—ay, at Birmingham,—about the time when they tried to murder Count Gal—"

"Oh, sir!" here cried Madam Hayes, dropping her voice at once from a tone of scorn to one of gentlest entreaty, "what is it you want with my husband? I know not, indeed, if ever I saw you before. For what do you seize him? How much will you take to release him, and let us go? Name the sum; he is rich, and—"

"RICH, Catherine!" cried Hayes. "Rich!—O heavens! Sir, I have nothing but my hands to support me: I am a poor carpenter, sir, working under my father!"

"He can give twenty guineas to be free; I know he can!" said Mrs. Cat.

"I have but a guinea to carry me home," sighed out Hayes.

"But you have twenty at home, John," said his wife. "Give these brave gentlemen a writing to your mother, and she will pay; and you will let us free then, gentlemen—won't you?"

"When the money's paid, yes," said the leader, Mr. Brock.

"Oh, in course," echoed the tall man with the halberd. "What's a thrifling detintion, my dear?" continued he, addressing Hayes. "We'll amuse you in your absence, and drink to the health of your pretty wife here."

This promise, to do the halberdier justice, he fulfilled. He called upon the landlady to produce the desired liquor; and when Mr. Hayes flung himself at that lady's feet, demanding succour from her, and asking whether there was no law in the land—

"There's no law at the 'Three Rooks' except THIS!" said Mr. Brock in reply, holding up a horse-pistol. To which the hostess, grinning, assented, and silently went her way.

After some further solicitations, John Hayes drew out the necessary letter to his father, stating that he was pressed, and would not be set free under a sum of twenty guineas; and that it would be of no use to detain the bearer of the letter, inasmuch as the gentlemen who had possession of him vowed that they would murder him should any harm befall their comrade. As a further proof of the authenticity of the letter, a token was added: a ring that Hayes wore, and that his mother had given him.

The missives were, after some consultation, entrusted to the care of the tall halberdier, who seemed to rank as second in command of the forces that marched under Corporal Brock. This gentleman was called indifferently Ensign, Mr., or even Captain Macshane; his intimates occasionally in sport called him Nosey, from the prominence of that feature in his countenance; or Spindleshins, for the very reason which brought on the first Edward a similar nickname. Mr. Macshane then quitted Worcester, mounted on Hayes's horse; leaving all parties at the "Three Rooks" not a little anxious for his return.

This was not to be expected until the next morning; and a weary nuit de noces did Mr. Hayes pass. Dinner was served, and, according to promise, Mr. Brock and his two friends enjoyed the meal along with the bride and bridegroom. Punch followed, and this was taken in company; then came supper. Mr. Brock alone partook of this, the other two gentlemen preferring the society of their pipes and the landlady in the kitchen.

"It is a sorry entertainment, I confess," said the ex-corporal, "and a dismal way for a gentleman to spend his bridal night; but somebody must stay with you, my dears: for who knows but you might take a fancy to scream out of window, and then there would be murder, and the deuce and all to pay. One of us must stay, and my friends love a pipe, so you must put up with my company until they can relieve guard."

The reader will not, of course, expect that three people who were to pass the night, however unwillingly, together in an inn-room, should sit there dumb and moody, and without any personal communication; on the contrary, Mr. Brock, as an old soldier, entertained his prisoners with the utmost courtesy, and did all that lay in his power, by the help of liquor and conversation, to render their durance tolerable. On the bridegroom his attentions were a good deal thrown away: Mr. Hayes consented to drink copiously, but could not be made to talk much; and, in fact, the fright of the seizure, the fate hanging over him should his parents refuse a ransom, and the tremendous outlay of money which would take place should they accede to it, weighed altogether on his mind so much as utterly to unman it.

As for Mrs. Cat, I don't think she was at all sorry in her heart to see the old Corporal: for he had been a friend of old times—dear times to her; she had had from him, too, and felt for him, not a little kindness; and there was really a very tender, innocent friendship subsisting between this pair of rascals, who relished much a night's conversation together.

The Corporal, after treating his prisoners to punch in great quantities, proposed the amusement of cards: over which Mr. Hayes had not been occupied more than an hour, when he found himself so excessively sleepy as to be persuaded to fling himself down on the bed dressed as he was, and there to snore away until morning.

Mrs. Catherine had no inclination for sleep; and the Corporal, equally wakeful, plied incessantly the bottle, and held with her a great deal of conversation. The sleep, which was equivalent to the absence, of John Hayes took all restraint from their talk. She explained to Brock the circumstances of her marriage, which we have already described; they wondered at the chance which had brought them together at the "Three Rooks;" nor did Brock at all hesitate to tell her at once that his calling was quite illegal, and that his intention was simply to extort money. The worthy Corporal had not the slightest shame regarding his own profession, and cut many jokes with Mrs. Cat about her late one; her attempt to murder the Count, and her future prospects as a wife.

And here, having brought him upon the scene again, we may as well shortly narrate some of the principal circumstances which befell him after his sudden departure from Birmingham; and which he narrated with much candour to Mrs. Catherine.

He rode the Captain's horse to Oxford (having exchanged his military dress for a civil costume on the road), and at Oxford he disposed of "George of Denmark," a great bargain, to one of the heads of colleges. As soon as Mr. Brock, who took on himself the style and title of Captain Wood, had sufficiently examined the curiosities of the University, he proceeded at once to the capital: the only place for a gentleman of his fortune and figure.

Here he read, with a great deal of philosophical indifference, in the Daily Post, the Courant, the Observator, the Gazette, and the chief journals of those days, which he made a point of examining at "Button's" and "Will's," an accurate description of his person, his clothes, and the horse he rode, and a promise of fifty guineas' reward to any person who would give an account of him (so that he might be captured) to Captain Count Galgenstein at Birmingham, to Mr. Murfey at the "Golden Ball" in the Savoy, or Mr. Bates at the "Blew Anchor in Pickadilly." But Captain Wood, in an enormous full-bottomed periwig that cost him sixty pounds,[*] with high red heels to his shoes, a silver sword, and a gold snuff-box, and a large wound (obtained, he said, at the siege of Barcelona), which disfigured much of his countenance, and caused him to cover one eye, was in small danger, he thought, of being mistaken for Corporal Brock, the deserter of Cutts's; and strutted along the Mall with as grave an air as the very best nobleman who appeared there. He was generally, indeed, voted to be very good company; and as his expenses were unlimited ("A few convent candlesticks," my dear, he used to whisper, "melt into a vast number of doubloons"), he commanded as good society as he chose to ask for: and it was speedily known as a fact throughout town, that Captain Wood, who had served under His Majesty Charles III. of Spain, had carried off the diamond petticoat of Our Lady of Compostella, and lived upon the proceeds of the fraud. People were good Protestants in those days, and many a one longed to have been his partner in the pious plunder.

All surmises concerning his wealth, Captain Wood, with much discretion, encouraged. He contradicted no report, but was quite ready to confirm all; and when two different rumours were positively put to him, he used only to laugh, and say, "My dear sir, I don't make the stories; but I'm not called upon to deny them; and I give you fair warning, that I shall assent to every one of them; so you may believe them or not, as you please." And so he had the reputation of being a gentleman, not only wealthy, but discreet. In truth, it was almost a pity that worthy Brock had not been a gentleman born; in which case, doubtless, he would have lived and died as became his station; for he spent his money like a gentleman, he loved women like a gentleman, he would fight like a gentleman, he gambled and got drunk like a gentleman. What did he want else? Only a matter of six descents, a little money, and an estate, to render him the equal of St. John or Harley. "Ah, those were merry days!" would Mr. Brock say,—for he loved, in a good old age, to recount the story of his London fashionable campaign;—"and when I think how near I was to become a great man, and to die perhaps a general, I can't but marvel at the wicked obstinacy of my ill-luck."

"I will tell you what I did, my dear: I had lodgings in Piccadilly, as if I were a lord; I had two large periwigs, and three suits of laced clothes; I kept a little black dressed out like a Turk; I walked daily in the Mall; I dined at the politest ordinary in Covent Garden; I frequented the best of coffee-houses, and knew all the pretty fellows of the town; I cracked a bottle with Mr. Addison, and lent many a piece to Dick Steele (a sad debauched rogue, my dear); and, above all, I'll tell you what I did—the noblest stroke that sure ever a gentleman performed in my situation.

"One day, going into 'Will's,' I saw a crowd of gentlemen gathered together, and heard one of them say, 'Captain Wood! I don't know the man; but there was a Captain Wood in Southwell's regiment.' Egad, it was my Lord Peterborough himself who was talking about me. So, putting off my hat, I made a most gracious conge to my Lord, and said I knew HIM, and rode behind him at Barcelona on our entry into that town.

"'No doubt you did, Captain Wood,' says my Lord, taking my hand; 'and no doubt you know me: for many more know Tom Fool, than Tom Fool knows.' And with this, at which all of us laughed, my Lord called for a bottle, and he and I sat down and drank it together.

"Well, he was in disgrace, as you know, but he grew mighty fond of me, and—would you believe it?—nothing would satisfy him but presenting me at Court! Yes, to Her Sacred Majesty the Queen, and my Lady Marlborough, who was in high feather. Ay, truly, the sentinels on duty used to salute me as if I were Corporal John himself! I was on the high road to fortune. Charley Mordaunt used to call me Jack, and drink canary at my chambers; I used to make one at my Lord Treasurer's levee; I had even got Mr. Army-Secretary Walpole to take a hundred guineas as a compliment: and he had promised me a majority: when bad luck turned, and all my fine hopes were overthrown in a twinkling.

"You see, my dear, that after we had left that gaby, Galgenstein,—ha, ha—with a gag in his mouth, and twopence-halfpenny in his pocket, the honest Count was in the sorriest plight in the world; owing money here and there to tradesmen, a cool thousand to the Warwickshire Squire: and all this on eighty pounds a year! Well, for a little time the tradesmen held their hands; while the jolly Count moved heaven and earth to catch hold of his dear Corporal and his dear money-bags over again, and placarded every town from London to Liverpool with descriptions of my pretty person. The bird was flown, however,—the money clean gone,—and when there was no hope of regaining it, what did the creditors do but clap my gay gentleman into Shrewsbury gaol: where I wish he had rotted, for my part.

"But no such luck for honest Peter Brock, or Captain Wood, as he was in those days. One blessed Monday I went to wait on Mr. Secretary, and he squeezed my hand and whispered to me that I was to be Major of a regiment in Virginia—the very thing: for you see, my dear, I didn't care about joining my Lord Duke in Flanders; being pretty well known to the army there. The Secretary squeezed my hand (it had a fifty-pound bill in it) and wished me joy, and called me Major, and bowed me out of his closet into the ante-room; and, as gay as may be, I went off to the 'Tilt-yard Coffee-house' in Whitehall, which is much frequented by gentlemen of our profession, where I bragged not a little of my good luck.

"Amongst the company were several of my acquaintance, and amongst them a gentleman I did not much care to see, look you! I saw a uniform that I knew—red and yellow facings—Cutts's, my dear; and the wearer of this was no other than his Excellency Gustavus Adolphus Maximilian, whom we all know of!

"He stared me full in the face, right into my eye (t'other one was patched, you know), and after standing stock-still with his mouth open, gave a step back, and then a step forward, and then screeched out, 'It's Brock!'

"'I beg your pardon, sir,' says I; 'did you speak to me?'

"'I'll SWEAR it's Brock,' cries Gal, as soon as he hears my voice, and laid hold of my cuff (a pretty bit of Mechlin as ever you saw, by the way).

"'Sirrah!' says I, drawing it back, and giving my Lord a little touch of the fist (just at the last button of the waistcoat, my dear,—a rare place if you wish to prevent a man from speaking too much: it sent him reeling to the other end of the room). 'Ruffian!' says I. 'Dog!' says I. 'Insolent puppy and coxcomb! what do you mean by laying your hand on me?'

"'Faith, Major, you giv him his BILLYFUL,' roared out a long Irish unattached ensign, that I had treated with many a glass of Nantz at the tavern. And so, indeed, I had; for the wretch could not speak for some minutes, and all the officers stood laughing at him, as he writhed and wriggled hideously.

"'Gentlemen, this is a monstrous scandal,' says one officer. 'Men of rank and honour at fists like a parcel of carters!'

"'Men of honour!' says the Count, who had fetched up his breath by this time. (I made for the door, but Macshane held me and said, 'Major, you are not going to shirk him, sure?' Whereupon I gripped his hand and vowed I would have the dog's life.)

"'Men of honour!' says the Count. 'I tell you the man is a deserter, a thief, and a swindler! He was my corporal, and ran away with a thou—'

"'Dog, you lie!' I roared out, and made another cut at him with my cane; but the gentlemen rushed between us.

"'O bluthanowns!' says honest Macshane, 'the lying scounthrel this fellow is! Gentlemen, I swear be me honour that Captain Wood was wounded at Barcelona; and that I saw him there; and that he and I ran away together at the battle of Almanza, and bad luck to us.'

"You see, my dear, that these Irish have the strongest imaginations in the world; and that I had actually persuaded poor Mac that he and I were friends in Spain. Everybody knew Mac, who was a character in his way, and believed him.

"'Strike a gentleman,' says I. 'I'll have your blood, I will.'

"'This instant,' says the Count, who was boiling with fury; 'and where you like.'

"'Montague House,' says I. 'Good,' says he. And off we went. In good time too, for the constables came in at the thought of such a disturbance, and wanted to take us in charge.

"But the gentlemen present, being military men, would not hear of this. Out came Mac's rapier, and that of half-a-dozen others; and the constables were then told to do their duty if they liked, or to take a crown-piece, and leave us to ourselves. Off they went; and presently, in a couple of coaches, the Count and his friends, I and mine, drove off to the fields behind Montague House. Oh that vile coffee-house! why did I enter it?

"We came to the ground. Honest Macshane was my second, and much disappointed because the second on the other side would not make a fight of it, and exchange a few passes with him; but he was an old major, a cool old hand, as brave as steel, and no fool. Well, the swords are measured, Galgenstein strips off his doublet, and I my handsome cut-velvet in like fashion. Galgenstein flings off his hat, and I handed mine over—the lace on it cost me twenty pounds. I longed to be at him, for—curse him!—I hate him, and know that he has no chance with me at sword's-play.

"'You'll not fight in that periwig, sure?' says Macshane. 'Of course not,' says I, and took it off.

"May all barbers be roasted in flames; may all periwigs, bobwigs, scratchwigs, and Ramillies cocks, frizzle in purgatory from this day forth to the end of time! Mine was the ruin of me: what might I not have been now but for that wig!

"I gave it over to Ensign Macshane, and with it went what I had quite forgotten, the large patch which I wore over one eye, which popped out fierce, staring, and lively as was ever any eye in the world.

"'Come on!' says I, and made a lunge at my Count; but he sprang back (the dog was as active as a hare, and knew, from old times, that I was his master with the small-sword), and his second, wondering, struck up my blade.

"'I will not fight that man,' says he, looking mighty pale. 'I swear upon my honour that his name is Peter Brock: he was for two years my corporal, and deserted, running away with a thousand pounds of my moneys. Look at the fellow! What is the matter with his eye? why did he wear a patch over it? But stop!' says he. 'I have more proof. Hand me my pocket-book.' And from it, sure enough, he produced the infernal proclamation announcing my desertion! 'See if the fellow has a scar across his left ear' (and I can't say, my dear, but what I have: it was done by a cursed Dutchman at the Boyne). 'Tell me if he has not got C.R. in blue upon his right arm' (and there it is sure enough). 'Yonder swaggering Irishman may be his accomplice for what I know; but I will have no dealings with Mr. Brock, save with a constable for a second.'

"'This is an odd story, Captain Wood,' said the old Major who acted for the Count.

"'A scounthrelly falsehood regarding me and my friend!' shouted out Mr. Macshane; 'and the Count shall answer for it.'

"'Stop, stop!' says the Major. 'Captain Wood is too gallant a gentleman, I am sure, not to satisfy the Count; and will show us that he has no such mark on his arm as only private soldiers put there.'

"'Captain Wood,' says I, 'will do no such thing, Major. I'll fight that scoundrel Galgenstein, or you, or any of you, like a man of honour; but I won't submit to be searched like a thief!'

"'No, in coorse,' said Macshane.

"'I must take my man off the ground,' says the Major.

"'Well, take him, sir,' says I, in a rage; 'and just let me have the pleasure of telling him that he's a coward and a liar; and that my lodgings are in Piccadilly, where, if ever he finds courage to meet me, he may hear of me!'

"'Faugh! I shpit on ye all,' cries my gallant ally Macshane. And sure enough he kept his word, or all but—suiting the action to it at any rate.

"And so we gathered up our clothes, and went back in our separate coaches, and no blood spilt.

"'And is it thrue now,' said Mr. Macshane, when we were alone—'is it thrue now, all these divvles have been saying?' 'Ensign,' says I, 'you're a man of the world?'

"'"Deed and I am, and insign these twenty-two years.'

"'Perhaps you'd like a few pieces?' says I.

"'Faith and I should; for to tell you the secred thrut, I've not tasted mate these four days.'

"'Well then, Ensign, it IS true,' says I; 'and as for meat, you shall have some at the first cook-shop.' I bade the coach stop until he bought a plateful, which he ate in the carriage, for my time was precious. I just told him the whole story: at which he laughed, and swore that it was the best piece of GENERALSHIP he ever heard on. When his belly was full, I took out a couple of guineas and gave them to him. Mr. Macshane began to cry at this, and kissed me, and swore he never would desert me: as, indeed, my dear, I don't think he will; for we have been the best of friends ever since, and he's the only man I ever could trust, I think.

"I don't know what put it into my head, but I had a scent of some mischief in the wind; so stopped the coach a little before I got home, and, turning into a tavern, begged Macshane to go before me to my lodging, and see if the coast was clear: which he did; and came back to me as pale as death, saying that the house was full of constables. The cursed quarrel at the Tilt-yard had, I suppose, set the beaks upon me; and a pretty sweep they made of it. Ah, my dear! five hundred pounds in money, five suits of laced clothes, three periwigs, besides laced shirts, swords, canes, and snuff-boxes; and all to go back to that scoundrel Count.

"It was all over with me, I saw—no more being a gentleman for me; and if I remained to be caught, only a choice between Tyburn and a file of grenadiers. My love, under such circumstances, a gentleman can't be particular, and must be prompt; the livery-stable was hard by where I used to hire my coach to go to Court,—ha! ha!—and was known as a man of substance. Thither I went immediately. 'Mr. Warmmash,' says I, 'my gallant friend here and I have a mind for a ride and a supper at Twickenham, so you must lend us a pair of your best horses.' Which he did in a twinkling, and off we rode.

"We did not go into the Park, but turned off and cantered smartly up towards Kilburn; and, when we got into the country, galloped as if the devil were at our heels. Bless you, my love, it was all done in a minute: and the Ensign and I found ourselves regular knights of the road, before we knew where we were almost. Only think of our finding you and your new husband at the 'Three Rooks'! There's not a greater fence than the landlady in all the country. It was she that put us on seizing your husband, and introduced us to the other two gentlemen, whose names I don't know any more than the dead."

"And what became of the horses?" said Mrs. Catherine to Mr. Brock, when his tale was finished.

"Rips, madam," said he; "mere rips. We sold them at Stourbridge fair, and got but thirteen guineas for the two."

"And—and—the Count, Max; where is he, Brock?" sighed she.

"Whew!" whistled Mr. Brock. "What, hankering after him still? My dear, he is off to Flanders with his regiment; and, I make no doubt, there have been twenty Countesses of Galgenstein since your time."

"I don't believe any such thing, sir," said Mrs. Catherine, starting up very angrily.

"If you did, I suppose you'd laudanum him; wouldn't you?"

"Leave the room, fellow," said the lady. But she recollected herself speedily again; and, clasping her hands, and looking very wretched at Brock, at the ceiling, at the floor, at her husband (from whom she violently turned away her head), she began to cry piteously: to which tears the Corporal set up a gentle accompaniment of whistling, as they trickled one after another down her nose.

I don't think they were tears of repentance; but of regret for the time when she had her first love, and her fine clothes, and her white hat and blue feather. Of the two, the Corporal's whistle was much more innocent than the girl's sobbing: he was a rogue; but a good-natured old fellow when his humour was not crossed. Surely our novel-writers make a great mistake in divesting their rascals of all gentle human qualities: they have such—and the only sad point to think of is, in all private concerns of life, abstract feelings, and dealings with friends, and so on, how dreadfully like a rascal is to an honest man. The man who murdered the Italian boy, set him first to play with his children whom he loved, and who doubtless deplored his loss.

CHAPTER VI

If we had not been obliged to follow history in all respects, it is probable that we should have left out the last adventure of Mrs. Catherine and her husband, at the inn at Worcester, altogether; for, in truth, very little came of it, and it is not very romantic or striking. But we are bound to stick closely, above all, by THE TRUTH—the truth, though it be not particularly pleasant to read of or to tell. As anybody may read in the "Newgate Calendar," Mr. and Mrs. Hayes were taken at an inn at Worcester; were confined there; were swindled by persons who pretended to impress the bridegroom for military service. What is one to do after that? Had we been writing novels instead of authentic histories, we might have carried them anywhere else we chose: and we had a great mind to make Hayes philosophising with Bolingbroke, like a certain Devereux; and Mrs. Catherine maitresse en titre to Mr. Alexander Pope, Doctor Sacheverel, Sir John Reade the oculist, Dean Swift, or Marshal Tallard; as the very commonest romancer would under such circumstances. But alas and alas! truth must be spoken, whatever else is in the wind; and the excellent "Newgate Calendar," which contains the biographies and thanatographies of Hayes and his wife, does not say a word of their connections with any of the leading literary or military heroes of the time of Her Majesty Queen Anne. The "Calendar" says, in so many words, that Hayes was obliged to send to his father in Warwickshire for money to get him out of the scrape, and that the old gentleman came down to his aid. By this truth must we stick; and not for the sake of the most brilliant episode,—no, not for a bribe of twenty extra guineas per sheet, would we depart from it.

Mr. Brock's account of his adventure in London has given the reader some short notice of his friend, Mr Macshane. Neither the wits nor the principles of that worthy Ensign were particularly firm: for drink, poverty, and a crack on the skull at the battle of Steenkirk had served to injure the former; and the Ensign was not in his best days possessed of any share of the latter. He had really, at one period, held such a rank in the army, but pawned his half-pay for drink and play; and for many years past had lived, one of the hundred thousand miracles of our city, upon nothing that anybody knew of, or of which he himself could give any account. Who has not a catalogue of these men in his list? who can tell whence comes the occasional clean shirt, who supplies the continual means of drunkenness, who wards off the daily-impending starvation? Their life is a wonder from day to day: their breakfast a wonder; their dinner a miracle; their bed an interposition of Providence. If you and I, my dear sir, want a shilling tomorrow, who will give it us? Will OUR butchers give us mutton-chops? will OUR laundresses clothe us in clean linen?—not a bone or a rag. Standing as we do (may it be ever so) somewhat removed from want,[*] is there one of us who does not shudder at the thought of descending into the lists to combat with it, and expect anything but to be utterly crushed in the encounter?

* The author, it must be remembered, has his lodgings and food provided for him by the government of his country.

Not a bit of it, my dear sir. It takes much more than you think for to starve a man. Starvation is very little when you are used to it. Some people I know even, who live on it quite comfortably, and make their daily bread by it. It had been our friend Macshane's sole profession for many years; and he did not fail to draw from it such a livelihood as was sufficient, and perhaps too good, for him. He managed to dine upon it a certain or rather uncertain number of days in the week, to sleep somewhere, and to get drunk at least three hundred times a year. He was known to one or two noblemen who occasionally helped him with a few pieces, and whom he helped in turn—never mind how. He had other acquaintances whom he pestered undauntedly; and from whom he occasionally extracted a dinner, or a crown, or mayhap, by mistake, a goldheaded cane, which found its way to the pawnbroker's. When flush of cash, he would appear at the coffee-house; when low in funds, the deuce knows into what mystic caves and dens he slunk for food and lodging. He was perfectly ready with his sword, and when sober, or better still, a very little tipsy, was a complete master of it; in the art of boasting and lying he had hardly any equals; in shoes he stood six feet five inches; and here is his complete signalement. It was a fact that he had been in Spain as a volunteer, where he had shown some gallantry, had had a brain-fever, and was sent home to starve as before.

Mr. Macshane had, however, like Mr. Conrad, the Corsair, one virtue in the midst of a thousand crimes,—he was faithful to his employer for the time being: and a story is told of him, which may or may not be to his credit, viz. that being hired on one occasion by a certain lord to inflict a punishment upon a roturier who had crossed his lordship in his amours, he, Macshane, did actually refuse from the person to be belaboured, and who entreated his forbearance, a larger sum of money than the nobleman gave him for the beating; which he performed punctually, as bound in honour and friendship. This tale would the Ensign himself relate, with much self-satisfaction; and when, after the sudden flight from London, he and Brock took to their roving occupation, he cheerfully submitted to the latter as his commanding officer, called him always Major, and, bating blunders and drunkenness, was perfectly true to his leader. He had a notion—and, indeed, I don't know that it was a wrong one—that his profession was now, as before, strictly military, and according to the rules of honour. Robbing he called plundering the enemy; and hanging was, in his idea, a dastardly and cruel advantage that the latter took, and that called for the sternest reprisals.

The other gentlemen concerned were strangers to Mr. Brock, who felt little inclined to trust either of them upon such a message, or with such a large sum to bring back. They had, strange to say, a similar mistrust on their side; but Mr. Brock lugged out five guineas, which he placed in the landlady's hand as security for his comrade's return; and Ensign Macshane, being mounted on poor Hayes's own horse, set off to visit the parents of that unhappy young man. It was a gallant sight to behold our thieves' ambassador, in a faded sky-blue suit with orange facings, in a pair of huge jack-boots unconscious of blacking, with a mighty basket-hilted sword by his side, and a little shabby beaver cocked over a large tow-periwig, ride out from the inn of the "Three Rooks" on his mission to Hayes's paternal village.

It was eighteen miles distant from Worcester; but Mr. Macshane performed the distance in safety, and in sobriety moreover (for such had been his instructions), and had no difficulty in discovering the house of old Hayes: towards which, indeed, John's horse trotted incontinently. Mrs. Hayes, who was knitting at the house-door, was not a little surprised at the appearance of the well-known grey gelding, and of the stranger mounted upon it.

Flinging himself off the steed with much agility, Mr. Macshane, as soon as his feet reached the ground, brought them rapidly together, in order to make a profound and elegant bow to Mrs. Hayes; and slapping his greasy beaver against his heart, and poking his periwig almost into the nose of the old lady, demanded whether he had the "shooprame honour of adthressing Misthriss Hees?"

Having been answered in the affirmative, he then proceeded to ask whether there was a blackguard boy in the house who would take "the horse to the steeble;" whether "he could have a dthrink of small-beer or buthermilk, being, faith, uncommon dthry;" and whether, finally, "he could be feevored with a few minutes' private conversation with her and Mr. Hees, on a matther of consitherable impartance." All these preliminaries were to be complied with before Mr. Macshane would enter at all into the subject of his visit. The horse and man were cared for; Mr. Hayes was called in; and not a little anxious did Mrs. Hayes grow, in the meanwhile, with regard to the fate of her darling son. "Where is he? How is he? Is he dead?" said the old lady. "Oh yes, I'm sure he's dead!"

"Indeed, madam, and you're misteeken intirely: the young man is perfectly well in health."

"Oh, praised be Heaven!"

"But mighty cast down in sperrits. To misfortunes, madam, look you, the best of us are subject; and a trifling one has fell upon your son."

And herewith Mr. Macshane produced a letter in the handwriting of young Hayes, of which we have had the good luck to procure a copy. It ran thus:—

"HONORED FATHER AND MOTHER,—The bearer of this is a kind gentleman, who has left me in a great deal of trouble. Yesterday, at this towne, I fell in with some gentlemen of the queene's servas; after drinking with whom, I accepted her Majesty's mony to enliste. Repenting thereof, I did endeavour to escape; and, in so doing, had the misfortune to strike my superior officer, whereby I made myself liable to Death, according to the rules of warr. If, however, I pay twenty ginnys, all will be wel. You must give the same to the barer, els I shall be shott without fail on Tewsday morning. And so no more from your loving son,

"JOHN HAYES.

"From my prison at Bristol, this unhappy Monday."

When Mrs. Hayes read this pathetic missive, its success with her was complete, and she was for going immediately to the cupboard, and producing the money necessary for her darling son's release. But the carpenter Hayes was much more suspicious. "I don't know you, sir," said he to the ambassador.

"Do you doubt my honour, sir?" said the Ensign, very fiercely.

"Why, sir," replied Mr. Hayes "I know little about it one way or other, but shall take it for granted, if you will explain a little more of this business."

"I sildom condescind to explean," said Mr. Macshane, "for it's not the custom in my rank; but I'll explean anything in reason."

"Pray, will you tell me in what regiment my son is enlisted?"

"In coorse. In Colonel Wood's fut, my dear; and a gallant corps it is as any in the army."

"And you left him?"

"On me soul, only three hours ago, having rid like a horse-jockey ever since; as in the sacred cause of humanity, curse me, every man should."

As Hayes's house was seventy miles from Bristol, the old gentleman thought this was marvellous quick riding, and so, cut the conversation short. "You have said quite enough, sir," said he, "to show me there is some roguery in the matter, and that the whole story is false from beginning to end."

At this abrupt charge the Ensign looked somewhat puzzled, and then spoke with much gravity. "Roguery," said he, "Misthur Hees, is a sthrong term; and which, in consideration of my friendship for your family, I shall pass over. You doubt your son's honour, as there wrote by him in black and white?"

"You have forced him to write," said Mr. Hayes.

"The sly old divvle's right," muttered Mr. Macshane, aside. "Well, sir, to make a clean breast of it, he HAS been forced to write it. The story about the enlistment is a pretty fib, if you will, from beginning to end. And what then, my dear? Do you think your son's any better off for that?"

"Oh, where is he?" screamed Mrs. Hayes, plumping down on her knees. "We WILL give him the money, won't we, John?"

"I know you will, madam, when I tell you where he is. He is in the hands of some gentlemen of my acquaintance, who are at war with the present government, and no more care about cutting a man's throat than they do a chicken's. He is a prisoner, madam, of our sword and spear. If you choose to ransom him, well and good; if not, peace be with him! for never more shall you see him."

"And how do I know you won't come back to-morrow for more money?" asked Mr. Hayes.

"Sir, you have my honour; and I'd as lieve break my neck as my word," said Mr. Macshane, gravely. "Twenty guineas is the bargain. Take ten minutes to talk of it—take it then, or leave it; it's all the same to me, my dear." And it must be said of our friend the Ensign, that he meant every word he said, and that he considered the embassy on which he had come as perfectly honourable and regular.

"And pray, what prevents us," said Mr. Hayes, starting up in a rage, "from taking hold of you, as a surety for him?"

"You wouldn't fire on a flag of truce, would ye, you dishonourable ould civilian?" replied Mr. Macshane. "Besides," says he, "there's more reasons to prevent you: the first is this," pointing to his sword; "here are two more"—and these were pistols; "and the last and the best of all is, that you might hang me and dthraw me and quarther me, an yet never see so much as the tip of your son's nose again. Look you, sir, we run mighty risks in our profession—it's not all play, I can tell you. We're obliged to be punctual, too, or it's all up with the thrade. If I promise that your son will die as sure as fate to-morrow morning, unless I return home safe, our people MUST keep my promise; or else what chance is there for me? You would be down upon me in a moment with a posse of constables, and have me swinging before Warwick gaol. Pooh, my dear! you never would sacrifice a darling boy like John Hayes, let alone his lady, for the sake of my long carcass. One or two of our gentlemen have been taken that way already, because parents and guardians would not believe them."

"AND WHAT BECAME OF THE POOR CHILDREN?" said Mrs. Hayes, who began to perceive the gist of the argument, and to grow dreadfully frightened.

"Don't let's talk of them, ma'am: humanity shudthers at the thought!" And herewith Mr. Macshane drew his finger across his throat in such a dreadful way as to make the two parents tremble. "It's the way of war, madam, look you. The service I have the honour to belong to is not paid by the Queen; and so we're obliged to make our prisoners pay, according to established military practice."

No lawyer could have argued his case better than Mr. Macshane so far; and he completely succeeded in convincing Mr. and Mrs. Hayes of the necessity of ransoming their son. Promising that the young man should be restored to them next morning, along with his beautiful lady, he courteously took leave of the old couple, and made the best of his way back to Worcester again. The elder Hayes wondered who the lady could be of whom the ambassador had spoken, for their son's elopement was altogether unknown to them; but anger or doubt about this subject was overwhelmed by their fears for their darling John's safety. Away rode the gallant Macshane with the money necessary to effect this; and it must be mentioned, as highly to his credit, that he never once thought of appropriating the sum to himself, or of deserting his comrades in any way.

His ride from Worcester had been a long one. He had left that city at noon, but before his return thither the sun had gone down; and the landscape, which had been dressed like a prodigal, in purple and gold, now appeared like a Quaker, in dusky grey; and the trees by the road-side grew black as undertakers or physicians, and, bending their solemn heads to each other, whispered ominously among themselves; and the mists hung on the common; and the cottage lights went out one by one; and the earth and heaven grew black, but for some twinkling useless stars, which freckled the ebon countenance of the latter; and the air grew colder; and about two o'clock the moon appeared, a dismal pale-faced rake, walking solitary through the deserted sky; and about four, mayhap, the Dawn (wretched 'prentice-boy!) opened in the east the shutters of the Day:—in other words, more than a dozen hours had passed. Corporal Brock had been relieved by Mr. Redcap, the latter by Mr. Sicklop, the one-eyed gentleman; Mrs. John Hayes, in spite of her sorrows and bashfulness, had followed the example of her husband, and fallen asleep by his side—slept for many hours—and awakened still under the guardianship of Mr. Brock's troop; and all parties began anxiously to expect the return of the ambassador, Mr. Macshane.

That officer, who had performed the first part of his journey with such distinguished prudence and success, found the night, on his journey homewards, was growing mighty cold and dark; and as he was thirsty and hungry, had money in his purse, and saw no cause to hurry, he determined to take refuge at an alehouse for the night, and to make for Worcester by dawn the next morning. He accordingly alighted at the first inn on his road, consigned his horse to the stable, and, entering the kitchen, called for the best liquor in the house.

A small company was assembled at the inn, among whom Mr. Macshane took his place with a great deal of dignity; and, having a considerable sum of money in his pocket, felt a mighty contempt for his society, and soon let them know the contempt he felt for them. After a third flagon of ale, he discovered that the liquor was sour, and emptied, with much spluttering and grimaces, the remainder of the beer into the fire. This process so offended the parson of the parish (who in those good old times did not disdain to take the post of honour in the chimney-nook), that he left his corner, looking wrathfully at the offender; who without any more ado instantly occupied it. It was a fine thing to hear the jingling of the twenty pieces in his pocket, the oaths which he distributed between the landlord, the guests, and the liquor—to remark the sprawl of his mighty jack-boots, before the sweep of which the timid guests edged farther and farther away; and the languishing leers which he cast on the landlady, as with wide-spread arms he attempted to seize upon her.

When the ostler had done his duties in the stable, he entered the inn, and whispered the landlord that "the stranger was riding John Hayes's horse:" of which fact the host soon convinced himself, and did not fail to have some suspicions of his guest. Had he not thought that times were unquiet, horses might be sold, and one man's money was as good as another's, he probably would have arrested the Ensign immediately, and so lost all the profit of the score which the latter was causing every moment to be enlarged.

In a couple of hours, with that happy facility which one may have often remarked in men of the gallant Ensign's nation, he had managed to disgust every one of the landlord's other guests, and scare them from the kitchen. Frightened by his addresses, the landlady too had taken flight; and the host was the only person left in the apartment; who there stayed for interest's sake merely, and listened moodily to his tipsy guest's conversation. In an hour more, the whole house was awakened by a violent noise of howling, curses, and pots clattering to and fro. Forth issued Mrs. Landlady in her night-gear, out came John Ostler with his pitchfork, downstairs tumbled Mrs. Cook and one or two guests, and found the landlord and ensign on the kitchen-floor—the wig of the latter lying, much singed and emitting strange odours, in the fireplace, his face hideously distorted, and a great quantity of his natural hair in the partial occupation of the landlord; who had drawn it and the head down towards him, in order that he might have the benefit of pummelling the latter more at his ease. In revenge, the landlord was undermost, and the Ensign's arms were working up and down his face and body like the flaps of a paddle-wheel: the man of war had clearly the best of it.

The combatants were separated as soon as possible; but, as soon as the excitement of the fight was over, Ensign Macshane was found to have no further powers of speech, sense, or locomotion, and was carried by his late antagonist to bed. His sword and pistols, which had been placed at his side at the commencement of the evening, were carefully put by, and his pocket visited. Twenty guineas in gold, a large knife—used, probably, for the cutting of bread-and-cheese—some crumbs of those delicacies and a paper of tobacco found in the breeches-pockets, and in the bosom of the sky-blue coat, the leg of a cold fowl and half of a raw onion, constituted his whole property.

These articles were not very suspicious; but the beating which the landlord had received tended greatly to confirm his own and his wife's doubts about their guest; and it was determined to send off in the early morning to Mr. Hayes, informing him how a person had lain at their inn who had ridden thither mounted upon young Hayes's horse. Off set John Ostler at earliest dawn; but on his way he woke up Mr. Justice's clerk, and communicated his suspicions to him; and Mr. Clerk consulted with the village baker, who was always up early; and the clerk, the baker, the butcher with his cleaver, and two gentlemen who were going to work, all adjourned to the inn.

Accordingly, when Ensign Macshane was in a truckle-bed, plunged in that deep slumber which only innocence and drunkenness enjoy in this world, and charming the ears of morn by the regular and melodious music of his nose, a vile plot was laid against him; and when about seven of the clock he woke, he found, on sitting up in his bed, three gentlemen on each side of it, armed, and looking ominous. One held a constable's staff, and albeit unprovided with a warrant, would take upon himself the responsibility of seizing Mr. Macshane and of carrying him before his worship at the hall.

"Taranouns, man!" said the Ensign, springing up in bed, and abruptly breaking off a loud sonorous yawn, with which he had opened the business of the day, "you won't deteen a gentleman who's on life and death? I give ye my word, an affair of honour."

"How came you by that there horse?" said the baker.

"How came you by these here fifteen guineas?" said the landlord, in whose hands, by some process, five of the gold pieces had disappeared.

"What is this here idolatrous string of beads?" said the clerk.

Mr. Macshane, the fact is, was a Catholic, but did not care to own it: for in those days his religion was not popular.

"Baids? Holy Mother of saints! give me back them baids," said Mr. Macshane, clasping his hands. "They were blest, I tell you, by his holiness the po—psha! I mane they belong to a darling little daughter I had that's in heaven now: and as for the money and the horse, I should like to know how a gentleman is to travel in this counthry without them."

"Why, you see, he may travel in the country to GIT 'em," here shrewdly remarked the constable; "and it's our belief that neither horse nor money is honestly come by. If his worship is satisfied, why so, in course, shall we be; but there is highwaymen abroad, look you; and, to our notion, you have very much the cut of one."

Further remonstrances or threats on the part of Mr. Macshane were useless. Although he vowed that he was first cousin to the Duke of Leinster, an officer in Her Majesty's service, and the dearest friend Lord Marlborough had, his impudent captors would not believe a word of his statement (which, further, was garnished with a tremendous number of oaths); and he was, about eight o'clock, carried up to the house of Squire Ballance, the neighbouring justice of the peace.

When the worthy magistrate asked the crime of which the prisoner had been guilty, the captors looked somewhat puzzled for the moment; since, in truth, it could not be shown that the Ensign had committed any crime at all; and if he had confined himself to simple silence, and thrown upon them the onus of proving his misdemeanours, Justice Ballance must have let him loose, and soundly rated his clerk and the landlord for detaining an honest gentleman on so frivolous a charge.

But this caution was not in the Ensign's disposition; and though his accusers produced no satisfactory charge against him, his own words were quite enough to show how suspicious his character was. When asked his name, he gave it in as Captain Geraldine, on his way to Ireland, by Bristol, on a visit to his cousin the Duke of Leinster. He swore solemnly that his friends, the Duke of Marlborough and Lord Peterborough, under both of whom he had served, should hear of the manner in which he had been treated; and when the justice,—a sly old gentleman, and one that read the Gazettes, asked him at what battles he had been present, the gallant Ensign pitched on a couple in Spain and in Flanders, which had been fought within a week of each other, and vowed that he had been desperately wounded at both; so that, at the end of his examination, which had been taken down by the clerk, he had been made to acknowledge as follows:—Captain Geraldine, six feet four inches in height; thin, with a very long red nose, and red hair; grey eyes, and speaks with a strong Irish accent; is the first-cousin of the Duke of Leinster, and in constant communication with him: does not know whether his Grace has any children; does not know whereabouts he lives in London; cannot say what sort of a looking man his Grace is: is acquainted with the Duke of Marlborough, and served in the dragoons at the battle of Ramillies; at which time he was with my Lord Peterborough before Barcelona. Borrowed the horse which he rides from a friend in London, three weeks since. Peter Hobbs, ostler, swears that it was in his master's stable four days ago, and is the property of John Hayes, carpenter. Cannot account for the fifteen guineas found on him by the landlord; says there were twenty; says he won them at cards, a fortnight since, at Edinburgh; says he is riding about the country for his amusement: afterwards says he is on a matter of life and death, and going to Bristol; declared last night, in the hearing of several witnesses, that he was going to York; says he is a man of independent property, and has large estates in Ireland, and a hundred thousand pounds in the Bank of England. Has no shirt or stockings, and the coat he wears is marked "S.S." In his boots is written "Thomas Rodgers," and in his hat is the name of the "Rev. Doctor Snoffler."

Doctor Snoffler lived at Worcester, and had lately advertised in the Hue and Cry a number of articles taken from his house. Mr. Macshane said, in reply to this, that his hat had been changed at the inn, and he was ready to take his oath that he came thither in a gold-laced one. But this fact was disproved by the oaths of many persons who had seen him at the inn. And he was about to be imprisoned for the thefts which he had not committed (the fact about the hat being, that he had purchased it from a gentleman at the "Three Rooks" for two pints of beer)—he was about to be remanded, when, behold, Mrs. Hayes the elder made her appearance; and to her it was that the Ensign was indebted for his freedom.

Old Hayes had gone to work before the ostler arrived; but when his wife heard the lad's message, she instantly caused her pillion to be placed behind the saddle, and mounting the grey horse, urged the stable-boy to gallop as hard as ever he could to the justice's house.

She entered panting and alarmed. "Oh, what is your honour going to do to this honest gentleman?" said she. "In the name of Heaven, let him go! His time is precious—he has important business—business of life and death."

"I tould the jidge so," said the Ensign, "but he refused to take my word—the sacred wurrd of honour of Captain Geraldine."

Macshane was good at a single lie, though easily flustered on an examination; and this was a very creditable stratagem to acquaint Mrs. Hayes with the name that he bore.

"What! you know Captain Geraldine?" said Mr. Ballance, who was perfectly well acquainted with the carpenter's wife.

"In coorse she does. Hasn't she known me these tin years? Are we not related? Didn't she give me the very horse which I rode, and, to make belave, tould you I'd bought in London?"

"Let her tell her own story. Are you related to Captain Geraldine, Mrs. Hayes?"

"Yes—oh, yes!"

"A very elegant connection! And you gave him the horse, did you, of your own free-will?"

"Oh yes! of my own will—I would give him anything. Do, do, your honour, let him go! His child is dying," said the old lady, bursting into tears. "It may be dead before he gets to—before he gets there. Oh, your honour, your honour, pray, pray, don't detain him!"

The justice did not seem to understand this excessive sympathy on the part of Mrs. Hayes; nor did the father himself appear to be nearly so affected by his child's probable fate as the honest woman who interested herself for him. On the contrary, when she made this passionate speech, Captain Geraldine only grinned, and said, "Niver mind, my dear. If his honour will keep an honest gentleman for doing nothing, why, let him—the law must settle between us; and as for the child, poor thing, the Lord deliver it!"

At this, Mrs. Hayes fell to entreating more loudly than ever; and as there was really no charge against him, Mr. Ballance was constrained to let him go.

The landlord and his friends were making off, rather confused, when Ensign Macshane called upon the former in a thundering voice to stop, and refund the five guineas which he had stolen from him. Again the host swore there were but fifteen in his pocket. But when, on the Bible, the Ensign solemnly vowed that he had twenty, and called upon Mrs. Hayes to say whether yesterday, half-an-hour before he entered the inn, she had not seen him with twenty guineas, and that lady expressed herself ready to swear that she had, Mr. Landlord looked more crestfallen than ever, and said that he had not counted the money when he took it; and though he did in his soul believe that there were only fifteen guineas, rather than be suspected of a shabby action, he would pay the five guineas out of his own pocket: which he did, and with the Ensign's, or rather Mrs. Hayes's, own coin.

As soon as they were out of the justice's house, Mr. Macshane, in the fulness of his gratitude, could not help bestowing an embrace upon Mrs. Hayes. And when she implored him to let her ride behind him to her darling son, he yielded with a very good grace, and off the pair set on John Hayes's grey.

"Who has Nosey brought with him now?" said Mr. Sicklop, Brock's one-eyed confederate, who, about three hours after the above adventure, was lolling in the yard of the "Three Rooks." It was our Ensign, with the mother of his captive. They had not met with any accident in their ride.

"I shall now have the shooprame bliss," said Mr. Macshane, with much feeling, as he lifted Mrs. Hayes from the saddle—"the shooprame bliss of intwining two harrts that are mead for one another. Ours, my dear, is a dismal profession; but ah! don't moments like this make aminds for years of pain? This way, my dear. Turn to your right, then to your left—mind the stip—and the third door round the corner."

All these precautions were attended to; and after giving his concerted knock, Mr. Macshane was admitted into an apartment, which he entered holding his gold pieces in the one hand, and a lady by the other.

We shall not describe the meeting which took place between mother and son. The old lady wept copiously; the young man was really glad to see his relative, for he deemed that his troubles were over. Mrs. Cat bit her lips, and stood aside, looking somewhat foolish; Mr. Brock counted the money; and Mr. Macshane took a large dose of strong waters, as a pleasing solace for his labours, dangers, and fatigue.

When the maternal feelings were somewhat calmed, the old lady had leisure to look about her, and really felt a kind of friendship and goodwill for the company of thieves in which she found herself. It seemed to her that they had conferred an actual favour on her, in robbing her of twenty guineas, threatening her son's life, and finally letting him go.

"Who is that droll old gentleman?" said she; and being told that it was Captain Wood, she dropped him a curtsey, and said, with much respect, "Captain, your very humble servant;" which compliment Mr. Brock acknowledged by a gracious smile and bow. "And who is this pretty young lady?" continued Mrs. Hayes.

"Why—hum—oh—mother, you must give her your blessing. She is Mrs. John Hayes." And herewith Mr. Hayes brought forward his interesting lady, to introduce her to his mamma.

The news did not at all please the old lady; who received Mrs. Catherine's embrace with a very sour face indeed. However, the mischief was done; and she was too glad to get back her son to be, on such an occasion, very angry with him. So, after a proper rebuke, she told Mrs. John Hayes that though she never approved of her son's attachment, and thought he married below his condition, yet as the evil was done, it was their duty to make the best of it; and she, for her part, would receive her into her house, and make her as comfortable there as she could.

"I wonder whether she has any more money in that house?" whispered Mr. Sicklop to Mr. Redcap; who, with the landlady, had come to the door of the room, and had been amusing themselves by the contemplation of this sentimental scene.

"What a fool that wild Hirishman was not to bleed her for more!" said the landlady; "but he's a poor ignorant Papist. I'm sure my man" (this gentleman had been hanged), "wouldn't have come away with such a beggarly sum."

"Suppose we have some more out of 'em?" said Mr. Redcap. "What prevents us? We have got the old mare, and the colt too,—ha! ha!—and the pair of 'em ought to be worth at least a hundred to us."

This conversation was carried on sotto voce; and I don't know whether Mr. Brock had any notion of the plot which was arranged by the three worthies. The landlady began it. "Which punch, madam, will you take?" says she. "You must have something for the good of the house, now you are in it."

"In coorse," said the Ensign.

"Certainly," said the other three. But the old lady said she was anxious to leave the place; and putting down a crown-piece, requested the hostess to treat the gentlemen in her absence. "Good-bye, Captain," said the old lady.

"Ajew!" cried the Ensign, "and long life to you, my dear. You got me out of a scrape at the justice's yonder; and, split me! but Insign Macshane will remimber it as long as he lives."

And now Hayes and the two ladies made for the door; but the landlady placed herself against it, and Mr. Sicklop said, "No, no, my pretty madams, you ain't a-going off so cheap as that neither; you are not going out for a beggarly twenty guineas, look you,—we must have more."

Mr. Hayes starting back, and cursing his fate, fairly burst into tears; the two women screamed; and Mr. Brock looked as if the proposition both amused and had been expected by him: but not so Ensign Macshane.

"Major!" said he, clawing fiercely hold of Brock's arms.

"Ensign," said Mr. Brock, smiling.

"Arr we, or arr we not, men of honour?"

"Oh, in coorse," said Brock, laughing, and using Macshane's favourite expression.

"If we ARR men of honour, we are bound to stick to our word; and, hark ye, you dirty one-eyed scoundrel, if you don't immediately make way for these leedies, and this lily-livered young jontleman who's crying so, the Meejor here and I will lug out and force you." And so saying, he drew his great sword and made a pass at Mr. Sicklop; which that gentleman avoided, and which caused him and his companion to retreat from the door. The landlady still kept her position at it, and with a storm of oaths against the Ensign, and against two Englishmen who ran away from a wild Hirishman, swore she would not budge a foot, and would stand there until her dying day.

"Faith, then, needs must," said the Ensign, and made a lunge at the hostess, which passed so near the wretch's throat, that she screamed, sank on her knees, and at last opened the door.

Down the stairs, then, with great state, Mr. Macshane led the elder lady, the married couple following; and having seen them to the street, took an affectionate farewell of the party, whom he vowed that he would come and see. "You can walk the eighteen miles aisy, between this and nightfall," said he.

"WALK!" exclaimed Mr. Hayes. "Why, haven't we got Ball, and shall ride and tie all the way?"

"Madam!" cried Macshane, in a stern voice, "honour before everything. Did you not, in the presence of his worship, vow and declare that you gave me that horse, and now d'ye talk of taking it back again? Let me tell you, madam, that such paltry thricks ill become a person of your years and respectability, and ought never to be played with Insign Timothy Macshane."

He waved his hat and strutted down the street; and Mrs. Catherine Hayes, along with her bridegroom and mother-in-law, made the best of their way homeward on foot.

CHAPTER VII

WHICH EMBRACES A PERIOD OF SEVEN YEARS

The recovery of so considerable a portion of his property from the clutches of Brock was, as may be imagined, no trifling source of joy to that excellent young man, Count Gustavus Adolphus de Galgenstein; and he was often known to say, with much archness, and a proper feeling of gratitude to the Fate which had ordained things so, that the robbery was, in reality, one of the best things that could have happened to him: for, in event of Mr. Brock's NOT stealing the money, his Excellency the Count would have had to pay the whole to the Warwickshire Squire, who had won it from him at play. He was enabled, in the present instance, to plead his notorious poverty as an excuse; and the Warwickshire conqueror got off with nothing, except a very badly written autograph of the Count's, simply acknowledging the debt.

This point his Excellency conceded with the greatest candour; but (as, doubtless, the reader may have remarked in the course of his experience) to owe is not quite the same thing as to pay; and from the day of his winning the money until the day of his death the Warwickshire Squire did never, by any chance, touch a single bob, tizzy, tester, moidore, maravedi, doubloon, tomaun, or rupee, of the sum which Monsieur de Galgenstein had lost to him.

That young nobleman was, as Mr. Brock hinted in the little autobiographical sketch which we gave in a former chapter, incarcerated for a certain period, and for certain other debts, in the donjons of Shrewsbury; but he released himself from them by that noble and consolatory method of whitewashing which the law has provided for gentlemen in his oppressed condition; and he had not been a week in London, when he fell in with, and overcame, or put to flight, Captain Wood, alias Brock, and immediately seized upon the remainder of his property. After receiving this, the Count, with commendable discretion, disappeared from England altogether for a while; nor are we at all authorised to state that any of his debts to his tradesmen were discharged, any more than his debts of honour, as they are pleasantly called.

Having thus settled with his creditors, the gallant Count had interest enough with some of the great folk to procure for himself a post abroad, and was absent in Holland for some time. It was here that he became acquainted with the lovely Madam Silverkoop, the widow of a deceased gentleman of Leyden; and although the lady was not at that age at which tender passions are usually inspired—being sixty—and though she could not, like Mademoiselle Ninon de l'Enclos, then at Paris, boast of charms which defied the progress of time,—for Mrs. Silverkoop was as red as a boiled lobster, and as unwieldy as a porpoise; and although her mental attractions did by no means make up for her personal deficiencies,—for she was jealous, violent, vulgar, drunken, and stingy to a miracle: yet her charms had an immediate effect on Monsieur de Galgenstein; and hence, perhaps, the reader (the rogue! how well he knows the world!) will be led to conclude that the honest widow was RICH.

Such, indeed, she was; and Count Gustavus, despising the difference between his twenty quarterings and her twenty thousand pounds, laid the most desperate siege to her, and finished by causing her to capitulate; as I do believe, after a reasonable degree of pressing, any woman will do to any man: such, at least, has been MY experience in the matter.

The Count then married; and it was curious to see how he—who, as we have seen in the case of Mrs. Cat, had been as great a tiger and domestic bully as any extant—now, by degrees, fell into a quiet submission towards his enormous Countess; who ordered him up and down as a lady orders her footman, who permitted him speedily not to have a will of his own, and who did not allow him a shilling of her money without receiving for the same an accurate account.

How was it that he, the abject slave of Madam Silverkoop, had been victorious over Mrs. Cat? The first blow is, I believe, the decisive one in these cases, and the Countess had stricken it a week after their marriage;—establishing a supremacy which the Count never afterwards attempted to question.

We have alluded to his Excellency's marriage, as in duty bound, because it will be necessary to account for his appearance hereafter in a more splendid fashion than that under which he has hitherto been known to us; and just comforting the reader by the knowledge that the union, though prosperous in a worldly point of view, was, in reality, extremely unhappy, we must say no more from this time forth of the fat and legitimate Madam de Galgenstein. Our darling is Mrs. Catherine, who had formerly acted in her stead; and only in so much as the fat Countess did influence in any way the destinies of our heroine, or those wise and virtuous persons who have appeared and are to follow her to her end, shall we in any degree allow her name to figure here. It is an awful thing to get a glimpse, as one sometimes does, when the time is past, of some little little wheel which works the whole mighty machinery of FATE, and see how our destinies turn on a minute's delay or advance, or on the turning of a street, or on somebody else's turning of a street, or on somebody else's doing of something else in Downing Street or in Timbuctoo, now or a thousand years ago. Thus, for instance, if Miss Poots, in the year 1695, had never been the lovely inmate of a Spielhaus at Amsterdam, Mr. Van Silverkoop would never have seen her; if the day had not been extraordinarily hot, the worthy merchant would never have gone thither; if he had not been fond of Rhenish wine and sugar, he never would have called for any such delicacies; if he had not called for them, Miss Ottilia Poots would never have brought them, and partaken of them; if he had not been rich, she would certainly have rejected all the advances made to her by Silverkoop; if he had not been so fond of Rhenish and sugar, he never would have died; and Mrs. Silverkoop would have been neither rich nor a widow, nor a wife to Count von Galgenstein. Nay, nor would this history have ever been written; for if Count Galgenstein had not married the rich widow, Mrs. Catherine would never have—

Oh, my dear madam! you thought we were going to tell you. Pooh! nonsense!—no such thing! not for two or three and seventy pages or so,—when, perhaps, you MAY know what Mrs. Catherine never would have done.

The reader will remember, in the second chapter of these Memoirs, the announcement that Mrs. Catherine had given to the world a child, who might bear, if he chose, the arms of Galgenstein, with the further adornment of a bar-sinister. This child had been put out to nurse some time before its mother's elopement from the Count; and as that nobleman was in funds at the time (having had that success at play which we duly chronicled), he paid a sum of no less than twenty guineas, which was to be the yearly reward of the nurse into whose charge the boy was put. The woman grew fond of the brat; and when, after the first year, she had no further news or remittances from father or mother, she determined, for a while at least, to maintain the infant at her own expense; for, when rebuked by her neighbours on this score, she stoutly swore that no parents could ever desert their children, and that some day or other she should not fail to be rewarded for her trouble with this one.

Under this strange mental hallucination poor Goody Billings, who had five children and a husband of her own, continued to give food and shelter to little Tom for a period of no less than seven years; and though it must be acknowledged that the young gentleman did not in the slightest degree merit the kindnesses shown to him, Goody Billings, who was of a very soft and pitiful disposition, continued to bestow them upon him: because, she said, he was lonely and unprotected, and deserved them more than other children who had fathers and mothers to look after them. If, then, any difference was made between Tom's treatment and that of her own brood, it was considerably in favour of the former; to whom the largest proportions of treacle were allotted for his bread, and the handsomest supplies of hasty pudding. Besides, to do Mrs. Billings justice, there WAS a party against him; and that consisted not only of her husband and her five children, but of every single person in the neighbourhood who had an opportunity of seeing and becoming acquainted with Master Tom.

A celebrated philosopher—I think Miss Edgeworth—has broached the consolatory doctrine, that in intellect and disposition all human beings are entirely equal, and that circumstance and education are the causes of the distinctions and divisions which afterwards unhappily take place among them. Not to argue this question, which places Jack Howard and Jack Thurtell on an exact level,—which would have us to believe that Lord Melbourne is by natural gifts and excellences a man as honest, brave, and farsighted as the Duke of Wellington,—which would make out that Lord Lyndhurst is, in point of principle, eloquence, and political honesty, no better than Mr. O'Connell,—not, I say, arguing this doctrine, let us simply state that Master Thomas Billings (for, having no other, he took the name of the worthy people who adopted him) was in his long-coats fearfully passionate, screaming and roaring perpetually, and showing all the ill that he COULD show. At the age of two, when his strength enabled him to toddle abroad, his favourite resort was the coal-hole or the dung-heap: his roarings had not diminished in the least, and he had added to his former virtues two new ones,—a love of fighting and stealing; both which amiable qualities he had many opportunities of exercising every day. He fought his little adoptive brothers and sisters; he kicked and cuffed his father and mother; he fought the cat, stamped upon the kittens, was worsted in a severe battle with the hen in the backyard; but, in revenge, nearly beat a little sucking-pig to death, whom he caught alone and rambling near his favourite haunt, the dung-hill. As for stealing, he stole the eggs, which he perforated and emptied; the butter, which he ate with or without bread, as he could find it; the sugar, which he cunningly secreted in the leaves of a "Baker's Chronicle," that nobody in the establishment could read; and thus from the pages of history he used to suck in all he knew—thieving and lying namely; in which, for his years, he made wonderful progress. If any followers of Miss Edgeworth and the philosophers are inclined to disbelieve this statement, or to set it down as overcharged and distorted, let them be assured that just this very picture was, of all the pictures in the world, taken from nature. I, Ikey Solomons, once had a dear little brother who could steal before he could walk (and this not from encouragement,—for, if you know the world, you must know that in families of our profession the point of honour is sacred at home,—but from pure nature)—who could steal, I say, before he could walk, and lie before he could speak; and who, at four and a half years of age, having attacked my sister Rebecca on some question of lollipops, had smitten her on the elbow with a fire-shovel, apologising to us by saying simply, "— her, I wish it had been her head!" Dear, dear Aminadab! I think of you, and laugh these philosophers to scorn. Nature made you for that career which you fulfilled: you were from your birth to your dying a scoundrel; you COULDN'T have been anything else, however your lot was cast; and blessed it was that you were born among the prigs,—for had you been of any other profession, alas! alas! what ills might you have done! As I have heard the author of "Richelieu," "Siamese Twins," etc. say "Poeta nascitur non fit," which means that though he had tried ever so much to be a poet, it was all moonshine: in the like manner, I say, "ROAGUS nascitur, non fit." We have it from nature, and so a fig for Miss Edgeworth.

In this manner, then, while his father, blessed with a wealthy wife, was leading, in a fine house, the life of a galley-slave; while his mother, married to Mr. Hayes, and made an honest women of, as the saying is, was passing her time respectably in Warwickshire, Mr. Thomas Billings was inhabiting the same county, not cared for by either of them; but ordained by Fate to join them one day, and have a mighty influence upon the fortunes of both. For, as it has often happened to the traveller in the York or the Exeter coach to fall snugly asleep in his corner, and on awaking suddenly to find himself sixty or seventy miles from the place where Somnus first visited him: as, we say, although you sit still, Time, poor wretch, keeps perpetually running on, and so must run day and night, with never a pause or a halt of five minutes to get a drink, until his dying day; let the reader imagine that since he left Mrs. Hayes and all the other worthy personages of this history, in the last chapter, seven years have sped away; during which, all our heroes and heroines have been accomplishing their destinies.

Seven years of country carpentering, or rather trading, on the part of a husband, of ceaseless scolding, violence, and discontent on the part of a wife, are not pleasant to describe: so we shall omit altogether any account of the early married life of Mr. and Mrs. John Hayes. The "Newgate Calendar" (to which excellent compilation we and the OTHER popular novelists of the day can never be sufficiently grateful) states that Hayes left his house three or four times during this period, and, urged by the restless humours of his wife, tried several professions: returning, however, as he grew weary of each, to his wife and his paternal home. After a certain time his parents died, and by their demise he succeeded to a small property, and the carpentering business, which he for some time followed.

What, then, in the meanwhile, had become of Captain Wood, or Brock, and Ensign Macshane?—the only persons now to be accounted for in our catalogue. For about six months after their capture and release of Mr. Hayes, those noble gentlemen had followed, with much prudence and success, that trade which the celebrated and polite Duval, the ingenious Sheppard, the dauntless Turpin, and indeed many other heroes of our most popular novels, had pursued,—or were pursuing, in their time. And so considerable were said to be Captain Wood's gains, that reports were abroad of his having somewhere a buried treasure; to which he might have added more, had not Fate suddenly cut short his career as a prig. He and the Ensign were—shame to say—transported for stealing three pewter-pots off a railing at Exeter; and not being known in the town, which they had only reached that morning, they were detained by no further charges, but simply condemned on this one. For this misdemeanour, Her Majesty's Government vindictively sent them for seven years beyond the sea; and, as the fashion then was, sold the use of their bodies to Virginian planters during that space of time. It is thus, alas! that the strong are always used to deal with the weak, and many an honest fellow has been led to rue his unfortunate difference with the law.

Thus, then, we have settled all scores. The Count is in Holland with his wife; Mrs. Cat in Warwickshire along with her excellent husband; Master Thomas Billings with his adoptive parents in the same county; and the two military gentlemen watching the progress and cultivation of the tobacco and cotton plant in the New World. All these things having passed between the acts, dingaring-a-dingaring-a-dingledingleding, the drop draws up, and the next act begins. By the way, the play ENDS with a drop: but that is neither here nor there.

(Here, as in a theatre, the orchestra is supposed to play something melodious. The people get up, shake themselves, yawn, and settle down in their seats again. "Porter, ale, ginger-beer, cider," comes round, squeezing through the legs of the gentlemen in the pit. Nobody takes anything, as usual; and lo! the curtain rises again. "Sh, 'shsh, 'shshshhh! Hats off!" says everybody.)

Mrs. Hayes had now been for six years the adored wife of Mr. Hayes, and no offspring had arisen to bless their loves and perpetuate their name. She had obtained a complete mastery over her lord and master; and having had, as far as was in that gentleman's power, every single wish gratified that she could demand, in the way of dress, treats to Coventry and Birmingham, drink, and what not—for, though a hard man, John Hayes had learned to spend his money pretty freely on himself and her—having had all her wishes gratified, it was natural that she should begin to find out some more; and the next whim she hit upon was to be restored to her child. It may be as well to state that she had never informed her husband of the existence of that phenomenon, although he was aware of his wife's former connection with the Count,—Mrs. Hayes, in their matrimonial quarrels, invariably taunting him with accounts of her former splendour and happiness, and with his own meanness of taste in condescending to take up with his Excellency's leavings.

She determined, then (but as yet had not confided her determination to her husband), she would have her boy; although in her seven years' residence within twenty miles of him she had never once thought of seeing him: and the kind reader knows that when his excellent lady determines on a thing—a shawl, or an opera-box, or a new carriage, or twenty-four singing-lessons from Tamburini, or a night at the "Eagle Tavern," City Road, or a ride in a 'bus to Richmond and tea and brandy-and-water at "Rose

Cottage Hotel"—the reader, high or low, knows that when Mrs. Reader desires a thing have it she will; you may just as well talk of avoiding her as of avoiding gout, bills, or grey hairs—and that, you know, is impossible. I, for my part, have had all three—ay, and a wife too.

I say that when a woman is resolved on a thing, happen it will; if husbands refuse, Fate will interfere (flectere si nequeo, etc.; but quotations are odious). And some hidden power was working in the case of Mrs. Hayes, and, for its own awful purposes, lending her its aid.

Who has not felt how he works—the dreadful conquering Spirit of Ill? Who cannot see, in the circle of his own society, the fated and foredoomed to woe and evil? Some call the doctrine of destiny a dark creed; but, for me, I would fain try and think it a consolatory one. It is better, with all one's sins upon one's head, to deem oneself in the hands of Fate, than to think—with our fierce passions and weak repentances; with our resolves so loud, so vain, so ludicrously, despicably weak and frail; with our dim, wavering, wretched conceits about virtue, and our irresistible propensity to wrong,—that we are the workers of our future sorrow or happiness. If we depend on our strength, what is it against mighty circumstance? If we look to ourselves, what hope have we? Look back at the whole of your life, and see how Fate has mastered you and it. Think of your disappointments and your successes. Has YOUR striving influenced one or the other? A fit of indigestion puts itself between you and honours and reputation; an apple plops on your nose and makes you a world's wonder and glory; a fit of poverty makes a rascal of you, who were, and are still, an honest man; clubs, trumps, or six lucky mains at dice, make an honest man for life of you, who ever were, will be, and are a rascal. Who sends the illness? who causes the apple to fall? who deprives you of your worldly goods? or who shuffles the cards, and brings trumps, honour, virtue, and prosperity back again? You call it chance; ay, and so it is chance that when the floor gives way, and the rope stretches tight, the poor wretch before St. Sepulchre's clock dies. Only with us, clear-sighted mortals as we are, we can't SEE the rope by which we hang, and know not when or how the drop may fall.

But revenons a nos moutons: let us return to that sweet lamb Master Thomas, and the milk-white ewe Mrs. Cat. Seven years had passed away, and she began to think that she should very much like to see her child once more. It was written that she should; and you shall hear how, soon after, without any great exertions of hers, back he came to her.

In the month of July, in the year 1715, there came down a road about ten miles from the city of Worcester, two gentlemen; not mounted, Templar-like, upon one horse, but having a horse between them—a sorry bay, with a sorry saddle, and a large pack behind it; on which each by turn took a ride. Of the two, one was a man of excessive stature, with red hair, a very prominent nose, and a faded military dress; while the other, an old weather-beaten, sober-looking personage, wore the costume of a civilian—both man and dress appearing to have reached the autumnal, or seedy state. However, the pair seemed, in spite of their apparent poverty, to be passably merry. The old gentleman rode the horse; and had, in the course of their journey, ridden him two miles at least in every three. The tall one walked with immense strides by his side; and seemed, indeed, as if he could have quickly outstripped the four-footed animal, had he chosen to exert his speed, or had not affection for his comrade retained him at his stirrup.

A short time previously the horse had cast a shoe; and this the tall man on foot had gathered up, and was holding in his hand: it having been voted that the first blacksmith to whose shop they should come should be called upon to fit it again upon the bay horse.

"Do you remimber this counthry, Meejor?" said the tall man, who was looking about him very much pleased, and sucking a flower. "I think thim green cornfields is prettier looking at than the devil tobacky out yondther, and bad lack to it!"

"I recollect the place right well, and some queer pranks we played here seven years agone," responded the gentleman addressed as Major. "You remember that man and his wife, whom we took in pawn at the 'Three Rooks'?"

"And the landlady only hung last Michaelmas?" said the tall man, parenthetically.

"Hang the landlady!—we've got all we ever would out of HER, you know. But about the man and woman. You went after the chap's mother, and, like a jackass, as you are, let him loose. Well, the woman was that Catherine that you've often heard me talk about. I like the wench, — her, for I almost brought her up; and she was for a year or two along with that scoundrel Galgenstein, who has been the cause of my ruin."

"The infernal blackguard and ruffian!" said the tall man; who, with his companion, has no doubt been recognised by the reader.

"Well, this Catherine had a child by Galgenstein; and somewhere here hard by the woman lived to whom we carried the brat to nurse. She was the wife of a blacksmith, one Billings: it won't be out of the way to get our horse shod at his house, if he is alive still, and we may learn something about the little beast. I should be glad to see the mother well enough."

"Do I remember her?" said the Ensign. "Do I remember whisky? Sure I do, and the snivelling sneak her husband, and the stout old lady her mother-in-law, and the dirty one-eyed ruffian who sold me the parson's hat that had so nearly brought me into trouble. Oh but it was a rare rise we got out of them chaps, and the old landlady that's hanged too!" And here both Ensign Macshane and Major Brock, or Wood, grinned, and showed much satisfaction.

It will be necessary to explain the reason of it. We gave the British public to understand that the landlady of the "Three Rooks," at Worcester, was a notorious fence, or banker of thieves; that is, a purchaser of their merchandise. In her hands Mr. Brock and his companion had left property to the amount of sixty or seventy pounds, which was secreted in a cunning recess in a chamber of the "Three Rooks" known only to the landlady and the gentlemen who banked with her; and in this place, Mr. Sicklop, the one-eyed man who had joined in the Hayes adventure, his comrade, and one or two of the topping prigs of the county, were free. Mr. Sicklop had been shot dead in a night attack near Bath: the landlady had been suddenly hanged, as an accomplice in another case of robbery; and when, on their return from Virginia, our two heroes, whose hopes of livelihood depended upon it, had bent their steps towards Worcester, they were not a little frightened to hear of the cruel fate of the hostess and many of the amiable frequenters of the "Three Rooks." All the goodly company were separated; the house was no longer an inn. Was the money gone too? At least it was worth while to look—which Messrs. Brock and Macshane determined to do.

The house being now a private one, Mr. Brock, with a genius that was above his station, visited its owner, with a huge portfolio under his arm, and, in the character of a painter, requested permission to take a particular sketch from a particular window. The Ensign followed with the artist's materials (consisting simply of a screwdriver and a crowbar); and it is hardly necessary to say that, when admission was granted to them, they opened the well-known door, and to their inexpressible satisfaction discovered, not their own peculiar savings exactly, for these had been appropriated instantly, on hearing of their transportation, but stores of money and goods to the amount of near three hundred pounds: to which Mr. Macshane said they had as just and honourable a right as anybody else. And so they had as just a right as anybody—except the original owners: but who was to discover them?

With this booty they set out on their journey—anywhere, for they knew not whither; and it so chanced that when their horse's shoe came off, they were within a few furlongs of the cottage of Mr. Billings, the blacksmith. As they came near, they were saluted by tremendous roars issuing from the smithy. A small boy was held across the bellows, two or three children of smaller and larger growth were holding him down, and many others of the village were gazing in at the window, while a man, half-naked, was lashing the little boy with a whip, and occasioning the cries heard by the travellers. As the horse drew up, the operator looked at the new-comers for a moment, and then proceeded incontinently with his work; belabouring the child more fiercely than ever.

When he had done, he turned round to the new-comers and asked how he could serve them? whereupon Mr. Wood (for such was the name he adopted, and by such we shall call him to the end) wittily remarked that however he might wish to serve THEM, he seemed mightily inclined to serve that young gentleman first.

"It's no joking matter," said the blacksmith: "if I don't serve him so now, he'll be worse off in his old age. He'll come to the gallows, as sure as his name is Bill—never mind what his name is." And so saying, he gave the urchin another cut; which elicited, of course, another scream.

"Oh! his name is Bill?" said Captain Wood.

"His name's NOT Bill!" said the blacksmith, sulkily. "He's no name; and no heart, neither. My wife took the brat in, seven years ago, from a beggarly French chap to nurse, and she kept him, for she was a good soul" (here his eyes began to wink), "and she's—she's gone now" (here he began fairly to blubber). "And damn him, out of love for her, I kept him too, and the scoundrel is a liar and a thief. This blessed day, merely to vex me and my boys here, he spoke ill of her, he did, and I'll—cut—his—life—out—I—will!" and with each word honest Mulciber applied a whack on the body of little Tom Billings; who, by shrill shrieks, and oaths in treble, acknowledged the receipt of the blows.

"Come, come," said Mr. Wood, "set the boy down, and the bellows a-going; my horse wants shoeing, and the poor lad has had strapping enough."

The blacksmith obeyed, and cast poor Master Thomas loose. As he staggered away and looked back at his tormentor, his countenance assumed an expression which made Mr. Wood say, grasping hold of Macshane's arm, "It's the boy, it's the boy! When his mother gave Galgenstein the laudanum, she had the self-same look with her!"

"Had she really now?" said Mr. Macshane. "And pree, Meejor, who WAS his mother?"

"Mrs. Cat, you fool!" answered Wood.

"Then, upon my secred word of honour, she has a mighty fine KITTEN anyhow, my dear. Aha!"

"They don't DROWN such kittens," said Mr. Wood, archly; and Macshane, taking the allusion, clapped his finger to his nose in token of perfect approbation of his commander's sentiment.

While the blacksmith was shoeing the horse, Mr. Wood asked him many questions concerning the lad whom he had just been chastising, and succeeded, beyond a doubt, in establishing his identity with the child whom Catherine Hall had brought into the world seven years since. Billings told him of all the virtues of his wife, and the manifold crimes of the lad: how he stole, and fought, and lied, and swore; and though the youngest under his roof, exercised the most baneful influence over all the rest of his family. He was determined at last, he said, to put him to the parish, for he did not dare to keep him.

"He's a fine whelp, and would fetch ten pieces in Virginny," sighed the Ensign.

"Crimp, of Bristol, would give five for him," said Mr. Wood, ruminating.

"Why not take him?" said the Ensign.

"Faith, why not?" said Mr. Wood. "His keep, meanwhile, will not be sixpence a day." Then turning round to the blacksmith, "Mr. Billings," said he, "you will be surprised, perhaps, to hear that I know everything regarding that poor lad's history. His mother was an unfortunate lady of high family, now no more; his father a German nobleman, Count de Galgenstein by name."

"The very man!" said Billings: "a young, fair-haired man, who came here with the child, and a dragoon sergeant."

"Count de Galgenstein by name, who, on the point of death, recommended the infant to me."

"And did he pay you seven years' boarding?" said Mr. Billings, who was quite alive at the very idea.

"Alas, sir, not a jot! He died, sir, six hundred pounds in my debt; didn't he, Ensign?"

"Six hundred, upon my secred honour! I remember when he got into the house along with the poli—"

"Psha! what matters it?" here broke out Mr. Wood, looking fiercely at the Ensign. "Six hundred pounds he owes me: how was he to pay you? But he told me to take charge of this boy, if I found him; and found him I have, and WILL take charge of him, if you will hand him over."

"Send our Tom!" cried Billings. And when that youth appeared, scowling, and yet trembling, and prepared, as it seemed, for another castigation, his father, to his surprise, asked him if he was willing to go along with those gentlemen, or whether he would be a good lad and stay with him.

Mr. Tom replied immediately, "I won't be a good lad, and I'd rather go to — than stay with you!"

"Will you leave your brothers and sisters?" said Billings, looking very dismal.

"Hang my brothers and sisters—I hate 'em; and, besides, I haven't got any!"

"But you had a good mother, hadn't you, Tom?"

Tom paused for a moment.

"Mother's gone," said he, "and you flog me, and I'll go with these men."

"Well, then, go thy ways," said Billings, starting up in a passion: "go thy ways for a graceless reprobate; and if this gentleman will take you, he may do so."

After some further parley, the conversation ended, and the next morning Mr. Wood's party consisted of three: a little boy being mounted upon the bay horse, in addition to the Ensign or himself; and the whole company went journeying towards Bristol.

We have said that Mrs. Hayes had, on a sudden, taken a fit of maternal affection, and was bent upon being restored to her child; and that benign destiny which watched over the life of this lucky lady instantly set about gratifying her wish, and, without cost to herself of coach-hire or saddle-horse, sent the young gentleman very quickly to her arms. The village in which the Hayeses dwelt was but a very few miles out of the road from Bristol; whither, on the benevolent mission above, hinted at, our party of worthies were bound: and coming, towards the afternoon, in sight of the house of that very Justice Ballance who had been so nearly the ruin of Ensign Macshane, that officer narrated, for the hundredth time, and with much glee, the circumstances which had then befallen him, and the manner in which Mrs. Hayes the elder had come forward to his rescue.

"Suppose we go and see the old girl?" suggested Mr. Wood. "No harm can come to us now." And his comrade always assenting, they wound their way towards the village, and reached it as the evening came on. In the public-house where they rested, Wood made inquiries concerning the Hayes family; was informed of the death of the old couple, of the establishment of John Hayes and his wife in their place, and of the kind of life that these latter led together. When all these points had been imparted to him, he ruminated much: an expression of sublime triumph and exultation at length lighted up his features. "I think, Tim," said he at last, "that we can make more than five pieces of that boy."

"Oh, in coorse!" said Timothy Macshane, Esquire; who always agreed with his "Meejor."

"In coorse, you fool! and how? I'll tell you how. This Hayes is well to do in the world, and—"

"And we'll nab him again—ha, ha!" roared out Macshane. "By my secred honour, Meejor, there never was a gineral like you at a strathyjam!"

"Peace, you bellowing donkey, and don't wake the child. The man is well to do, his wife rules him, and they have no children. Now, either she will be very glad to have the boy back again, and pay for the finding of him, or else she has said nothing about him, and will pay us for being silent too: or, at any rate, Hayes himself will be ashamed at finding his wife the mother of a child a year older than his marriage, and will pay for the keeping of the brat away. There's profit, my dear, in any one of the cases, or my name's not Peter Brock."

When the Ensign understood this wondrous argument, he would fain have fallen on his knees and worshipped his friend and guide. They began operations, almost immediately, by an attack on Mrs. Hayes. On hearing, as she did in private interview with the ex-corporal the next morning, that her son was found, she was agitated by both of the passions which Wood attributed to her. She longed to have the boy back, and would give any reasonable sum to see him; but she dreaded exposure, and would pay equally to avoid that. How could she gain the one point and escape the other?

Mrs. Hayes hit upon an expedient which, I am given to understand, is not uncommon nowadays. She suddenly discovered that she had a dear brother, who had been obliged to fly the country in consequence of having joined the Pretender, and had died in France, leaving behind him an only son. This boy her brother had, with his last breath, recommended to her protection, and had confided him to the charge of a brother officer who was now in the country, and would speedily make his appearance; and, to put the story beyond a doubt, Mr. Wood wrote the letter from her brother stating all these particulars, and Ensign Macshane received full instructions how to perform the part of the "brother officer." What consideration Mr. Wood received for his services, we cannot say; only it is well known that Mr. Hayes caused to be committed to gaol a young apprentice in his service, charged with having broken open a cupboard in which Mr. Hayes had forty guineas in gold and silver, and to which none but he and his wife had access.

Having made these arrangements, the Corporal and his little party decamped to a short distance, and Mrs. Catherine was left to prepare her husband for a speedy addition to his family, in the shape of this darling nephew. John Hayes received the news with anything but pleasure. He had never heard of any brother of Catherine's; she had been bred at the workhouse, and nobody ever hinted that she had relatives: but it is easy for a lady of moderate genius to invent circumstances; and with lies, tears, threats, coaxings, oaths, and other blandishments, she compelled him to submit.

Two days afterwards, as Mr. Hayes was working in his shop with his lady seated beside him, the trampling of a horse was heard in his courtyard, and a gentleman, of huge stature, descended from it, and strode into the shop. His figure was wrapped in a large cloak; but Mr. Hayes could not help fancying that he had somewhere seen his face before.

"This, I preshoom," said the gentleman, "is Misther Hayes, that I have come so many miles to see, and this is his amiable lady? I was the most intimate frind, madam, of your laminted brother, who died in King Lewis's service, and whose last touching letthers I despatched to you two days ago. I have with me a further precious token of my dear friend, Captain Hall—it is HERE."

And so saying, the military gentleman, with one arm, removed his cloak, and stretching forward the other into Hayes's face almost, stretched likewise forward a little boy, grinning and sprawling in the air, and prevented only from falling to the ground by the hold which the Ensign kept of the waistband of his little coat and breeches.

"Isn't he a pretty boy?" said Mrs. Hayes, sidling up to her husband tenderly, and pressing one of Mr. Hayes's hands.

About the lad's beauty it is needless to say what the carpenter thought; but that night, and for many many nights after, the lad stayed at Mr. Hayes's.

CHAPTER VIII

We are obliged, in recording this history, to follow accurately that great authority, the "Calendarium Newgaticum Roagorumque Registerium," of which every lover of literature, in the present day knows the value; and as that remarkable work totally discards all the unities in its narratives, and reckons the life of its heroes only by their actions, and not by periods of time, we must follow in the wake of this mighty ark—a humble cock-boat. When it pauses, we pause; when it runs ten knots an hour, we run with the same celerity; and as, in order to carry the reader from the penultimate chapter of this work unto the last chapter, we were compelled to make him leap over a gap of seven blank years, ten years more must likewise be granted to us before we are at liberty to resume our history.

During that period, Master Thomas Billings had been under the especial care of his mother; and, as may be imagined, he rather increased than diminished the accomplishments for which he had been remarkable while under the roof of his foster-father. And with this advantage, that while at the blacksmith's, and only three or four years of age, his virtues were necessarily appreciated only in his family circle and among those few acquaintants of his own time of life whom a youth of three can be expected to meet in the alleys or over the gutters of a small country hamlet,—in his mothers residence, his circle extended with his own growth, and he began to give proofs of those powers of which in infancy there had been only encouraging indications. Thus it was nowise remarkable that a child of four years should not know his letters, and should have had a great disinclination to learn them; but when a young man of fifteen showed the same creditable ignorance, the same undeviating dislike, it was easy to see that he possessed much resolution and perseverance. When it was remarked, too, that, in case of any difference, he not only beat the usher, but by no means disdained to torment and bully the very smallest boys of the school, it was easy to see that his mind was comprehensive and careful, as well as courageous and grasping. As it was said of the Duke of Wellington, in the Peninsula, that he had a thought for everybody—from Lord Hill to the smallest drummer in the army—in like manner Tom Billings bestowed HIS attention on high and low; but in the shape of blows: he would fight the strongest and kick the smallest, and was always at work with one or the other. At thirteen, when he was removed from the establishment whither he had been sent, he was the cock of the school out of doors, and the very last boy in. He used to let the little boys and new-comers pass him by, and laugh; but he always belaboured them unmercifully afterwards; and then it was, he said, HIS turn to laugh. With such a pugnacious turn, Tom Billings ought to have been made a soldier, and might have died a marshal; but, by an unlucky ordinance of fate, he was made a tailor, and died a—never mind what for the present; suffice it to say, that he was suddenly cut off, at a very early period of his existence, by a disease which has exercised considerable ravages among the British youth.

By consulting the authority above mentioned, we find that Hayes did not confine himself to the profession of a carpenter, or remain long established in the country; but was induced, by the eager spirit of Mrs. Catherine most probably, to try his fortune in the metropolis; where he lived, flourished, and died. Oxford Road, Saint Giles's, and Tottenham Court were, at various periods of his residence in town, inhabited by him. At one place he carried on the business of greengrocer and small-coalman; in another, he was carpenter, undertaker, and lender of money to the poor; finally, he was a lodging-house keeper in the Oxford or Tyburn Road; but continued to exercise the last-named charitable profession.

Lending as he did upon pledges, and carrying on a pretty large trade, it was not for him, of course, to inquire into the pedigree of all the pieces of plate, the bales of cloth, swords, watches, wigs, shoe-buckles, etc. that were confided by his friends to his keeping; but it is clear that his friends had the requisite confidence in him, and that he enjoyed the esteem of a class of characters who still live in history, and are admired unto this very day. The mind loves to think that, perhaps, in Mr. Hayes's back parlour the gallant Turpin might have hob-and-nobbed with Mrs. Catherine; that here, perhaps, the noble Sheppard might have cracked his joke, or quaffed his pint of rum. Who knows but that Macheath and Paul Clifford may have crossed legs under Hayes's dinner-table? But why pause to speculate on things that might have been? why desert reality for fond imagination, or call up from their honoured graves the sacred dead? I know not: and yet, in sooth, I can never pass Cumberland Gate without a sigh, as I think of the gallant cavaliers who traversed that road in old time. Pious priests accompanied their triumphs; their chariots were surrounded by hosts of glittering javelin-men. As the slave at the car of the Roman conqueror shouted, "Remember thou art mortal!", before the eyes of the British warrior rode the undertaker and his coffin, telling him that he too must die! Mark well the spot! A hundred years ago Albion Street (where comic Power dwelt, Milesia's darling son)—Albion Street was a desert. The square of Connaught was without its penultimate, and, strictly speaking, NAUGHT. The Edgware Road was then a road, 'tis true; with tinkling waggons passing now and then, and fragrant walls of snowy hawthorn blossoms. The ploughman whistled over Nutford Place; down the green solitudes of Sovereign Street the merry milkmaid led the lowing kine. Here, then, in the midst of green fields and sweet air—before ever omnibuses were, and when Pineapple Turnpike and Terrace were alike unknown—here stood Tyburn: and on the road towards it, perhaps to enjoy the prospect, stood, in the year 1725, the habitation of Mr. John Hayes.

One fine morning in the year 1725, Mrs. Hayes, who had been abroad in her best hat and riding-hood; Mr. Hayes, who for a wonder had accompanied her; and Mrs. Springatt, a lodger, who for a remuneration had the honour of sharing Mrs. Hayes's friendship and table: all returned, smiling and rosy, at about half-past ten o'clock, from a walk which they had taken to Bayswater. Many thousands of people were likewise seen flocking down the Oxford Road; and you would rather have thought, from the smartness of their appearance and the pleasure depicted in their countenances, that they were just issuing from a sermon, than quitting the ceremony which they had been to attend.

The fact is, that they had just been to see a gentleman hanged,—a cheap pleasure, which the Hayes family never denied themselves; and they returned home with a good appetite to breakfast, braced by the walk, and tickled into hunger, as it were, by the spectacle. I can recollect, when I was a gyp at Cambridge, that the "men" used to have breakfast-parties for the very same purpose; and the exhibition of the morning acted infallibly upon the stomach, and caused the young students to eat with much voracity.

Well, Mrs. Catherine, a handsome, well-dressed, plump, rosy woman of three or four and thirty (and when, my dear, is a woman handsomer than at that age?), came in quite merrily from her walk, and entered the back-parlour, which looked into a pleasant yard, or garden, whereon the sun was shining very gaily; and where, at a table covered with a nice white cloth, laid out with some silver mugs, too, and knives, all with different crests and patterns, sat an old gentleman reading in an old book.

"Here we are at last, Doctor," said Mrs. Hayes, "and here's his speech." She produced the little halfpenny tract, which to this day is sold at the gallows-foot upon the death of every offender. "I've seen a many men turned off, to be sure; but I never did see one who bore it more like a man than he did."

"My dear," said the gentleman addressed as Doctor, "he was as cool and as brave as steel, and no more minded hanging than tooth-drawing."

"It was the drink that ruined him," said Mrs. Cat.

"Drink, and bad company. I warned him, my dear,—I warned him years ago: and directly he got into Wild's gang, I knew that he had not a year to run. Ah, why, my love, will men continue such dangerous courses," continued the Doctor, with a sigh, "and jeopardy their lives for a miserable watch or a snuff-box, of which Mr. Wild takes three-fourths of the produce? But here comes the breakfast; and, egad, I am as hungry as a lad of twenty."

Indeed, at this moment Mrs. Hayes's servant appeared with a smoking dish of bacon and greens; and Mr. Hayes himself ascended from the cellar (of which he kept the key), bearing with him a tolerably large jug of small-beer. To this repast the Doctor, Mrs. Springatt (the other lodger), and Mr. and Mrs. Hayes, proceeded with great alacrity. A fifth cover was laid, but not used; the company remarking that "Tom had very likely found some acquaintances at Tyburn, with whom he might choose to pass the morning."

Tom was Master Thomas Billings, now of the age of sixteen: slim, smart, five feet ten inches in height, handsome, sallow in complexion, black-eyed and black-haired. Mr. Billings was apprentice to a tailor, of tolerable practice, who was to take him into partnership at the end of his term. It was supposed, and with reason, that Tom would not fail to make a fortune in this business; of which the present head was one Beinkleider, a German. Beinkleider was skilful in his trade (after the manner of his nation, which in breeches and metaphysics—in inexpressibles and incomprehensibles—may instruct all Europe), but too fond of his pleasure. Some promissory notes of his had found their way into Hayes's hands, and had given him the means not only of providing Master Billings with a cheap apprenticeship, and a cheap partnership afterwards; but would empower him, in one or two years after the young partner had joined the firm, to eject the old one altogether. So that there was every prospect that, when Mr. Billings was twenty-one years of age, poor Beinkleider would have to act, not as his master, but his journeyman.

Tom was a very precocious youth; was supplied by a doting mother with plenty of pocket-money, and spent it with a number of lively companions of both sexes, at plays, bull-baitings, fairs, jolly parties on the river, and such-like innocent amusements. He could throw a main, too, as well as his elders; had pinked his man, in a row at Madam King's in the Piazza; and was much respected at the Roundhouse.

Mr. Hayes was not very fond of this promising young gentleman; indeed, he had the baseness to bear malice, because, in a quarrel which occurred about two years previously, he, Hayes, being desirous to chastise Mr. Billings, had found himself not only quite incompetent, but actually at the mercy of the boy; who struck him over the head with a joint-stool, felled him to the ground, and swore he would have his life. The Doctor, who was then also a lodger at Mr. Hayes's, interposed, and restored the combatants, not to friendship, but to peace. Hayes never afterwards attempted to lift his hand to the young man, but contented himself with hating him profoundly. In this sentiment Mr. Billings participated cordially; and, quite unlike Mr. Hayes, who never dared to show his dislike, used on every occasion when they met, by actions, looks, words, sneers, and curses, to let his stepfather know the opinion which he had of him. Why did not Hayes discard the boy altogether? Because, if he did so, he was really afraid of his life, and because he trembled before Mrs. Hayes, his lady, as the leaf trembles before the tempest in October. His breath was not his own, but hers; his money, too, had been chiefly of her getting,—for though he was as stingy and mean as mortal man can be, and so likely to save much, he had not the genius for GETTING which Mrs. Hayes possessed. She kept his books (for she had learned to read and write by this time), she made his bargains, and she directed the operations of the poor-spirited little capitalist. When bills became due, and debtors pressed for time, then she brought Hayes's own professional merits into play. The man was as deaf and cold as a rock; never did poor tradesmen gain a penny from him; never were the bailiffs delayed one single minute from their prey. The Beinkleider business, for instance, showed pretty well the genius of the two. Hayes was for closing with him at once; but his wife saw the vast profits which might be drawn out of him, and arranged the apprenticeship and the partnership before alluded to. The woman heartily scorned and spit upon her husband, who fawned upon her like a spaniel. She loved good cheer; she did not want for a certain kind of generosity. The only feeling that Hayes had for anyone except himself was for his wife, whom he held in a cowardly awe and attachment: he liked drink, too, which made him chirping and merry, and accepted willingly any treats that his acquaintances might offer him; but he would suffer agonies when his wife brought or ordered from the cellar a bottle of wine.

And now for the Doctor. He was about seventy years of age. He had been much abroad; he was of a sober, cheerful aspect; he dressed handsomely and quietly in a broad hat and cassock; but saw no company except the few friends whom he met at the coffee-house. He had an income of about one hundred pounds, which he promised to leave to young Billings. He was amused with the lad, and fond of his mother, and had boarded with them for some years past. The Doctor, in fact, was our old friend Corporal Brock, the Reverend Doctor Wood now, as he had been Major Wood fifteen years back.

Anyone who has read the former part of this history must have seen that we have spoken throughout with invariable respect of Mr. Brock; and that in every circumstance in which he has appeared, he has acted not only with prudence, but often with genius. The early obstacle to Mr. Brock's success was want of conduct simply. Drink, women, play—how many a brave fellow have they ruined!—had pulled Brock down as often as his merit had carried him up. When a man's passion for play has brought him to be a scoundrel, it at once ceases to be hurtful to him in a worldly point of view; he cheats, and wins. It is only for the idle and luxurious that women retain their fascinations to a very late period; and Brock's passions had been whipped out of him in Virginia; where much ill-health, ill-treatment, hard labour, and hard food, speedily put an end to them. He forgot there even how to drink; rum or wine made this poor declining gentleman so ill that he could indulge in them no longer; and so his three vices were cured.

Had he been ambitious, there is little doubt but that Mr. Brock, on his return from transportation, might have risen in the world; but he was old and a philosopher: he did not care about rising. Living was cheaper in those days, and interest for money higher: when he had amassed about six hundred pounds, he purchased an annuity of seventy-two pounds, and gave out—why should he not?—that he had the capital as well as the interest. After leaving the Hayes family in the country, he found them again in London: he took up his abode with them, and was attached to the mother and the son. Do you suppose that rascals have not affections like other people? hearts, madam—ay, hearts—and family ties which they cherish? As the Doctor lived on with this charming family he began to regret that he had sunk all his money in annuities, and could not, as he repeatedly vowed he would, leave his savings to his adopted children.

He felt an indescribable pleasure ("suave mari magno," etc.) in watching the storms and tempests of the Hayes menage. He used to encourage Mrs. Catherine into anger when, haply, that lady's fits of calm would last too long; he used to warm up the disputes between wife and husband, mother and son, and enjoy them beyond expression: they served him for daily amusement; and he used to laugh until the tears ran down his venerable cheeks at the accounts which young Tom continually brought him of his pranks abroad, among watchmen and constables, at taverns or elsewhere.

When, therefore, as the party were discussing their bacon and cabbage, before which the Reverend Doctor with much gravity said grace, Master Tom entered. Doctor Wood, who had before been rather gloomy, immediately brightened up, and made a place for Billings between himself and Mrs. Catherine.

"How do, old cock?" said that young gentleman familiarly. "How goes it, mother?" And so saying, he seized eagerly upon the jug of beer which Mr. Hayes had drawn, and from which the latter was about to help himself, and poured down his throat exactly one quart.

"Ah!" said Mr. Billings, drawing breath after a draught which he had learned accurately to gauge from the habit of drinking out of pewter measures which held precisely that quantity.—"Ah!" said Mr. Billings, drawing breath, and wiping his mouth with his sleeves, "this is very thin stuff, old Squaretoes; but my coppers have been red-hot since last night, and they wanted a sluicing."

"Should you like some ale, dear?" said Mrs. Hayes, that fond and judicious parent.

"A quart of brandy, Tom?" said Doctor Wood. "Your papa will run down to the cellar for it in a minute."

"I'll see him hanged first!" cried Mr. Hayes, quite frightened.

"Oh, fie, now, you unnatural father!" said the Doctor.

The very name of father used to put Mr. Hayes in a fury. "I'm not his father, thank Heaven!" said he.

"No, nor nobody else's," said Tom.

Mr. Hayes only muttered "Base-born brat!"

"His father was a gentleman,—that's more than you ever were!" screamed Mrs. Hayes. "His father was a man of spirit; no cowardly sneak of a carpenter, Mr Hayes! Tom has noble blood in his veins, for all he has a tailor's appearance; and if his mother had had her right, she would be now in a coach-and-six."

"I wish I could find my father," said Tom; "for I think Polly Briggs and I would look mighty well in a coach-and-six." Tom fancied that if his father was a count at the time of his birth, he must be a prince now; and, indeed, went among his companions by the latter august title.

"Ay, Tom, that you would," cried his mother, looking at him fondly.

"With a sword by my side, and a hat and feather there's never a lord at St. James's would cut a finer figure."

After a little more of this talk, in which Mrs. Hayes let the company know her high opinion of her son—who, as usual, took care to show his extreme contempt for his stepfather—the latter retired to his occupations; the lodger, Mrs. Springatt, who had never said a word all this time, retired to her apartment on the second floor; and, pulling out their pipes and tobacco, the old gentleman and the young one solaced themselves with half-an-hour's more talk and smoking; while the thrifty Mrs. Hayes, opposite to them, was busy with her books.

"What's in the confessions?" said Mr. Billings to Doctor Wood. "There were six of 'em besides Mac: two for sheep, four housebreakers; but nothing of consequence, I fancy."

"There's the paper," said Wood, archly. "Read for yourself, Tom."

Mr. Tom looked at the same time very fierce and very foolish; for, though he could drink, swear, and fight as well as any lad of his inches in England, reading was not among his accomplishments. "I tell you what, Doctor," said he, "— you! have no bantering with me,—for I'm not the man that will bear it, — me!" and he threw a tremendous swaggering look across the table.

"I want you to learn to read, Tommy dear. Look at your mother there over her books: she keeps them as neat as a scrivener now, and at twenty she could make never a stroke."

"Your godfather speaks for your good, child; and for me, thou knowest that I have promised thee a gold-headed cane and periwig on the first day that thou canst read me a column of the Flying Post."

"Hang the periwig!" said Mr. Tom, testily. "Let my godfather read the paper himself, if he has a liking for it."

Whereupon the old gentleman put on his spectacles, and glanced over the sheet of whity-brown paper, which, ornamented with a picture of a gallows at the top, contained the biographies of the seven unlucky individuals who had that morning suffered the penalty of the law. With the six heroes who came first in the list we have nothing to do; but have before us a copy of the paper containing the life of No. 7, and which the Doctor read in an audible voice.

"CAPTAIN MACSHANE.

"The seventh victim to his own crimes was the famous highwayman, Captain Macshane, so well known as the Irish Fire-eater.

"The Captain came to the ground in a fine white lawn shirt and nightcap; and, being a Papist in his religion, was attended by Father O'Flaherty, Popish priest, and chaplain to the Bavarian Envoy.

"Captain Macshane was born of respectable parents, in the town of Clonakilty, in Ireland, being descended from most of the kings in that country. He had the honour of serving their Majesties King William and Queen Mary, and Her Majesty Queen Anne, in Flanders and Spain, and obtained much credit from my Lords Marlborough and Peterborough for his valour.

"But being placed on half-pay at the end of the war, Ensign Macshane took to evil courses; and, frequenting the bagnios and dice-houses, was speedily brought to ruin.

"Being at this pass, he fell in with the notorious Captain Wood, and they two together committed many atrocious robberies in the inland counties; but these being too hot to hold them, they went into the west, where they were unknown. Here, however, the day of retribution arrived; for, having stolen three pewter-pots from a public-house, they, under false names, were tried at Exeter, and transported for seven years beyond the sea. Thus it is seen that Justice never sleeps; but, sooner or latter, is sure to overtake the criminal.

"On their return from Virginia, a quarrel about booty arose between these two, and Macshane killed Wood in a combat that took place between them near to the town of Bristol; but a waggon coming up, Macshane was obliged to fly without the ill-gotten wealth: so true is it, that wickedness never prospers.

"Two days afterwards, Macshane met the coach of Miss Macraw, a Scotch lady and heiress, going, for lumbago and gout, to the Bath. He at first would have robbed this lady; but such were his arts, that he induced her to marry him; and they lived together for seven years in the town of Eddenboro, in Scotland,—he passing under the name of Colonel Geraldine. The lady dying, and Macshane having expended all her wealth, he was obliged to resume his former evil courses, in order to save himself from starvation; whereupon he robbed a Scotch lord, by name the Lord of Whistlebinkie, of a mull of snuff; for which crime he was condemned to the Tolbooth prison at Eddenboro, in Scotland, and whipped many times in publick.

"These deserved punishments did not at all alter Captain Macshane's disposition; and on the 17th of February last, he stopped the Bavarian Envoy's coach on Blackheath, coming from Dover, and robbed his Excellency and his chaplain; taking from the former his money, watches, star, a fur-cloak, his sword (a very valuable one); and from the latter a Romish missal, out of which he was then reading, and a case-bottle."

"The Bavarian Envoy!" said Tom parenthetically. "My master, Beinkleider, was his Lordship's regimental tailor in Germany, and is now making a Court suit for him. It will be a matter of a hundred pounds to him, I warrant."

Doctor Wood resumed his reading. "Hum—hum! A Romish missal, out of which he was reading, and a case-bottle.

"By means of the famous Mr. Wild, this notorious criminal was brought to justice, and the case-bottle and missal have been restored to Father O'Flaherty.

"During his confinement in Newgate, Mr. Macshane could not be brought to express any contrition for his crimes, except that of having killed his commanding officer. For this Wood he pretended an excessive sorrow, and vowed that usquebaugh had been the cause of his death,—indeed, in prison he partook of no other liquor, and drunk a bottle of it on the day before his death.

"He was visited by several of the clergy and gentry in his cell; among others, by the Popish priest whom he had robbed, Father O'Flaherty, before mentioned, who attended him likewise in his last moments (if that idolatrous worship may be called attention), and likewise by the Father's patron, the Bavarian Ambassador, his Excellency Count Maximilian de Galgenstein."

As old Wood came to these words, he paused to give them utterance.

"What! Max?" screamed Mrs. Hayes, letting her ink-bottle fall over her ledgers.

"Why, be hanged if it ben't my father!" said Mr. Billings.

"Your father, sure enough, unless there be others of his name, and unless the scoundrel is hanged," said the Doctor—sinking his voice, however, at the end of the sentence.

Mr. Billings broke his pipe in an agony of joy. "I think we'll have the coach now, Mother," says he; "and I'm blessed if Polly Briggs shall not look as fine as a duchess."

"Polly Briggs is a low slut, Tom, and not fit for the likes of you, his Excellency's son. Oh, fie! You must be a gentleman now, sirrah; and I doubt whether I shan't take you away from that odious tailor's shop altogether."

To this proposition Mr. Billings objected altogether; for, besides Mrs. Briggs before alluded to, the young gentleman was much attached to his master's daughter, Mrs. Margaret Gretel, or Gretchen Beinkleider.

"No," says he. "There will be time to think of that hereafter, ma'am. If my pa makes a man of me, why, of course, the shop may go to the deuce, for what I care; but we had better wait, look you, for something certain before we give up such a pretty bird in the hand as this."

"He speaks like Solomon," said the Doctor.

"I always said he would be a credit to his old mother, didn't I, Brock?" cried Mrs. Cat, embracing her son very affectionately. "A credit to her; ay, I warrant, a real blessing! And dost thou want any money, Tom? for a lord's son must not go about without a few pieces in his pocket. And I tell thee, Tommy, thou must go and see his Lordship; and thou shalt have a piece of brocade for a waistcoat, thou shalt; ay, and the silver-hilted sword I told thee of; but oh, Tommy, Tommy! have a care, and don't be a-drawing of it in naughty company at the gaming-houses, or at the—"

"A drawing of fiddlesticks, Mother! If I go to see my father, I must have a reason for it; and instead of going with a sword in my hand, I shall take something else in it."

"The lad IS a lad of nous," cried Doctor Wood, "although his mother does spoil him so cruelly. Look you, Madam Cat: did you not hear what he said about Beinkleider and the clothes? Tommy will just wait on the Count with his Lordship's breeches. A man may learn a deal of news in the trying on of a pair of breeches."

And so it was agreed that in this manner the son should at first make his appearance before his father. Mrs. Cat gave him the piece of brocade, which, in the course of the day, was fashioned into a smart waistcoat (for Beinkleider's shop was close by, in Cavendish Square). Mrs. Gretel, with many blushes, tied a fine blue riband round his neck; and, in a pair of silk stockings, with gold buckles to his shoes, Master Billings looked a very proper young gentleman.

"And, Tommy," said his mother, blushing and hesitating, "should Max—should his Lordship ask after your—want to know if your mother is alive, you can say she is, and well, and often talks of old times. And, Tommy" (after another pause), "you needn't say anything about Mr. Hayes; only say I'm quite well."

Mrs. Hayes looked at him as he marched down the street, a long long way. Tom was proud and gay in his new costume, and was not unlike his father. As she looked, lo! Oxford Street disappeared, and she saw a green common, and a village, and a little inn. There was a soldier leading a pair of horses about on the green common; and in the inn sat a cavalier, so young, so merry, so beautiful! Oh, what slim white hands he had; and winning words, and tender, gentle blue eyes! Was it not an honour to a country lass that such a noble gentleman should look at her for a moment? Had he not some charm about him that she must needs obey when he whispered in her ear, "Come, follow me!" As she walked towards the lane that morning, how well she remembered each spot as she passed it, and the look it wore for the last time! How the smoke was rising from the pastures, how the fish were jumping and plashing in the mill-stream! There was the church, with all its windows lighted up with gold, and yonder were the reapers sweeping down the brown corn. She tried to sing as she went up the hill—what was it? She could not remember; but oh, how well she remembered the sound of the horse's hoofs, as they came quicker, quicker—nearer, nearer! How noble he looked on his great horse! Was he thinking of her, or were they all silly words which he spoke last night, merely to pass away the time and deceive poor girls with? Would he remember them,—would he?

"Cat my dear," here cried Mr. Brock, alias Captain, alias Doctor Wood, "here's the meat a-getting cold, and I am longing for my breakfast."

As they went in he looked her hard in the face. "What, still at it, you silly girl? I've been watching you these five minutes, Cat; and be hanged but I think a word from Galgenstein, and you would follow him as a fly does a treacle-pot!"

They went in to breakfast; but though there was a hot shoulder of mutton and onion-sauce—Mrs. Catherine's favourite dish—she never touched a morsel of it.

In the meanwhile Mr. Thomas Billings, in his new clothes which his mamma had given him, in his new riband which the fair Miss Beinkleider had tied round his neck, and having his Excellency's breeches wrapped in a silk handkerchief in his right hand, turned down in the direction of Whitehall, where the Bavarian Envoy lodged. But, before he waited on him, Mr. Billings, being excessively pleased with his personal appearance, made an early visit to Mrs. Briggs, who lived in the neighbourhood of Swallow Street; and who, after expressing herself with much enthusiasm regarding her Tommy's good looks, immediately asked him what he would stand to drink? Raspberry gin being suggested, a pint of that liquor was sent for; and so great was the confidence and intimacy subsisting between these two young people, that the reader will be glad to hear that Mrs. Polly accepted every shilling of the money which Tom Billings had received from his mamma the day before; nay, could with difficulty be prevented from seizing upon the cut-velvet breeches which he was carrying to the nobleman for whom they were made. Having paid his adieux to Mrs. Polly, Mr. Billings departed to visit his father.

CHAPTER IX

INTERVIEW BETWEEN COUNT GALGENSTEIN AND MASTER THOMAS BILLINGS, WHEN HE INFORMS THE COUNT OF HIS PARENTAGE

I don't know in all this miserable world a more miserable spectacle than that of a young fellow of five or six and forty. The British army, that nursery of valour, turns out many of the young fellows I mean: who, having flaunted in dragoon uniforms from seventeen to six-and-thirty; having bought, sold, or swapped during that period some two hundred horses; having played, say, fifteen thousand games at billiards; having drunk some six thousand bottles of wine; having consumed a reasonable number of Nugee coats, split many dozen pairs of high-heeled Hoby boots, and read the newspaper and the army-list duly, retire from the service when they have attained their eighth lustre, and saunter through the world, trailing from London to Cheltenham, and from Boulogne to Paris, and from Paris to Baden, their idleness, their ill-health, and their ennui. "In the morning of youth," and when seen along with whole troops of their companions, these flowers look gaudy and brilliant enough; but there is no object more dismal than one of them alone, and in its autumnal, or seedy state. My friend, Captain Popjoy, is one who has arrived at this condition, and whom everybody knows by his title of Father Pop. A kinder, simpler, more empty-headed fellow does not exist. He is forty-seven years old, and appears a young, good-looking man of sixty. At the time of the Army of Occupation he really was as good-looking a man as any in the Dragoons. He now uses all sorts of stratagems to cover the bald place on his head, by combing certain thin grey sidelocks over it. He has, in revenge, a pair of enormous moustaches, which he dyes of the richest blue-black. His nose is a good deal larger and redder than it used to be; his eyelids have grown flat and heavy; and a little pair of red, watery eyeballs float in the midst of them: it seems as if the light which was once in those sickly green pupils had extravasated into the white part of the eye. If Pop's legs are not so firm and muscular as they used to be in those days when he took such leaps into White's buckskins, in revenge his waist is much larger. He wears a very good coat, however, and a waistband, which he lets out after dinner. Before ladies he blushes, and is as silent as a schoolboy. He calls them "modest women." His society is chiefly among young lads belonging to his former profession. He knows the best wine to be had at each tavern or cafe, and the waiters treat him with much respectful familiarity. He knows the names of every one of them; and shouts out, "Send Markwell here!" or, "Tell Cuttriss to give us a bottle of the yellow seal!" or, "Dizzy voo, Monsure Borrel, noo donny shampang frappy," etc. He always makes the salad or the punch, and dines out three hundred days in the year: the other days you see him in a two-franc eating-house at Paris, or prowling about Rupert Street, or St. Martin's Court, where you get a capital cut of meat for eightpence. He has decent lodgings and scrupulously clean linen; his animal functions are still tolerably well preserved, his spiritual have evaporated long since; he sleeps well, has no conscience, believes himself to be a respectable fellow, and is tolerably happy on the days when he is asked out to dinner.

Poor Pop is not very high in the scale of created beings; but, if you fancy there is none lower, you are in egregious error. There was once a man who had a mysterious exhibition of an animal, quite unknown to naturalists, called "the wusser." Those curious individuals who desired to see the wusser were introduced into an apartment where appeared before them nothing more than a little lean shrivelled hideous blear-eyed mangy pig. Everyone cried out "Swindle!" and "Shame!" "Patience, gentlemen, be heasy," said the showman: "look at that there hanimal; it's a perfect phenomaly of hugliness: I engage you never see such a pig." Nobody ever had seen. "Now, gentlemen," said he, "I'll keep my promise, has per bill; and bad as that there pig is, look at this here" (he showed another). "Look at this here, and you'll see at once that it's A WUSSER." In like manner the Popjoy breed is bad enough, but it serves only to show off the Galgenstein race; which is WUSSER.

Galgenstein had led a very gay life, as the saying is, for the last fifteen years; such a gay one, that he had lost all capacity of enjoyment by this time, and only possessed inclinations without powers of gratifying them. He had grown to be exquisitely curious and fastidious about meat and drink, for instance, and all that he wanted was an appetite. He carried about with him a French cook, who could not make him eat; a doctor, who could not make him well; a mistress, of whom he was heartily sick after two days; a priest, who had been a favourite of the exemplary Dubois, and by turns used to tickle him by the imposition of penance, or by the repetition of a tale from the recueil of Noce, or La Fare. All his appetites were wasted and worn; only some monstrosity would galvanise them into momentary action. He was in that effete state to which many noblemen of his time had arrived; who were ready to believe in ghost-raising or in gold-making, or to retire into monasteries and wear hair-shirts, or to dabble in conspiracies, or to die in love with little cook-maids of fifteen, or to pine for the smiles or at the frowns of a prince of the blood, or to go mad at the refusal of a chamberlain's key. The last gratification he remembered to have enjoyed was that of riding bareheaded in a soaking rain for three hours by the side of his Grand Duke's mistress's coach; taking the pas of Count Krahwinkel, who challenged him, and was run through the body for this very dispute. Galgenstein gained a rheumatic gout by it, which put him to tortures for many months; and was further gratified with the post of English Envoy. He had a fortune, he asked no salary, and could look the envoy very well. Father O'Flaherty did all the duties, and furthermore acted as a spy over the ambassador—a sinecure post, for the man had no feelings, wishes, or opinions—absolutely none.

"Upon my life, father," said this worthy man, "I care for nothing. You have been talking for an hour about the Regent's death, and the Duchess of Phalaris, and sly old Fleury, and what not; and I care just as much as if you told me that one of my bauers at Galgenstein had killed a pig; or as if my lacquey, La Rose yonder, had made love to my mistress."

"He does!" said the reverend gentleman.

"Ah, Monsieur l'Abbe!" said La Rose, who was arranging his master's enormous Court periwig, "you are, helas! wrong. Monsieur le Comte will not be angry at my saying that I wish the accusation were true."

The Count did not take the slightest notice of La Rose's wit, but continued his own complaints.

"I tell you, Abbe, I care for nothing. I lost a thousand guineas t'other night at basset; I wish to my heart I could have been vexed about it. Egad! I remember the day when to lose a hundred made me half mad for a month. Well, next day I had my revenge at dice, and threw thirteen mains. There was some delay; a call for fresh bones, I think; and would you believe it?—I fell asleep with the box in my hand!"

"A desperate case, indeed," said the Abbe.

"If it had not been for Krahwinkel, I should have been a dead man, that's positive. That pinking him saved me."

"I make no doubt of it," said the Abbe. "Had your Excellency not run him through, he, without a doubt, would have done the same for you."

"Psha! you mistake my words, Monsieur l'Abbe" (yawning). "I mean—what cursed chocolate!—that I was dying for want of excitement. Not that I cared for dying; no, damn me if I do!"

"WHEN you do, your Excellency means," said the Abbe, a fat grey-haired Irishman, from the Irlandois College at Paris.

His Excellency did not laugh, nor understand jokes of any kind; he was of an undeviating stupidity, and only replied, "Sir, I mean what I say. I don't care for living: no, nor for dying either; but I can speak as well as another, and I'll thank you not to be correcting my phrases as if I were one of your cursed schoolboys, and not a gentleman of fortune and blood."

Herewith the Count, who had uttered four sentences about himself (he never spoke of anything else), sunk back on his pillows again, quite exhausted by his eloquence. The Abbe, who had a seat and a table by the bedside, resumed the labours which had brought him into the room in the morning, and busied himself with papers, which occasionally he handed over to his superior for approval.

Presently Monsieur la Rose appeared.

"Here is a person with clothes from Mr. Beinkleider's. Will your Excellency see him, or shall I bid him leave the clothes?"

The Count was very much fatigued by this time; he had signed three papers, and read the first half-a-dozen lines of a pair of them.

"Bid the fellow come in, La Rose; and, hark ye, give me my wig: one must show one's self to be a gentleman before these scoundrels." And he therefore mounted a large chestnut-coloured, orange-scented pyramid of horsehair, which was to awe the new-comer.

He was a lad of about seventeen, in a smart waistcoat and a blue riband: our friend Tom Billings, indeed. He carried under his arm the Count's destined breeches. He did not seem in the least awed, however, by his Excellency's appearance, but looked at him with a great degree of curiosity and boldness. In the same manner he surveyed the chaplain, and then nodded to him with a kind look of recognition.

"Where have I seen the lad?" said the father. "Oh, I have it! My good friend, you were at the hanging yesterday, I think?"

Mr. Billings gave a very significant nod with his head. "I never miss," said he.

"What a young Turk! And pray, sir, do you go for pleasure, or for business?"

"Business! what do you mean by business?"

"Oh, I did not know whether you might be brought up to the trade, or your relations be undergoing the operation."

"My relations," said Mr. Billings, proudly, and staring the Count full in the face, "was not made for no such thing. I'm a tailor now, but I'm a gentleman's son: as good a man, ay, as his lordship there: for YOU a'n't his lordship—you're the Popish priest you are; and we were very near giving you a touch of a few Protestant stones, master."

The Count began to be a little amused: he was pleased to see the Abbe look alarmed, or even foolish.

"Egad, Abbe," said he, "you turn as white as a sheet."

"I don't fancy being murdered, my Lord," said the Abbe, hastily; "and murdered for a good work. It was but to be useful to yonder poor Irishman, who saved me as a prisoner in Flanders, when Marlborough would have hung me up like poor Macshane himself was yesterday."

"Ah!" said the Count, bursting out with some energy, "I was thinking who the fellow could be, ever since he robbed me on the Heath. I recollect the scoundrel now: he was a second in a duel I had here in the year six."

"Along with Major Wood, behind Montague House," said Mr. Billings. "I'VE heard on it." And here he looked more knowing than ever.

"YOU!" cried the Count, more and more surprised. "And pray who the devil ARE you?"

"My name's Billings."

"Billings?" said the Count.

"I come out of Warwickshire," said Mr. Billings.

"Indeed!"

"I was born at Birmingham town."

"Were you, really!"

"My mother's name was Hayes," continued Billings, in a solemn voice. "I was put out to a nurse along with John Billings, a blacksmith; and my father run away. NOW do you know who I am?"

"Why, upon honour, now," said the Count, who was amused,—"upon honour, Mr. Billings, I have not that advantage."

"Well, then, my Lord, YOU'RE MY FATHER!"

Mr. Billings when he said this came forward to the Count with a theatrical air; and, flinging down the breeches of which he was the bearer, held out his arms and stared, having very little doubt but that his Lordship would forthwith spring out of bed and hug him to his heart. A similar piece of naivete many fathers of families have, I have no doubt, remarked in their children; who, not caring for their parents a single doit, conceive, nevertheless, that the latter are bound to show all sorts of affection for them. His lordship did move, but backwards towards the wall, and began pulling at the bell-rope with an expression of the most intense alarm.

"Keep back, sirrah!—keep back! Suppose I AM your father, do you want to murder me? Good heavens! how the boy smells of gin and tobacco! Don't turn away, my lad; sit down there at a proper distance. And, La Rose, give him some eau-de-Cologne, and get a cup of coffee. Well, now, go on with your story. Egad, my dear Abbe, I think it is very likely that what the lad says is true."

"If it is a family conversation," said the Abbe, "I had better leave you."

"Oh, for Heaven's sake, no! I could not stand the boy alone. Now, Mister ah!—What's-your-name? Have the goodness to tell your story."

Mr. Billings was woefully disconcerted; for his mother and he had agreed that as soon as his father saw him he would be recognised at once, and, mayhap, made heir to the estates and title; in which being disappointed, he very sulkily went on with his narrative, and detailed many of those events with which the reader has already been made acquainted. The Count asked the boy's mother's Christian name, and being told it, his memory at once returned to him.

"What! are you little Cat's son?" said his Excellency. "By heavens, mon cher Abbe, a charming creature, but a tigress—positively a tigress. I recollect the whole affair now. She's a little fresh black-haired woman, a'n't she? with a sharp nose and thick eyebrows, ay? Ah yes, yes!" went on my Lord, "I recollect her, I recollect her. It was at Birmingham I first met her: she was my Lady Trippet's woman, wasn't she?"

"She was no such thing," said Mr. Billings, hotly. "Her aunt kept the 'Bugle Inn' on Waltham Green, and your Lordship seduced her."

"Seduced her! Oh, 'gad, so I did. Stap me, now, I did. Yes, I made her jump on my black horse, and bore her off like—like Aeneas bore his wife away from the siege of Rome! hey, l'Abbe?"

"The events were precisely similar," said the Abbe. "It is wonderful what a memory you have!"

"I was always remarkable for it," continued his Excellency. "Well, where was I,—at the black horse? Yes, at the black horse. Well, I mounted her on the black horse, and rode her en croupe, egad—ha, ha!—to Birmingham; and there we billed and cooed together like a pair of turtle-doves: yes—ha!—that we did!"

"And this, I suppose, is the end of some of the BILLINGS?" said the Abbe, pointing to Mr. Tom.

"Billings! what do you mean? Yes—oh—ah—a pun, a calembourg. Fi donc, M. l'Abbe." And then, after the wont of very stupid people, M. de Galgenstein went on to explain to the Abbe his own pun. "Well, but to proceed," cries he. "We lived together at Birmingham, and I was going to be married to a rich heiress, egad! when what do you think this little Cat does? She murders me, egad! and makes me manquer the marriage. Twenty thousand, I think it was; and I wanted the money in those days. Now, wasn't she an abominable monster, that mother of yours, hey, Mr. a—What's-your-name?"

"She served you right!" said Mr. Billings, with a great oath, starting up out of all patience.

"Fellow!" said his Excellency, quite aghast, "do you know to whom you speak?—to a nobleman of seventy-eight descents; a count of the Holy Roman Empire; a representative of a sovereign? Ha, egad! Don't stamp, fellow, if you hope for my protection."

"Damn your protection!" said Mr. Billings, in a fury. "Curse you and your protection too! I'm a free-born Briton, and no — French Papist! And any man who insults my mother—ay, or calls me feller—had better look to himself and the two eyes in his head, I can tell him!" And with this Mr. Billings put himself into the most approved attitude of the Cockpit, and invited his father, the reverend gentleman, and Monsieur la Rose the valet, to engage with him in a pugilistic encounter. The two latter, the Abbe especially, seemed dreadfully frightened; but the Count now looked on with much interest; and, giving utterance to a feeble kind of chuckle, which lasted for about half a minute, said,—

"Paws off, Pompey! You young hangdog, you—egad, yes, aha! 'pon honour, you're a lad of spirit; some of your father's spunk in you, hey? I know him by that oath. Why, sir, when I was sixteen, I used to swear—to swear, egad, like a Thames waterman, and exactly in this fellow's way! Buss me, my lad; no, kiss my hand. That will do"—and he held out a very lean yellow hand, peering from a pair of yellow ruffles. It shook very much, and the shaking made all the rings upon it shine only the more.

"Well," says Mr. Billings, "if you wasn't a-going to abuse me nor mother, I don't care if I shake hands with you. I ain't proud!"

The Abbe laughed with great glee; and that very evening sent off to his Court a most ludicrous spicy description of the whole scene of meeting between this amiable father and child; in which he said that young Billings was the eleve favori of M. Kitch, Ecuyer, le bourreau de Londres, and which made the Duke's mistress laugh so much that she vowed that the Abbe should have a bishopric on his return: for, with such store of wisdom, look you, my son, was the world governed in those days.

The Count and his offspring meanwhile conversed with some cordiality. The former informed the latter of all the diseases to which he was subject, his manner of curing them, his great consideration as chamberlain to the Duke of Bavaria; how he wore his Court suits, and of a particular powder which he had invented for the hair; how, when he was seventeen, he had run away with a canoness, egad! who was afterwards locked up in a convent, and grew to be sixteen stone in weight; how he remembered the time when ladies did not wear patches; and how the Duchess of Marlborough boxed his ears when he was so high, because he wanted to kiss her.

All these important anecdotes took some time in the telling, and were accompanied by many profound moral remarks; such as, "I can't abide garlic, nor white-wine, stap me! nor Sauerkraut, though his Highness eats half a bushel per day. I ate it the first time at Court; but when they brought it me a second time, I refused—refused, split me and grill me if I didn't! Everybody stared; his Highness looked as fierce as a Turk; and that infernal Krahwinkel (my dear, I did for him afterwards)—that cursed Krahwinkel, I say, looked as pleased as possible, and whispered to Countess Fritsch, 'Blitzchen, Frau Grafinn,' says he, 'it's all over with Galgenstein.' What did I do? I had the entree, and demanded it. 'Altesse,' says I, falling on one knee, 'I ate no kraut at dinner to-day. You remarked it: I saw your Highness remark it.'

"'I did, M. le Comte,' said his Highness, gravely.

"I had almost tears in my eyes; but it was necessary to come to a resolution, you know. 'Sir,' said I, 'I speak with deep grief to your Highness, who are my benefactor, my friend, my father; but of this I am resolved, I WILL NEVER EAT SAUERKRAUT MORE: it don't agree with me. After being laid up for four weeks by the last dish of Sauerkraut of which I partook, I may say with confidence—IT DON'T agree with me. By impairing my health, it impairs my intellect, and weakens my strength; and both I would keep for your Highness's service.'

"'Tut, tut!' said his Highness. 'Tut, tut, tut!' Those were his very words.

"'Give me my sword or my pen,' said I. 'Give me my sword or my pen, and with these Maximilian de Galgenstein is ready to serve you; but sure,—sure, a great prince will pity the weak health of a faithful subject, who does not know how to eat Sauerkraut?' His Highness was walking about the room: I was still on my knees, and stretched forward my hand to seize his coat.

"'GEHT ZUM TEUFEL, Sir!' said he, in a loud voice (it means 'Go to the deuce,' my dear),—'Geht zum Teufel, and eat what you like!' With this he went out of the room abruptly; leaving in my hand one of his buttons, which I keep to this day. As soon as I was alone, amazed by his great goodness and bounty, I sobbed aloud—cried like a child" (the Count's eyes filled and winked at the very recollection), "and when I went back into the card-room, stepping up to Krahwinkel, 'Count,' says I, 'who looks foolish now?'—Hey there, La Rose, give me the diamond—Yes, that was the very pun I made, and very good it was thought. 'Krahwinkel,' says I, 'WHO LOOKS FOOLISH NOW?' and from that day to this I was never at a Court-day asked to eat Sauerkraut—NEVER!"

"Hey there, La Rose! Bring me that diamond snuff-box in the drawer of my secretaire;" and the snuff-box was brought. "Look at it, my dear," said the Count, "for I saw you seemed to doubt. There is the button—the very one that came off his Grace's coat."

Mr. Billings received it, and twisted it about with a stupid air. The story had quite mystified him; for he did not dare yet to think his father was a fool—his respect for the aristocracy prevented him.

When the Count's communications had ceased, which they did as soon as the story of the Sauerkraut was finished, a silence of some minutes ensued. Mr. Billings was trying to comprehend the circumstances above narrated; his Lordship was exhausted; the chaplain had quitted the room directly the word Sauerkraut was mentioned—he knew what was coming. His Lordship looked for some time at his son; who returned the gaze with his mouth wide open. "Well," said the Count—"well, sir? What are you sitting there for? If you have nothing to say, sir, you had better go. I had you here to amuse me—split me—and not to sit there staring!"

Mr. Billings rose in a fury.

"Hark ye, my lad," said the Count, "tell La Rose to give thee five guineas, and, ah—come again some morning. A nice well-grown young lad," mused the Count, as Master Tommy walked wondering out of the apartment; "a pretty fellow enough, and intelligent too."

"Well, he IS an odd fellow, my father," thought Mr. Billings, as he walked out, having received the sum offered to him. And he immediately went to call upon his friend Polly Briggs, from whom he had separated in the morning.

What was the result of their interview is not at all necessary to the progress of this history. Having made her, however, acquainted with the particulars of his visit to his father, he went to his mother's, and related to her all that had occurred.

Poor thing, she was very differently interested in the issue of it!

CHAPTER X

SHOWING HOW GALGENSTEIN AND MRS. CAT RECOGNISE EACH OTHER IN MARYLEBONE GARDENS—AND HOW THE COUNT DRIVES HER HOME IN HIS CARRIAGE

About a month after the touching conversation above related, there was given, at Marylebone Gardens, a grand concert and entertainment, at which the celebrated Madame Amenaide, a dancer of the theatre at Paris, was to perform, under the patronage of several English and foreign noblemen; among whom was his Excellency the Bavarian Envoy. Madame Amenaide was, in fact, no other than the maitresse en titre of the Monsieur de Galgenstein, who had her a great bargain from the Duke de Rohan-Chabot at Paris.

It is not our purpose to make a great and learned display here, otherwise the costumes of the company assembled at this fete might afford scope for at least half-a-dozen pages of fine writing; and we might give, if need were, specimens of the very songs and music sung on the occasion. Does not the Burney collection of music, at the British Museum, afford one an ample store of songs from which to choose? Are there not the memoirs of Colley Cibber? those of Mrs. Clark, the daughter of Colley? Is there not Congreve, and Farquhar—nay, and at a pinch, the "Dramatic Biography," or even the Spectator, from which the observant genius might borrow passages, and construct pretty antiquarian figments? Leave we these trifles to meaner souls! Our business is not with the breeches and periwigs, with the hoops and patches, but with the divine hearts of men, and the passions which agitate them. What need, therefore, have we to say that on this evening, after the dancing, the music, and the fireworks, Monsieur de Galgenstein felt the strange and welcome pangs of appetite, and was picking a cold chicken, along with some other friends in an arbour—a cold chicken, with an accompaniment of a bottle of champagne—when he was led to remark that a very handsome plump little person, in a gorgeous stiff damask gown and petticoat, was sauntering up and down the walk running opposite his supping-place, and bestowing continual glances towards his Excellency. The lady, whoever she was, was in a mask, such as ladies of high and low fashion wore at public places in those days, and had a male companion. He was a lad of only seventeen, marvellously well dressed—indeed, no other than the Count's own son, Mr. Thomas Billings; who had at length received from his mother the silver-hilted sword, and the wig, which that affectionate parent had promised to him.

In the course of the month which had elapsed since the interview that has been described in the former chapter, Mr. Billings had several times had occasion to wait on his father; but though he had, according to her wishes, frequently alluded to the existence of his mother, the Count had never at any time expressed the slightest wish to renew his acquaintance with that lady; who, if she had seen him, had only seen him by stealth.

The fact is, that after Billings had related to her the particulars of his first meeting with his Excellency; which ended, like many of the latter visits, in nothing at all; Mrs. Hayes had found some pressing business, which continually took her to Whitehall, and had been prowling from day to day about Monsieur de Galgenstein's lodgings. Four or five times in the week, as his Excellency stepped into his coach, he might have remarked, had he chosen, a woman in a black hood, who was looking most eagerly into his eyes: but those eyes had long since left off the practice of observing; and Madam Catherine's visits had so far gone for nothing.

On this night, however, inspired by gaiety and drink, the Count had been amazingly stricken by the gait and ogling of the lady in the mask. The Reverend O'Flaherty, who was with him, and had observed the figure in the black cloak, recognised, or thought he recognised, her. "It is the woman who dogs your Excellency every day," said he. "She is with that tailor lad who loves to see people hanged—your Excellency's son, I mean." And he was just about to warn the Count of a conspiracy evidently made against him, and that the son had brought, most likely, the mother to play her arts upon him—he was just about, I say, to show to the Count the folly and danger of renewing an old liaison with a woman such as he had described Mrs. Cat to be, when his Excellency, starting up, and interrupting his ghostly adviser at the very beginning of his sentence, said, "Egad, l'Abbe, you are right—it IS my son, and a mighty smart-looking creature with him. Hey! Mr. What's-your-name—Tom, you rogue, don't you know your own father?" And so saying, and cocking his beaver on one side, Monsieur de Galgenstein strutted jauntily after Mr. Billings and the lady.

It was the first time that the Count had formally recognised his son.

"Tom, you rogue," stopped at this, and the Count came up. He had a white velvet suit, covered over with stars and orders, a neat modest wig and bag, and peach-coloured silk-stockings with silver clasps. The lady in the mask gave a start as his Excellency came forward. "Law, mother, don't squeege so," said Tom. The poor woman was trembling in every limb, but she had presence of mind to "squeege" Tom a great deal harder; and the latter took the hint, I suppose, and was silent.

The splendid Count came up. Ye gods, how his embroidery glittered in the lamps! What a royal exhalation of musk and bergamot came from his wig, his handkerchief, and his grand lace ruffles and frills! A broad yellow riband passed across his breast, and ended at his hip in a shining diamond cross—a diamond cross, and a diamond sword-hilt! Was anything ever seen so beautiful? And might not a poor woman tremble when such a noble creature drew near to her, and deigned, from the height of his rank and splendour, to look down upon her? As Jove came down to Semele in state, in his habits of ceremony, with all the grand cordons of his orders blazing about his imperial person—thus dazzling, magnificent, triumphant, the great Galgenstein descended towards Mrs. Catherine. Her cheeks glowed red-hot under her coy velvet mask, her heart thumped against the whalebone prison of her stays. What a delicious storm of vanity was raging in her bosom! What a rush of long-pent recollections burst forth at the sound of that enchanting voice!

As you wind up a hundred-guinea chronometer with a twopenny watch-key—as by means of a dirty wooden plug you set all the waters of Versailles a-raging, and splashing, and storming—in like manner, and by like humble agents, were Mrs. Catherine's tumultuous passions set going. The Count, we have said, slipped up to his son, and merely saying, "How do, Tom?" cut the young gentleman altogether, and passing round to the lady's side, said, "Madam, 'tis a charming evening—egad it is!" She almost fainted: it was the old voice. There he was, after seventeen years, once more at her side!

Now I know what I could have done. I can turn out a quotation from Sophocles (by looking to the index) as well as another: I can throw off a bit of fine writing too, with passion, similes, and a moral at the end. What, pray, is the last sentence but one but the very finest writing? Suppose, for example, I had made Maximilian, as he stood by the side of Catherine, look up towards the clouds, and exclaim, in the words of the voluptuous Cornelius Nepos,

'Aenaoi nephelai
'Arthoomen phanerai
Droseran phusin euageetoi, k.t.l. [*]

* Anglicised version of the author's original Greek text.

Or suppose, again, I had said, in a style still more popular:—

The Count advanced towards the maiden. They both were mute for a while; and only the beating of her heart interrupted that thrilling and passionate silence. Ah, what years of buried joys and fears, hopes and disappointments, arose from their graves in the far past, and in those brief moments flitted before the united ones! How sad was that delicious retrospect, and oh, how sweet! The tears that rolled down the cheek of each were bubbles from the choked and moss-grown wells of youth; the sigh that heaved each bosom had some lurking odours in it—memories of the fragrance of boyhood, echoes of the hymns of the young heart! Thus is it ever—for these blessed recollections the soul always has a place; and while crime perishes, and sorrow is forgotten, the beautiful alone is eternal.

"O golden legends, written in the skies!" mused De Galgenstein, "ye shine as ye did in the olden days! WE change, but YE speak ever the same language. Gazing in your abysmal depths, the feeble ratioci—"

There, now, are six columns[*] of the best writing to be found in this or any other book. Galgenstein has quoted Euripides thrice, Plato once, Lycophron nine times, besides extracts from the Latin syntax and the minor Greek poets. Catherine's passionate embreathings are of the most fashionable order; and I call upon the ingenious critic of the X— newspaper to say whether they do not possess the real impress of the giants of the olden time—the real Platonic smack, in a word? Not that I want in the least to show off; but it is as well, every now and then, to show the public what one CAN do.

(* There WERE six columns, as mentioned by the accurate Mr. Solomons; but we have withdrawn two pages and three-quarters, because, although our correspondent has been excessively eloquent, according to custom, we were anxiousto come to the facts of the story.

Mr. Solomons, by sending to our office, may have the cancelled passages.—O.Y.)

Instead, however, of all this rant and nonsense, how much finer is the speech that the Count really did make! "It is a very fine evening,—egad it is!" The "egad" did the whole business: Mrs. Cat was as much in love with him now as ever she had been; and, gathering up all her energies, she said, "It is dreadful hot too, I think;" and with this she made a curtsey.

"Stifling, split me!" added his Excellency. "What do you say, madam, to a rest in an arbour, and a drink of something cool?"

"Sir!" said the lady, drawing back.

"Oh, a drink—a drink by all means," exclaimed Mr. Billings, who was troubled with a perpetual thirst. "Come, mo—, Mrs. Jones, I mean. you're fond of a glass of cold punch, you know; and the rum here is prime, I can tell you."

The lady in the mask consented with some difficulty to the proposal of Mr. Billings, and was led by the two gentlemen into an arbour, where she was seated between them; and some wax-candles being lighted, punch was brought.

She drank one or two glasses very eagerly, and so did her two companions; although it was evident to see, from the flushed looks of both of them, that they had little need of any such stimulus. The Count, in the midst of his champagne, it must be said, had been amazingly stricken and scandalised by the appearance of such a youth as Billings in a public place with a lady under his arm. He was, the reader will therefore understand, in the moral stage of liquor; and when he issued out, it was not merely with the intention of examining Mr. Billings's female companion, but of administering to him some sound correction for venturing, at his early period of life, to form any such acquaintances. On joining Billings, his Excellency's first step was naturally to examine the lady. After they had been sitting for a while over their punch, he bethought him of his original purpose, and began to address a number of moral remarks to his son.

We have already given some specimens of Monsieur de Galgenstein's sober conversation; and it is hardly necessary to trouble the reader with any further reports of his speeches. They were intolerably stupid and dull; as egotistical as his morning lecture had been, and a hundred times more rambling and prosy. If Cat had been in the possession of her sober senses, she would have seen in five minutes that her ancient lover was a ninny, and have left him with scorn; but she was under the charm of old recollections, and the sound of that silly voice was to her magical. As for Mr. Billings, he allowed his Excellency to continue his prattle; only frowning, yawning, cursing occasionally, but drinking continually.

So the Count descanted at length upon the enormity of young Billings's early liaisons; and then he told his own, in the year four, with a burgomaster's daughter at Ratisbon, when he was in the Elector of Bavaria's service—then, after Blenheim, when he had come over to the Duke of Marlborough, when a physician's wife at Bonn poisoned herself for him, etc. etc.; of a piece with the story of the canoness, which has been recorded before. All the tales were true. A clever, ugly man every now and then is successful with the ladies; but a handsome fool is irresistible. Mrs. Cat listened and listened. Good heavens! she had heard all these tales before, and recollected the place and the time—how she was hemming a handkerchief for Max; who came round and kissed her, vowing that the physician's wife was nothing compared to her—how he was tired, and lying on the sofa, just come home from shooting. How handsome he looked! Cat thought he was only the handsomer now; and looked more grave and thoughtful, the dear fellow!

The garden was filled with a vast deal of company of all kinds, and parties were passing every moment before the arbour where our trio sat. About half-an-hour after his Excellency had quitted his own box and party, the Rev. Mr. O'Flaherty came discreetly round, to examine the proceedings of his diplomatical chef. The lady in the mask was listening with all her might; Mr. Billings was drawing figures on the table with punch; and the Count talking incessantly. The Father Confessor listened for a moment; and then, with something resembling an oath, walked away to the entry of the gardens, where his Excellency's gilt coach, with three footmen, was waiting to carry him back to London. "Get me a chair, Joseph," said his Reverence, who infinitely preferred a seat gratis in the coach. "That fool," muttered he, "will not move for this hour." The reverend gentleman knew that, when the Count was on the subject of the physician's wife, his discourses were intolerably long; and took upon himself, therefore, to disappear, along with the rest of the Count's party; who procured other conveyances, and returned to their homes.

After this quiet shadow had passed before the Count's box, many groups of persons passed and repassed; and among them was no other than Mrs. Polly Briggs, to whom we have been already introduced. Mrs. Polly was in company with one or two other ladies, and leaning on the arm of a gentleman with large shoulders and calves, a fierce cock to his hat, and a shabby genteel air. His name was Mr. Moffat, and his present occupation was that of doorkeeper at a gambling-house in Covent Garden; where, though he saw many thousands pass daily under his eyes, his own salary amounted to no more than four-and-sixpence weekly,—a sum quite insufficient to maintain him in the rank which he held.

Mr. Moffat had, however, received some funds—amounting indeed, to a matter of twelve guineas—within the last month, and was treating Mrs. Briggs very generously to the concert. It may be as well to say that every one of the twelve guineas had come out of Mrs. Polly's own pocket; who, in return, had received them from Mr. Billings. And as the reader may remember that, on the day of Tommy's first interview with his father, he had previously paid a visit to Mrs. Briggs, having under his arm a pair of breeches, which Mrs. Briggs coveted—he should now be informed that she desired these breeches, not for pincushions, but for Mr. Moffat, who had long been in want of a pair.

Having thus episodically narrated Mr. Moffat's history, let us state that he, his lady, and their friends, passed before the Count's arbour, joining in a melodious chorus to a song which one of the society, an actor of Betterton's, was singing:

"'Tis my will, when I'm dead, that no tear shall be shed,
No 'Hic jacet' be graved on my stone;
But pour o'er my ashes a bottle of red,
And say a good fellow is gone,
My brave boys!
And say a good fellow is gone."

"My brave boys" was given with vast emphasis by the party; Mr. Moffat growling it in a rich bass, and Mrs. Briggs in a soaring treble. As to the notes, when quavering up to the skies, they excited various emotions among the people in the gardens. "Silence them blackguards!" shouted a barber, who was taking a pint of small beer along with his lady. "Stop that there infernal screeching!" said a couple of ladies, who were sipping ratafia in company with two pretty fellows.

"Dang it, it's Polly!" said Mr. Tom Billings, bolting out of the box, and rushing towards the sweet-voiced Mrs. Briggs. When he reached her, which he did quickly, and made his arrival known by tipping Mrs. Briggs slightly on the waist, and suddenly bouncing down before her and her friend, both of the latter drew back somewhat startled.

"Law, Mr. Billings!" says Mrs. Polly, rather coolly, "is it you? Who thought of seeing you here?"

"Who's this here young feller?" says towering Mr. Moffat, with his bass voice.

"It's Mr. Billings, cousin, a friend of mine," said Mrs. Polly, beseechingly.

"Oh, cousin, if it's a friend of yours, he should know better how to conduct himself, that's all. Har you a dancing-master, young feller, that you cut them there capers before gentlemen?" growled Mr. Moffat; who hated Mr. Billings, for the excellent reason that he lived upon him.

"Dancing-master be hanged!" said Mr. Billings, with becoming spirit: "if you call me dancing-master, I'll pull your nose."

"What!" roared Mr. Moffat, "pull my nose? MY NOSE! I'll tell you what, my lad, if you durst move me, I'll cut your throat, curse me!"

"Oh, Moffy—cousin, I mean—'tis a shame to treat the poor boy so. Go away, Tommy; do go away; my cousin's in liquor," whimpered Madam Briggs, who really thought that the great doorkeeper would put his threat into execution.

"Tommy!" said Mr. Moffat, frowning horribly; "Tommy to me too? Dog, get out of my ssss—" SIGHT was the word which Mr. Moffat intended to utter; but he was interrupted; for, to the astonishment of his friends and himself, Mr. Billings did actually make a spring at the monster's nose, and caught it so firmly, that the latter could not finish his sentence.

The operation was performed with amazing celerity; and, having concluded it, Mr. Billings sprang back, and whisked from out its sheath that new silver-hilted sword which his mamma had given him. "Now," said he, with a fierce kind of calmness, "now for the throat-cutting, cousin: I'm your man!"

How the brawl might have ended, no one can say, had the two gentlemen actually crossed swords; but Mrs. Polly, with a wonderful presence of mind, restored peace by exclaiming, "Hush, hush! the beaks, the beaks!" Upon which, with one common instinct, the whole party made a rush for the garden gates, and disappeared into the fields. Mrs. Briggs knew her company: there was something in the very name of a constable which sent them all a-flying.

After running a reasonable time, Mr. Billings stopped. But the great Moffat was nowhere to be seen, and Polly Briggs had likewise vanished. Then Tom bethought him that he would go back to his mother; but, arriving at the gate of the gardens, was refused admittance, as he had not a shilling in his pocket. "I've left," says Tommy, giving himself the airs of a gentleman, "some friends in the gardens. I'm with his Excellency the Bavarian henvy."

"Then you had better go away with him," said the gate people.

"But I tell you I left him there, in the grand circle, with a lady; and, what's more, in the dark walk, I have left a silver-hilted sword."

"Oh, my Lord, I'll go and tell him then," cried one of the porters, "if you will wait."

Mr. Billings seated himself on a post near the gate, and there consented to remain until the return of his messenger. The latter went straight to the dark walk, and found the sword, sure enough. But, instead of returning it to its owner this discourteous knight broke the trenchant blade at the hilt; and flinging the steel away, pocketed the baser silver metal, and lurked off by the private door consecrated to the waiters and fiddlers.

In the meantime, Mr. Billings waited and waited. And what was the conversation of his worthy parents inside the garden? I cannot say; but one of the waiters declared that he had served the great foreign Count with two bowls of rack-punch, and some biscuits, in No. 3: that in the box with him were first a young gentleman, who went away, and a lady, splendidly dressed and masked: that when the lady and his Lordship were alone, she edged away to the further end of the table, and they had much talk: that at last, when his Grace had pressed her very much, she took off her mask and said, "Don't you know me now, Max?" that he cried out, "My own Catherine, thou art more beautiful than ever!" and wanted to kneel down and vow eternal love to her; but she begged him not to do so in a place where all the world would see: that then his Highness paid, and they left the gardens, the lady putting on her mask again.

When they issued from the gardens, "Ho! Joseph la Rose, my coach!" shouted his Excellency, in rather a husky voice; and the men who had been waiting came up with the carriage. A young gentleman, who was dosing on one of the posts at the entry, woke up suddenly at the blaze of the torches and the noise of the footmen. The Count gave his arm to the lady in the mask, who slipped in; and he was whispering La Rose, when the lad who had been sleeping hit his Excellency on the shoulder, and said, "I say, Count, you can give ME a cast home too," and jumped into the coach.

When Catherine saw her son, she threw herself into his arms, and kissed him with a burst of hysterical tears; of which Mr. Billings was at a loss to understand the meaning. The Count joined them, looking not a little disconcerted; and the pair were landed at their own door, where stood Mr. Hayes, in his nightcap, ready to receive them, and astounded at the splendour of the equipage in which his wife returned to him.

CHAPTER XI

OF SOME DOMESTIC QUARRELS, AND THE CONSEQUENCE THEREOF

An ingenious magazine-writer, who lived in the time of Mr. Brock and the Duke of Marlborough, compared the latter gentleman's conduct in battle, when he

"In peaceful thought the field of death surveyed,
To fainting squadrons lent the timely aid;
Inspired repulsed battalions to engage,
And taught the doubtful battle where to rage"—

Mr. Joseph Addison, I say, compared the Duke of Marlborough to an angel, who is sent by Divine command to chastise a guilty people—

"And pleased his Master's orders to perform,
Rides on the whirlwind, and directs the storm."

The first four of these novel lines touch off the Duke's disposition and genius to a tittle. He had a love for such scenes of strife: in the midst of them his spirit rose calm and supreme, soaring (like an angel or not, but anyway the compliment is a very pretty one) on the battle-clouds majestic, and causing to ebb or to flow the mighty tide of war.

But as this famous simile might apply with equal propriety—to a bad angel as to a good one, it may in like manner be employed to illustrate small quarrels as well as great—a little family squabble, in which two or three people are engaged, as well as a vast national dispute, argued on each side by the roaring throats of five hundred angry cannon. The poet means, in fact, that the Duke of Marlborough had an immense genius for mischief.

Our friend Brock, or Wood (whose actions we love to illustrate by the very handsomest similes), possessed this genius in common with his Grace; and was never so happy, or seen to so much advantage, as when he was employed in setting people by the ears. His spirits, usually dull, then rose into the utmost gaiety and good-humour. When the doubtful battle flagged, he by his art would instantly restore it. When, for instance, Tom's repulsed battalions of rhetoric fled from his mamma's fire, a few words of apt sneer or encouragement on Wood's part would bring the fight round again; or when Mr. Hayes's fainting squadrons of abuse broke upon the stubborn squares of Tom's bristling obstinacy, it was Wood's delight to rally the former, and bring him once more to the charge. A great share had this man in making those bad people worse. Many fierce words and bad passions, many falsehoods and knaveries on Tom's part, much bitterness, scorn, and jealousy on the part of Hayes and Catherine, might be attributed to this hoary old tempter, whose joy and occupation it was to raise and direct the domestic storms and whirlwinds of the family of which he was a member. And do not let us be accused of an undue propensity to use sounding words, because we compare three scoundrels in the

Tyburn Road to so many armies, and Mr. Wood to a mighty field-marshal. My dear sir, when you have well studied the world—how supremely great the meanest thing in this world is, and how infinitely mean the greatest—I am mistaken if you do not make a strange and proper jumble of the sublime and the ridiculous, the lofty and the low. I have looked at the world, for my part, and come to the conclusion that I know not which is which.

Well, then, on the night when Mrs Hayes, as recorded by us, had been to the Marylebone Gardens, Mr. Wood had found the sincerest enjoyment in plying her husband with drink; so that, when Catherine arrived at home, Mr. Hayes came forward to meet her in a manner which showed he was not only surly, but drunk. Tom stepped out of the coach first; and Hayes asked him, with an oath, where he had been? The oath Mr. Billings sternly flung back again (with another in its company), and at the same time refused to give his stepfather any sort of answer to his query.

"The old man is drunk, mother," said he to Mrs. Hayes, as he handed that lady out of the coach (before leaving which she had to withdraw her hand rather violently from the grasp of the Count, who was inside). Hayes instantly showed the correctness of his surmise by slamming the door courageously in Tom's face, when he attempted to enter the house with his mother. And when Mrs. Catherine remonstrated, according to her wont, in a very angry and supercilious tone, Mr. Hayes replied with equal haughtiness, and a regular quarrel ensued.

People were accustomed in those days to use much more simple and expressive terms of language than are now thought polite; and it would be dangerous to give, in this present year 1840, the exact words of reproach which passed between Hayes and his wife in 1726. Mr. Wood sat near, laughing his sides out. Mr. Hayes swore that his wife should not go abroad to tea-gardens in search of vile Popish noblemen; to which Mrs. Hayes replied, that Mr. Hayes was a pitiful, lying, sneaking cur, and that she would go where she pleased. Mr. Hayes rejoined that if she said much more he would take a stick to her. Mr. Wood whispered, "And serve her right." Mrs. Hayes thereupon swore she had stood his cowardly blows once or twice before, but that if ever he did so again, as sure as she was born, she would stab him. Mr. Wood said, "Curse me, but I like her spirit."

Mr. Hayes took another line of argument, and said, "The neighbours would talk, madam."

"Ay, that they will, no doubt," said Mr. Wood.

"Then let them," said Catherine. "What do we care about the neighbours? Didn't the neighbours talk when you sent Widow Wilkins to gaol? Didn't the neighbours talk when you levied on poor old Thomson? You didn't mind THEN, Mr. Hayes."

"Business, ma'am, is business; and if I did distrain on Thomson, and lock up Wilkins, I think you knew about it as much as I."

"I'faith, I believe you're a pair," said Mr. Wood.

"Pray, sir, keep your tongue to yourself. Your opinion isn't asked anyhow—no, nor your company wanted neither," cried Mrs. Catherine, with proper spirit.

At which remark Mr. Wood only whistled.

"I have asked this here gentleman to pass this evening along with me. We've been drinking together, ma'am."

"That we have", said Mr. Wood, looking at Mrs. Cat with the most perfect good-humour.

"I say, ma'am, that we've been a-drinking together; and when we've been a-drinking together, I say that a man is my friend. Doctor Wood is my friend, madam—the Reverend Doctor Wood. We've passed the evening in company, talking about politics, madam—politics and riddle-iddle-igion. We've not been flaunting in tea-gardens, and ogling the men."

"It's a lie!" shrieked Mrs. Hayes. "I went with Tom—you know I did: the boy wouldn't let me rest till I promised to go."

"Hang him, I hate him," said Mr. Hayes: "he's always in my way."

"He's the only friend I have in the world, and the only being I care a pin for," said Catherine.

"He's an impudent idle good-for-nothing scoundrel, and I hope to see him hanged!" shouted Mr. Hayes. "And pray, madam, whose carriage was that as you came home in? I warrant you paid something for the ride—ha, ha!"

"Another lie!" screamed Cat, and clutched hold of a supper-knife. "Say it again, John Hayes, and, by — I'll do for you."

"Do for me? Hang me," said Mr. Hayes, flourishing a stick, and perfectly pot-valiant, "do you think I care for a bastard and a—?"

He did not finish the sentence, for the woman ran at him like a savage, knife in hand. He bounded back, flinging his arms about wildly, and struck her with his staff sharply across the forehead. The woman went down instantly. A lucky blow was it for Hayes and her: it saved him from death, perhaps, and her from murder.

All this scene—a very important one of our drama—might have been described at much greater length; but, in truth, the author has a natural horror of dwelling too long upon such hideous spectacles: nor would the reader be much edified by a full and accurate knowledge of what took place. The quarrel, however, though not more violent than many that had previously taken place between Hayes and his wife, was about to cause vast changes in the condition of this unhappy pair.

Hayes was at the first moment of his victory very much alarmed; he feared that he had killed the woman; and Wood started up rather anxiously too, with the same fancy. But she soon began to recover. Water was brought; her head was raised and bound up; and in a short time Mrs. Catherine gave vent to a copious fit of tears, which relieved her somewhat. These did not affect Hayes much—they rather pleased him, for he saw he had got the better; and although Cat fiercely turned upon him when he made some small attempt towards reconciliation, he did not heed her anger, but smiled and winked in a self-satisfied way at Wood. The coward was quite proud of his victory; and finding Catherine asleep, or apparently so, when he followed her to bed, speedily gave himself up to slumber too, and had some pleasant dreams to his portion.

Mr. Wood also went sniggering and happy upstairs to his chamber. The quarrel had been a real treat to him; it excited the old man—tickled him into good-humour; and he promised himself a rare continuation of the fun when Tom should be made acquainted with the circumstances of the dispute. As for his Excellency the Count, the ride from Marylebone Gardens, and a tender squeeze of the hand, which Catherine permitted to him on parting, had so inflamed the passions of the nobleman, that, after sleeping for nine hours, and taking his chocolate as usual the next morning, he actually delayed to read the newspaper, and kept waiting a toy-shop lady from Cornhill (with the sweetest bargain of Mechlin lace), in order to discourse to his chaplain on the charms of Mrs. Hayes.

She, poor thing, never closed her lids, except when she would have had Mr. Hayes imagine that she slumbered; but lay beside him, tossing and tumbling, with hot eyes wide open and heart thumping, and pulse of a hundred and ten, and heard the heavy hours tolling; and at last the day came peering, haggard, through the window-curtains, and found her still wakeful and wretched.

Mrs. Hayes had never been, as we have seen, especially fond of her lord; but now, as the day made visible to her the sleeping figure and countenance of that gentleman, she looked at him with a contempt and loathing such as she had never felt even in all the years of her wedded life. Mr. Hayes was snoring profoundly: by his bedside, on his ledger, stood a large greasy tin candlestick, containing a lank tallow-candle, turned down in the shaft; and in the lower part, his keys, purse, and tobacco-pipe; his feet were huddled up in his greasy threadbare clothes; his head and half his sallow face muffled up in a red woollen nightcap; his beard was of several days' growth; his mouth was wide open, and he was snoring profoundly: on a more despicable little creature the sun never shone. And to this sordid wretch was Catherine united for ever. What a pretty rascal history might be read in yonder greasy day-book, which never left the miser!—he never read in any other. Of what a treasure were yonder keys and purse the keepers! not a shilling they guarded but was picked from the pocket of necessity, plundered from needy wantonness, or pitilessly squeezed from starvation. "A fool, a miser, and a coward! Why was I bound to this wretch?" thought Catherine: "I, who am high-spirited and beautiful (did not HE tell me so?); I who, born a beggar, have raised myself to competence, and might have mounted—who knows whither?—if cursed Fortune had not baulked me!"

As Mrs. Cat did not utter these sentiments, but only thought them, we have a right to clothe her thoughts in the genteelest possible language; and, to the best of our power, have done so. If the reader examines Mrs. Hayes's train of reasoning, he will not, we should think, fail to perceive how ingeniously she managed to fix all the wrong upon her husband, and yet to twist out some consolatory arguments for her own vanity. This perverse argumentation we have all of us, no doubt, employed in our time. How often have we,—we poets, politicians, philosophers, family-men,—found charming excuses for our own rascalities in the monstrous wickedness of the world about us; how loudly have we abused the times and our neighbours! All this devil's logic did Mrs. Catherine, lying wakeful in her bed on the night of the Marylebone fete, exert in gloomy triumph.

It must, however, be confessed, that nothing could be more just than Mrs. Hayes's sense of her husband's scoundrelism and meanness; for if we have not proved these in the course of this history, we have proved nothing. Mrs. Cat had a shrewd observing mind; and if she wanted for proofs against Hayes, she had but to look before and about her to find them. This amiable pair were lying in a large walnut-bed, with faded silk furniture, which had been taken from under a respectable old invalid widow, who had become security for a prodigal son; the room was hung round with an antique tapestry (representing Rebecca at the Well, Bathsheba Bathing, Judith and Holofernes, and other subjects from Holy Writ), which had been many score times sold for fifty pounds, and bought back by Mr. Hayes for two, in those accommodating bargains which he made with young gentlemen, who received fifty pounds of money and fifty of tapestry in consideration of their hundred-pound bills. Against this tapestry, and just cutting off Holofernes's head, stood an enormous ominous black clock, the spoil of some other usurious transaction. Some chairs, and a dismal old black cabinet, completed the furniture of this apartment: it wanted but a ghost to render its gloom complete.

Mrs. Hayes sat up in the bed sternly regarding her husband. There is, be sure, a strong magnetic influence in wakeful eyes so examining a sleeping person (do not you, as a boy, remember waking of bright summer mornings and finding your mother looking over you? had not the gaze of her tender eyes stolen into your senses long before you woke, and cast over your slumbering spirit a sweet spell of peace, and love, and fresh springing joy?) Some such influence had Catherine's looks upon her husband: for, as he slept under them, the man began to writhe about uneasily, and to burrow his head in the pillow, and to utter quick, strange moans and cries, such as have often jarred one's ear while watching at the bed of the feverish sleeper. It was just upon six, and presently the clock began to utter those dismal grinding sounds, which issue from clocks at such periods, and which sound like the death-rattle of the departing hour. Then the bell struck the knell of it; and with this Mr. Hayes awoke, and looked up, and saw Catherine gazing at him.

Their eyes met for an instant, and Catherine turned away, burning red, and looking as if she had been caught in the commission of a crime.

A kind of blank terror seized upon old Hayes's soul: a horrible icy fear, and presentiment of coming evil; and yet the woman had but looked at him. He thought rapidly over the occurrences of the last night, the quarrel, and the end of it. He had often struck her before when angry, and heaped all kinds of bitter words upon her; but, in the morning, she bore no malice, and the previous quarrel was forgotten, or, at least, passed over. Why should the last night's dispute not have the same end? Hayes calculated all this, and tried to smile.

"I hope we're friends, Cat?" said he. "You know I was in liquor last night, and sadly put out by the loss of that fifty pound. They'll ruin me, dear—I know they will."

Mrs. Hayes did not answer.

"I should like to see the country again, dear," said he, in his most wheedling way. "I've a mind, do you know, to call in all our money? It's you who've made every farthing of it, that's sure; and it's a matter of two thousand pound by this time. Suppose we go into Warwickshire, Cat, and buy a farm, and live genteel. Shouldn't you like to live a lady in your own county again? How they'd stare at Birmingham! hey, Cat?"

And with this Mr. Hayes made a motion as if he would seize his wife's hand, but she flung his back again.

"Coward!" said she, "you want liquor to give you courage, and then you've only heart enough to strike women."

"It was only in self-defence, my dear," said Hayes, whose courage had all gone. "You tried, you know, to—to—"

"To STAB you, and I wish I had!" said Mrs. Hayes, setting her teeth, and glaring at him like a demon; and so saying she sprung out of bed. There was a great stain of blood on her pillow. "Look at it," said she. "That blood's of your shedding!" and at this Hayes fairly began to weep, so utterly downcast and frightened was the miserable man. The wretch's tears only inspired his wife with a still greater rage and loathing; she cared not so much for the blow, but she hated the man: the man to whom she was tied for ever—for ever! The bar between her and wealth, happiness, love, rank perhaps. "If I were free," thought Mrs. Hayes (the thought had been sitting at her pillow all night, and whispering ceaselessly into her ear)—, "If I were free, Max would marry me; I know he would:—he said so yesterday!"

As if by a kind of intuition, old Wood seemed to read all this woman's thoughts; for he said that day with a sneer, that he would wager she was thinking how much better it would be to be a Count's lady than a poor miser's wife. "And faith," said he, "a Count and a chariot-and-six is better than an old skinflint with a cudgel." And then he asked her if her head was better, and supposed that she was used to beating; and cut sundry other jokes, which made the poor wretch's wounds of mind and body feel a thousand times sorer.

Tom, too, was made acquainted with the dispute, and swore his accustomed vengeance against his stepfather. Such feelings, Wood, with a dexterous malice, would never let rest; it was his joy, at first quite a disinterested one, to goad Catherine and to frighten Hayes: though, in truth, that unfortunate creature had no occasion for incitements from without to keep up the dreadful state of terror and depression into which he had fallen.

For, from the morning after the quarrel, the horrible words and looks of Catherine never left Hayes's memory; but a cold fear followed him—a dreadful prescience. He strove to overcome this fate as a coward would—to kneel to it for compassion—to coax and wheedle it into forgiveness. He was slavishly gentle to Catherine, and bore her fierce taunts with mean resignation. He trembled before young Billings, who was now established in the house (his mother said, to protect her against the violence of her husband), and suffered his brutal language and conduct without venturing to resist.

The young man and his mother lorded over the house: Hayes hardly dared to speak in their presence; seldom sat with the family except at meals; but slipped away to his chamber (he slept apart now from his wife) or passed the evening at the public-house, where he was constrained to drink—to spend some of his beloved sixpences for drink!

And, of course, the neighbours began to say, "John Hayes neglects his wife." "He tyrannises over her, and beats her." "Always at the public-house, leaving an honest woman alone at home!"

The unfortunate wretch did NOT hate his wife. He was used to her—fond of her as much as he could be fond—sighed to be friends with her again—repeatedly would creep, whimpering, to Wood's room, when the latter was alone, and begged him to bring about a reconciliation. They WERE reconciled, as much as ever they could be. The woman looked at him, thought what she might be but for him, and scorned and loathed him with a feeling that almost amounted to insanity. What nights she lay awake, weeping, and cursing herself and him! His humility and beseeching looks only made him more despicable and hateful to her.

If Hayes did not hate the mother, however, he hated the boy—hated and feared him dreadfully. He would have poisoned him if he had had the courage; but he dared not: he dared not even look at him as he sat there, the master of the house, in insolent triumph. O God! how the lad's brutal laughter rung in

Hayes's ears; and how the stare of his fierce bold black eyes pursued him! Of a truth, if Mr. Wood loved mischief, as he did, honestly and purely for mischief's sake, he had enough here. There was mean malice, and fierce scorn, and black revenge, and sinful desire, boiling up in the hearts of these wretched people, enough to content Mr. Wood's great master himself.

Hayes's business, as we have said, was nominally that of a carpenter; but since, for the last few years, he had added to it that of a lender of money, the carpenter's trade had been neglected altogether for one so much more profitable. Mrs. Hayes had exerted herself, with much benefit to her husband, in his usurious business. She was a resolute, clear-sighted, keen woman, that did not love money, but loved to be rich and push her way in the world. She would have nothing to do with the trade now, however, and told her husband to manage it himself. She felt that she was separated from him for ever, and could no more be brought to consider her interests as connected with his own.

The man was well fitted for the creeping and niggling of his dastardly trade; and gathered his moneys, and busied himself with his lawyer, and acted as his own bookkeeper and clerk, not without satisfaction. His wife's speculations, when they worked in concert, used often to frighten him. He never sent out his capital without a pang, and only because he dared not question her superior judgment and will. He began now to lend no more: he could not let the money out of his sight. His sole pleasure was to creep up into his room, and count and recount it. When Billings came into the house, Hayes had taken a room next to that of Wood. It was a protection to him; for Wood would often rebuke the lad for using Hayes ill: and both Catherine and Tom treated the old man with deference.

At last—it was after he had collected a good deal of his money—Hayes began to reason with himself, "Why should I stay?—stay to be insulted by that boy, or murdered by him? He is ready for any crime." He determined to fly. He would send Catherine money every year. No—she had the furniture; let her let lodgings—that would support her. He would go, and live away, abroad in some cheap place—away from that boy and his horrible threats. The idea of freedom was agreeable to the poor wretch; and he began to wind up his affairs as quickly as he could.

Hayes would now allow no one to make his bed or enter his room; and Wood could hear him through the panels fidgeting perpetually to and fro, opening and shutting of chests, and clinking of coin. At the least sound he would start up, and would go to Billings's door and listen. Wood used to hear him creeping through the passages, and returning stealthily to his own chamber.

One day the woman and her son had been angrily taunting him in the presence of a neighbour. The neighbour retired soon; and Hayes, who had gone with him to the door, heard, on returning, the voice of Wood in the parlour. The old man laughed in his usual saturnine way, and said, "Have a care, Mrs. Cat; for if Hayes were to die suddenly, by the laws, the neighbours would accuse thee of his death."

Hayes started as if he had been shot. "He too is in the plot," thought he. "They are all leagued against me: they WILL kill me: they are only biding their time." Fear seized him, and he thought of flying that instant and leaving all; and he stole into his room and gathered his money together. But only a half of it was there: in a few weeks all would have come in. He had not the heart to go. But that night Wood heard Hayes pause at HIS door, before he went to listen at Mrs. Catherine's. "What is the man thinking of?" said Wood. "He is gathering his money together. Has he a hoard yonder unknown to us all?"

Wood thought he would watch him. There was a closet between the two rooms: Wood bored a hole in the panel, and peeped through. Hayes had a brace of pistols, and four or five little bags before him on the table. One of these he opened, and placed, one by one, five-and-twenty guineas into it. Such a sum had been due that day—Catherine spoke of it only in the morning; for the debtor's name had by chance been mentioned in the conversation. Hayes commonly kept but a few guineas in the house. For what was he amassing all these? The next day, Wood asked for change for a twenty-pound bill. Hayes said he had but three guineas. And, when asked by Catherine where the money was that was paid the day before, said that it was at the banker's. "The man is going to fly," said Wood; "that is sure: if he does, I know him—he will leave his wife without a shilling."

He watched him for several days regularly: two or three more bags were added to the former number. "They are pretty things, guineas," thought Wood, "and tell no tales, like bank-bills." And he thought over the days when he and Macshane used to ride abroad in search of them.

I don't know what thoughts entered into Mr. Wood's brain; but the next day, after seeing young Billings, to whom he actually made a present of a guinea, that young man, in conversing with his mother, said, "Do you know, mother, that if you were free, and married the Count, I should be a lord? It's the German law, Mr. Wood says; and you know he was in them countries with Marlborough."

"Ay, that he would," said Mr. Wood, "in Germany: but Germany isn't England; and it's no use talking of such things."

"Hush, child!" said Mrs. Hayes, quite eagerly: "how can I marry the Count? Besides, a'n't I married, and isn't he too great a lord for me?"

"Too great a lord?—not a whit, mother. If it wasn't for Hayes, I might be a lord now. He gave me five guineas only last week; but curse the skinflint who never will part with a shilling."

"It's not so bad as his striking your mother, Tom. I had my stick up, and was ready to fell him t'other night," added Mr. Wood. And herewith he smiled, and looked steadily in Mrs. Catherine's face. She dared not look again; but she felt that the old man knew a secret that she had been trying to hide from herself. Fool! he knew it; and Hayes knew it dimly: and never, never, since that day of the gala, had it left her, sleeping or waking. When Hayes, in his fear, had proposed to sleep away from her, she started with joy: she had been afraid that she might talk in her sleep, and so let slip her horrible confession.

Old Wood knew all her history since the period of the Marylebone fete. He had wormed it out of her, day by day; he had counselled her how to act; warned her not to yield; to procure, at least, a certain provision for her son, and a handsome settlement for herself, if she determined on quitting her husband. The old man looked on the business in a proper philosophical light, told her bluntly that he saw she was bent upon going off with the Count, and bade her take precautions: else she might be left as she had been before.

Catherine denied all these charges; but she saw the Count daily, notwithstanding, and took all the measures which Wood had recommended to her. They were very prudent ones. Galgenstein grew hourly more in love: never had he felt such a flame; not in the best days of his youth; not for the fairest princess, countess, or actress, from Vienna to Paris.

At length—it was the night after he had seen Hayes counting his money-bags—old Wood spoke to Mrs. Hayes very seriously. "That husband of yours, Cat," said he, "meditates some treason; ay, and fancies we are about such. He listens nightly at your door and at mine: he is going to leave you, be sure on't; and if he leaves you, he leaves you to starve."

"I can be rich elsewhere," said Mrs. Cat.

"What, with Max?"

"Ay, with Max: and why not?" said Mrs. Hayes.

"Why not, fool! Do you recollect Birmingham? Do you think that Galgenstein, who is so tender now because he HASN'T won you, will be faithful because he HAS? Psha, woman, men are not made so! Don't go to him until you are sure: if you were a widow now, he would marry you; but never leave yourself at his mercy: if you were to leave your husband to go to him, he would desert you in a fortnight!"

She might have been a Countess! she knew she might, but for this cursed barrier between her and her fortune. Wood knew what she was thinking of, and smiled grimly.

"Besides," he continued, "remember Tom. As sure as you leave Hayes without some security from Max, the boy's ruined: he who might be a lord, if his mother had but—Psha! never mind: that boy will go on the road, as sure as my name's Wood. He's a Turpin cock in his eye, my dear,—a regular Tyburn look. He knows too many of that sort already; and is too fond of a bottle and a girl to resist and be honest when it comes to the pinch."

"It's all true," said Mrs. Hayes. "Tom's a high mettlesome fellow, and would no more mind a ride on Hounslow Heath than he does a walk now in the Mall."

"Do you want him hanged, my dear?" said Wood.

"Ah, Doctor!"

"It IS a pity, and that's sure," concluded Mr. Wood, knocking the ashes out of his pipe, and closing this interesting conversation. "It is a pity that that old skinflint should be in the way of both your fortunes; and he about to fling you over, too!"

Mrs. Catherine retired musing, as Mr. Billings had previously done; a sweet smile of contentment lighted up the venerable features of Doctor Wood, and he walked abroad into the streets as happy a fellow as any in London.

CHAPTER XII

TREATS OF LOVE, AND PREPARES FOR DEATH

And to begin this chapter, we cannot do better than quote a part of a letter from M. l'Abbe O'Flaherty to Madame la Comtesse de X—at Paris:

"MADAM,—The little Arouet de Voltaire, who hath come 'hither to take a turn in England,' as I see by the Post of this morning, hath brought me a charming pacquet from your Ladyship's hands, which ought to render a reasonable man happy; but, alas! makes your slave miserable. I think of dear Paris (and something more dear than all Paris, of which, Madam, I may not venture to speak further)—I think of dear Paris, and find myself in this dismal Vitehall, where, when the fog clears up, I can catch a glimpse of muddy Thames, and of that fatal palace which the kings of England have been obliged to exchange for your noble castle of Saint Germains, that stands so stately by silver Seine. Truly, no bad bargain. For my part, I would give my grand ambassadorial saloons, hangings, gildings, feasts, valets, ambassadors and all, for a bicoque in sight of the Thuilleries' towers, or my little cell in the Irlandois.

"My last sheets have given you a pretty notion of our ambassador's public doings; now for a pretty piece of private scandal respecting that great man. Figure to yourself, Madam, his Excellency is in love; actually in love, talking day and night about a certain fair one whom he hath picked out of a gutter; who is well nigh forty years old; who was his mistress when he was in England a captain of dragoons, some sixty, seventy, or a hundred years since; who hath had a son by him, moreover, a sprightly lad, apprentice to a tailor of eminence that has the honour of making his Excellency's breeches.

"Since one fatal night when he met this fair creature at a certain place of publique resort, called Marylebone Gardens, our Cyrus hath been an altered creature. Love hath mastered this brainless ambassador, and his antics afford me food for perpetual mirth. He sits now opposite to me at a table inditing a letter to his Catherine, and copying it from—what do you think?—from the 'Grand Cyrus.' 'I swear, madam, that my happiness would be to offer you this hand, as I have my heart long ago, and I beg you to bear in mind this declaration.' I have just dictated to him the above tender words; for our Envoy, I need not tell you, is not strong at writing or thinking.

"The fair Catherine, I must tell you, is no less than a carpenter's wife, a well-to-do bourgeois, living at the Tyburn, or Gallows Road. She found out her ancient lover very soon after our arrival, and hath a marvellous hankering to be a Count's lady. A pretty little creature is this Madam Catherine. Billets, breakfasts, pretty walks, presents of silks and satins, pass daily between the pair; but, strange to say, the lady is as virtuous as Diana, and hath resisted all my Count's cajoleries hitherto. The poor fellow told me, with tears in his eyes, that he believed he should have carried her by storm on the very first night of their meeting, but that her son stepped into the way; and he or somebody else hath been in the way ever since. Madam will never appear alone. I believe it is this wondrous chastity of the lady that has elicited this wondrous constancy of the gentleman. She is holding out for a settlement; who knows if not for a marriage? Her husband, she says, is ailing; her lover is fool enough, and she herself conducts her negotiations, as I must honestly own, with a pretty notion of diplomacy."

This is the only part of the reverend gentleman's letter that directly affects this history. The rest contains some scandal concerning greater personages about the Court, a great share of abuse of the Elector of Hanover, and a pretty description of a boxing-match at Mr. Figg's amphitheatre in Oxford Road, where John Wells, of Edmund Bury (as by the papers may be seen), master of the noble science of self-defence, did engage with Edward Sutton, of Gravesend, master of the said science; and the issue of the combat.

"N. B."—adds the Father, in a postscript—"Monsieur Figue gives a hat to be cudgelled for before the Master mount; and the whole of this fashionable information hath been given me by Monseigneur's son, Monsieur Billings, garcon-tailleur, Chevalier de Galgenstein."

Mr. Billings was, in fact, a frequent visitor at the Ambassador's house; to whose presence he, by a general order, was always admitted. As for the connection between Mrs. Catherine and her former admirer, the Abbe's history of it is perfectly correct; nor can it be said that this wretched woman, whose tale now begins to wear a darker hue, was, in anything but SOUL, faithless to her husband. But she hated him, longed to leave him, and loved another: the end was coming quickly, and every one of our unknowing actors and actresses were to be implicated, more or less, in the catastrophe.

It will be seen that Mrs. Cat had followed pretty closely the injunctions of Mr. Wood in regard to her dealings with the Count; who grew more heart-stricken and tender daily, as the completion of his wishes was delayed, and his desires goaded by contradiction. The Abbe has quoted one portion of a letter written by him; here is the entire performance, extracted, as the holy father said, chiefly from the romance of the "Grand Cyrus".

"Unhappy Maximilian unto unjust Catherina.

"MADAM,—It must needs be that I love you better than any ever did, since, notwithstanding your injustice in calling me perfidious, I love you no less than I did before. On the contrary, my passion is so violent, and your unjust accusation makes me so sensible of it, that if you did but know the resentments of my soule, you would confess your selfe the most cruell and unjust woman in the world. You shall, ere long, Madam, see me at your feete; and as you were my first passion, so you will be my last.

"On my knees I will tell you, at the first handsom opportunity, that the grandure of my passion can only be equalled by your beauty; it hath driven me to such a fatall necessity, as that I cannot hide the misery which you have caused. Sure, the hostil goddes have, to plague me, ordayned that fatal marridge, by which you are bound to one so infinitly below you in degree. Were that bond of ill-omind Hymen cut in twayn witch binds you, I swear, Madam, that my happiniss woulde be to offer you this hande, as I have my harte long agoe. And I praye you to beare in minde this declaracion, which I here sign with my hande, and witch I pray you may one day be called upon to prove the truth on. Beleave me, Madam, that there is none in the World who doth more honor to your vertue than myselfe, nor who wishes your happinesse with more zeal than—MAXIMILIAN.

"From my lodgings in Whitehall, this 25th of February.

"To the incomparable Catherina, these, with a scarlet satten petticoat."

The Count had debated about the sentence promising marriage in event of Hayes's death; but the honest Abbe cut these scruples very short, by saying, justly, that, because he wrote in that manner, there was no need for him to act so; that he had better not sign and address the note in full; and that he presumed his Excellency was not quite so timid as to fancy that the woman would follow him all the way to Germany, when his diplomatic duties would be ended; as they would soon.

The receipt of this billet caused such a flush of joy and exultation to unhappy happy Mrs. Catherine, that Wood did not fail to remark it, and speedily learned the contents of the letter. Wood had no need to bid the poor wretch guard it very carefully: it never from that day forth left her; it was her title of nobility,—her pass to rank, wealth, happiness. She began to look down on her neighbours; her manner to her husband grew more than ordinarily scornful; the poor vain wretch longed to tell her secret, and to take her place openly in the world. She a Countess, and Tom a Count's son! She felt that she should royally become the title!

About this time—and Hayes was very much frightened at the prevalence of the rumour—it suddenly began to be about in his quarter that he was going to quit the country. The story was in everybody's mouth; people used to sneer when he turned pale, and wept, and passionately denied it.

It was said, too, that Mrs. Hayes was not his wife, but his mistress—everybody had this story—his mistress, whom he treated most cruelly, and was about to desert. The tale of the blow which had felled her to the ground was known in all quarters. When he declared that the woman tried to stab him, nobody believed him: the women said he would have been served right if she had done so. How had these stories gone abroad? "Three days more, and I WILL fly," thought Hayes; "and the world may say what it pleases."

Ay, fool, fly—away so swiftly that Fate cannot overtake thee: hide so cunningly that Death shall not find thy place of refuge!

CHAPTER XIII

BEING A PREPARATION FOR THE END

The reader, doubtless, doth now partly understand what dark acts of conspiracy are beginning to gather around Mr. Hayes; and possibly hath comprehended—

1. That if the rumour was universally credited which declared that Mrs. Catherine was only Hayes's mistress, and not his wife,

She might, if she so inclined, marry another person; and thereby not injure her fame and excite wonderment, but actually add to her reputation.

2. That if all the world did steadfastly believe that Mr. Hayes intended to desert this woman, after having cruelly maltreated her,

The direction which his journey might take would be of no consequence; and he might go to Highgate, to Edinburgh, to Constantinople, nay, down a well, and no soul would care to ask whither he had gone.

These points Mr. Hayes had not considered duly. The latter case had been put to him, and annoyed him, as we have seen; the former had actually been pressed upon him by Mrs. Hayes herself; who, in almost the only communication she had had with him since their last quarrel, had asked him, angrily, in the presence of Wood and her son, whether he had dared to utter such lies, and how it came to pass that the neighbours looked scornfully at her, and avoided her?

To this charge Mr. Hayes pleaded, very meekly, that he was not guilty; and young Billings, taking him by the collar, and clinching his fist in his face, swore a dreadful oath that he would have the life of him if he dared abuse his mother. Mrs. Hayes then spoke of the general report abroad, that he was going to desert her; which, if he attempted to do, Mr. Billings vowed that he would follow him to Jerusalem and have his blood. These threats, and the insolent language of young Billings, rather calmed Hayes than agitated him: he longed to be on his journey; but he began to hope that no obstacle would be placed in the way of it. For the first time since many days, he began to enjoy a feeling something akin to security, and could look with tolerable confidence towards a comfortable completion of his own schemes of treason.

These points being duly settled, we are now arrived, O public, at a point for which the author's soul hath been yearning ever since this history commenced. We are now come, O critic, to a stage of the work when this tale begins to assume an appearance so interestingly horrific, that you must have a heart of stone if you are not interested by it. O candid and discerning reader, who art sick of the hideous scenes of brutal bloodshed which have of late come forth from pens of certain eminent wits,[*] if you turn away disgusted from the book, remember that this passage hath not been written for you, or such as you, who have taste to know and hate the style in which it hath been composed; but for the public, which hath no such taste:—for the public, which can patronise four different representations of Jack Sheppard,—for the public whom its literary providers have gorged with blood and foul Newgate garbage,—and to whom we poor creatures, humbly following at the tail of our great high-priests and prophets of the press, may, as in duty bound, offer some small gift of our own: a little mite truly, but given with good-will. Come up, then, fair Catherine and brave Count;—appear, gallant Brock, and faultless Billings;—hasten hither, honest John Hayes: the former chapters are but flowers in which we have been decking you for the sacrifice. Ascend to the altar, ye innocent lambs, and prepare for the final act: lo! the knife is sharpened, and the sacrificer ready! Stretch your throats, sweet ones,—for the public is thirsty, and must have blood!

* This was written in 1840.

CHAPTER THE LAST

That Mr. Hayes had some notion of the attachment of Monsieur de Galgenstein for his wife is very certain: the man could not but perceive that she was more gaily dressed, and more frequently absent than usual; and must have been quite aware that from the day of the quarrel until the present period, Catherine had never asked him for a shilling for the house expenses. He had not the heart to offer, however; nor, in truth, did she seem to remember that money was due.

She received, in fact, many sums from the tender Count. Tom was likewise liberally provided by the same personage; who was, moreover, continually sending presents of various kinds to the person on whom his affections were centred.

One of these gifts was a hamper of choice mountain-wine, which had been some weeks in the house, and excited the longing of Mr. Hayes, who loved wine very much. This liquor was generally drunk by Wood and Billings, who applauded it greatly; and many times, in passing through the back-parlour,—which he had to traverse in order to reach the stair, Hayes had cast a tender eye towards the drink; of which, had he dared, he would have partaken.

On the 1st of March, in the year 1726, Mr. Hayes had gathered together almost the whole sum with which he intended to decamp; and having on that very day recovered the amount of a bill which he thought almost hopeless, he returned home in tolerable good-humour; and feeling, so near was his period of departure, something like security. Nobody had attempted the least violence on him: besides, he was armed with pistols, had his money in bills in a belt about his person, and really reasoned with himself that there was no danger for him to apprehend.

He entered the house about dusk, at five o'clock. Mrs. Hayes was absent with Mr. Billings; only Mr. Wood was smoking, according to his wont, in the little back-parlour; and as Mr. Hayes passed, the old gentleman addressed him in a friendly voice, and, wondering that he had been such a stranger, invited him to sit and take a glass of wine. There was a light and a foreman in the shop; Mr. Hayes gave his injunctions to that person, and saw no objection to Mr. Wood's invitation.

The conversation, at first a little stiff between the two gentlemen, began speedily to grow more easy and confidential: and so particularly bland and good-humoured was Mr., or Doctor Wood, that his companion was quite caught, and softened by the charm of his manner; and the pair became as good friends as in the former days of their intercourse.

"I wish you would come down sometimes of evenings," quoth Doctor Wood; "for, though no book-learned man, Mr. Hayes, look you, you are a man of the world, and I can't abide the society of boys. There's Tom, now, since this tiff with Mrs. Cat, the scoundrel plays the Grank Turk here! The pair of 'em, betwixt them, have completely gotten the upper hand of you. Confess that you are beaten, Master Hayes, and don't like the boy?"

"No more I do," said Hayes; "and that's the truth on't. A man doth not like to have his wife's sins flung in his face, nor to be perpetually bullied in his own house by such a fiery sprig as that."

"Mischief, sir,—mischief only," said Wood: "'tis the fun of youth, sir, and will go off as age comes to the lad. Bad as you may think him—and he is as skittish and fierce, sure enough, as a young colt—there is good stuff in him; and though he hath, or fancies he hath, the right to abuse every one, by the Lord he will let none others do so! Last week, now, didn't he tell Mrs. Cat that you served her right in the last beating matter? and weren't they coming to knives, just as in your case? By my faith, they were. Ay, and at the "Braund's Head," when some fellow said that you were a bloody Bluebeard, and would murder your wife, stab me if Tom wasn't up in an instant and knocked the fellow down for abusing of you!"

The first of these stories was quite true; the second was only a charitable invention of Mr. Wood, and employed, doubtless, for the amiable purpose of bringing the old and young men together. The scheme partially succeeded; for, though Hayes was not so far mollified towards Tom as to entertain any affection for a young man whom he had cordially detested ever since he knew him, yet he felt more at ease and cheerful regarding himself: and surely not without reason. While indulging in these benevolent sentiments, Mrs. Catherine and her son arrived, and found, somewhat to their astonishment, Mr. Hayes seated in the back-parlour, as in former times; and they were invited by Mr. Wood to sit down and drink.

We have said that certain bottles of mountain-wine were presented by the Count to Mrs. Catherine: these were, at Mr. Wood's suggestion, produced; and Hayes, who had long been coveting them, was charmed to have an opportunity to drink his fill. He forthwith began bragging of his great powers as a drinker, and vowed that he could manage eight bottles without becoming intoxicated.

Mr. Wood grinned strangely, and looked in a peculiar way at Tom Billings, who grinned too. Mrs. Cat's eyes were turned towards the ground: but her face was deadly pale.

The party began drinking. Hayes kept up his reputation as a toper, and swallowed one, two, three bottles without wincing. He grew talkative and merry, and began to sing songs and to cut jokes; at which Wood laughed hugely, and Billings after him. Mrs. Cat could not laugh; but sat silent.

What ailed her? Was she thinking of the Count? She had been with Max that day, and had promised him, for the next night at ten, an interview near his lodgings at Whitehall. It was the first time that she would see him alone. They were to meet (not a very cheerful place for a love-tryst) at St. Margaret's churchyard, near Westminster Abbey. Of this, no doubt, Cat was thinking; but what could she mean by whispering to Wood, "No, no! for God's sake, not tonight!"

"She means we are to have no more liquor," said Wood to Mr. Hayes; who heard this sentence, and seemed rather alarmed.

"That's it,—no more liquor," said Catherine eagerly; "you have had enough to-night. Go to bed, and lock your door, and sleep, Mr. Hayes."

"But I say I've NOT had enough drink!" screamed Hayes; "I'm good for five bottles more, and wager I will drink them too."

"Done, for a guinea!" said Wood.

"Done, and done!" said Billings.

"Be YOU quiet!" growled Hayes, scowling at the lad. "I will drink what I please, and ask no counsel of yours." And he muttered some more curses against young Billings, which showed what his feelings were towards his wife's son; and which the latter, for a wonder, only received with a scornful smile, and a knowing look at Wood.

Well! the five extra bottles were brought, and drunk by Mr. Hayes; and seasoned by many songs from the recueil of Mr. Thomas d'Urfey and others. The chief part of the talk and merriment was on Hayes's part; as, indeed, was natural,—for, while he drank bottle after bottle of wine, the other two gentlemen confined themselves to small beer,—both pleading illness as an excuse for their sobriety.

And now might we depict, with much accuracy, the course of Mr. Hayes's intoxication, as it rose from the merriment of the three-bottle point to the madness of the four—from the uproarious quarrelsomeness of the sixth bottle to the sickly stupidity of the seventh; but we are desirous of bringing this tale to a conclusion, and must pretermit all consideration of a subject so curious, so instructive, and so delightful. Suffice it to say, as a matter of history, that Mr. Hayes did actually drink seven bottles of mountain-wine; and that Mr. Thomas Billings went to the "Braund's Head," in Bond Street, and purchased another, which Hayes likewise drank.

"That'll do," said Mr. Wood to young Billings; and they led Hayes up to bed, whither, in truth, he was unable to walk himself.

Mrs. Springatt, the lodger, came down to ask what the noise was. "'Tis only Tom Billings making merry with some friends from the country," answered Mrs. Hayes; whereupon Springatt retired, and the house was quiet.

Some scuffling and stamping was heard about eleven o'clock.

After they had seen Mr. Hayes to bed, Billings remembered that he had a parcel to carry to some person in the neighbourhood of the Strand; and, as the night was remarkably fine, he and Mr. Wood agreed to walk together, and set forth accordingly.

(Here follows a description of the THAMES AT MIDNIGHT, in a fine historical style; with an account of Lambeth, Westminster, the Savoy, Baynard's Castle, Arundel House, the Temple; of Old London Bridge, with its twenty arches, "on which be houses builded, so that it seemeth rather a continuall street than a bridge;"—of Bankside, and the "Globe" and the "Fortune" Theatres; of the ferries across the river, and of the pirates who infest the same—namely, tinklermen, petermen, hebbermen, trawlermen; of the fleet of barges that lay at the Savoy steps; and of the long lines of slim wherries sleeping on the river banks and basking and shining in the moonbeams. A combat on the river is described, that takes place between the crews of a tinklerman's boat and the water-bailiffs. Shouting his war-cry, "St. Mary Overy a la rescousse!" the water-bailiff sprung at the throat of the tinklerman captain. The crews of both vessels, as if aware that the struggle of their chiefs would decide the contest, ceased hostilities, and awaited on their respective poops the issue of the death-shock. It was not long coming. "Yield, dog!" said the water-bailiff. The tinklerman could not answer—for his throat was grasped too tight in the iron clench of the city champion; but drawing his snickersnee, he plunged it seven times in the bailiff's chest: still the latter fell not. The death-rattle gurgled in the throat of his opponent; his arms fell heavily to his side. Foot to foot, each standing at the side of his boat, stood the brave men—THEY WERE BOTH DEAD! "In the name of St. Clement Danes," said the master, "give way, my men!" and, thrusting forward his halberd (seven feet long, richly decorated with velvet and brass nails, and having the city arms, argent, a cross gules, and in the first quarter a dagger displayed of the second), he thrust the tinklerman's boat away from his own; and at once the bodies of the captains plunged down, down, down, down in the unfathomable waters.

After this follows another episode. Two masked ladies quarrel at the door of a tavern overlooking the Thames: they turn out to be Stella and Vanessa, who have followed Swift thither; who is in the act of reading "Gulliver's Travels" to Gay, Arbuthnot, Bolingbroke, and Pope. Two fellows are sitting shuddering under a doorway; to one of them Tom Billings flung a sixpence. He little knew that the names of those two young men were—Samuel Johnson and Richard Savage.)

ANOTHER LAST CHAPTER

Mr. Hayes did not join the family the next day; and it appears that the previous night's reconciliation was not very durable; for when Mrs. Springatt asked Wood for Hayes, Mr. Wood stated that Hayes had gone away without saying whither he was bound, or how long he might be absent. He only said, in rather a sulky tone, that he should probably pass the night at a friend's house. "For my part, I know of no friend he hath," added Mr. Wood; "and pray Heaven that he may not think of deserting his poor wife, whom he hath beaten and ill-used so already!" In this prayer Mrs. Springatt joined; and so these two worthy people parted.

What business Billings was about cannot be said; but he was this night bound towards Marylebone Fields, as he was the night before for the Strand and Westminster; and, although the night was very stormy and rainy, as the previous evening had been fine, old Wood good-naturedly resolved upon accompanying him; and forth they sallied together.

Mrs. Catherine, too, had HER business, as we have seen; but this was of a very delicate nature. At nine o'clock, she had an appointment with the Count; and faithfully, by that hour, had found her way to Saint Margaret's churchyard, near Westminster Abbey, where she awaited Monsieur de Galgenstein.

The spot was convenient, being very lonely, and at the same time close to the Count's lodgings at Whitehall. His Excellency came, but somewhat after the hour; for, to say the truth, being a freethinker, he had the most firm belief in ghosts and demons, and did not care to pace a churchyard alone. He was comforted, therefore, when he saw a woman muffled in a cloak, who held out her hand to him at the gate, and said, "Is that you?" He took her hand,—it was very clammy and cold; and at her desire he bade his confidential footman, who had attended him with a torch, to retire, and leave him to himself.

The torch-bearer retired, and left them quite in darkness; and the pair entered the little cemetery, cautiously threading their way among the tombs. They sat down on one, underneath a tree it seemed to be; the wind was very cold, and its piteous howling was the only noise that broke the silence of the place. Catherine's teeth were chattering, for all her wraps; and when Max drew her close to him, and encircled her waist with one arm, and pressed her hand, she did not repulse him, but rather came close to him, and with her own damp fingers feebly returned his pressure.

The poor thing was very wretched and weeping. She confided to Max the cause of her grief. She was alone in the world,—alone and penniless. Her husband had left her; she had that very day received a letter from him which confirmed all that she had suspected so long. He had left her, carried away all his property, and would not return!

If we say that a selfish joy filled the breast of Monsieur de Galgenstein, the reader will not be astonished. A heartless libertine, he felt glad at the prospect of Catherine's ruin; for he hoped that necessity would make her his own. He clasped the poor thing to his heart, and vowed that he would replace the husband she had lost, and that his fortune should be hers.

"Will you replace him?" said she.

"Yes, truly, in everything but the name, dear Catherine; and when he dies, I swear you shall be Countess of Galgenstein."

"Will you swear?" she cried, eagerly.

"By everything that is most sacred: were you free now, I would" (and here he swore a terrific oath) "at once make you mine."

We have seen before that it cost Monsieur de Galgenstein nothing to make these vows. Hayes was likely, too, to live as long as Catherine—as long, at least, as the Count's connection with her; but he was caught in his own snare.

She took his hand and kissed it repeatedly, and bathed it in her tears, and pressed it to her bosom. "Max," she said, "I AM FREE! Be mine, and I will love you as I have done for years and years."

Max started back. "What, is he dead?" he said.

"No, no, not dead: but he never was my husband."

He let go her hand, and, interrupting her, said sharply, "Indeed, madam, if this carpenter never was your husband, I see no cause why I should be. If a lady, who hath been for twenty years the mistress of a miserable country boor, cannot find it in her heart to put up with the protection of a nobleman—a sovereign's representative—she may seek a husband elsewhere!"

"I was no man's mistress except yours," sobbed Catherine, wringing her hands and sobbing wildly; "but, O Heaven! I deserved this. Because I was a child, and you saw, and ruined, and left me—because, in my sorrow and repentance, I wished to repair my crime, and was touched by that man's love, and married him—because he too deceives and leaves me—because, after loving you—madly loving you for twenty years—I will not now forfeit your respect, and degrade myself by yielding to your will, you too must scorn me! It is too much—too much—O Heaven!" And the wretched woman fell back almost fainting.

Max was almost frightened by this burst of sorrow on her part, and was coming forward to support her; but she motioned him away, and, taking from her bosom a letter, said, "If it were light, you could see, Max, how cruelly I have been betrayed by that man who called himself my husband. Long before he married me, he was married to another. This woman is still living, he says; and he says he leaves me for ever."

At this moment the moon, which had been hidden behind Westminster Abbey, rose above the vast black mass of that edifice, and poured a flood of silver light upon the little church of St. Margaret's, and the spot where the lovers stood. Max was at a little distance from Catherine, pacing gloomily up and down the flags. She remained at her old position at the tombstone under the tree, or pillar, as it seemed to be, as the moon got up. She was leaning against the pillar, and holding out to Max, with an arm beautifully white and rounded, the letter she had received from her husband: "Read it, Max," she said: "I asked for light, and here is Heaven's own, by which you may read."

But Max did not come forward to receive it. On a sudden his face assumed a look of the most dreadful surprise and agony. He stood still, and stared with wild eyes starting from their sockets; he stared upwards, at a point seemingly above Catherine's head. At last he raised up his finger slowly and said, "Look, Cat—THE HEAD—THE HEAD!" Then uttering a horrible laugh, he fell down grovelling among the stones, gibbering and writhing in a fit of epilepsy.

Catherine started forward and looked up. She had been standing against a post, not a tree—the moon was shining full on it now; and on the summit strangely distinct, and smiling ghastly, was a livid human head.

The wretched woman fled—she dared look no more. And some hours afterwards, when, alarmed by the Count's continued absence, his confidential servant came back to seek for him in the churchyard, he was found sitting on the flags, staring full at the head, and laughing, and talking to it wildly, and nodding at it. He was taken up a hopeless idiot, and so lived for years and years; clanking the chain, and moaning under the lash, and howling through long nights when the moon peered through the bars of his solitary cell, and he buried his face in the straw.

There—the murder is out! And having indulged himself in a chapter of the very finest writing, the author begs the attention of the British public towards it; humbly conceiving that it possesses some of those peculiar merits which have rendered the fine writing in other chapters of the works of other authors so famous.

Without bragging at all, let us just point out the chief claims of the above pleasing piece of composition. In the first place, it is perfectly stilted and unnatural; the dialogue and the sentiments being artfully arranged, so as to be as strong and majestic as possible. Our dear Cat is but a poor illiterate country wench, who has come from cutting her husband's throat; and yet, see! she talks and looks like a tragedy princess, who is suffering in the most virtuous blank verse. This is the proper end of fiction, and one of the greatest triumphs that a novelist can achieve: for to make people sympathise with virtue is a vulgar trick that any common fellow can do; but it is not everybody who can take a scoundrel, and cause us to weep and whimper over him as though he were a very saint. Give a young lady of five years old a skein of silk and a brace of netting-needles, and she will in a short time turn you out a decent silk purse—anybody can; but try her with a sow's ear, and see whether she can make a silk purse out of THAT. That is the work for your real great artist; and pleasant it is to see how many have succeeded in these latter days.

The subject is strictly historical, as anyone may see by referring to the Daily Post of March 3, 1726, which contains the following paragraph:

"Yesterday morning, early, a man's head, that by the freshness of it seemed to have been newly cut off from the body, having its own hair on, was found by the river's side, near Millbank, Westminster, and was afterwards exposed to public view in St. Margaret's churchyard, where thousands of people have seen it; but none could tell who the unhappy person was, much less who committed such a horrid and barbarous action. There are various conjectures relating to the deceased; but there being nothing certain, we omit them. The head was much hacked and mangled in the cutting off."

The head which caused such an impression upon Monsieur de Galgenstein was, indeed, once on the shoulders of Mr. John Hayes, who lost it under the following circumstances. We have seen how Mr. Hayes was induced to drink. Mr. Hayes having been encouraged in drinking the wine, and growing very merry therewith, he sang and danced about the room; but his wife, fearing the quantity he had drunk would not have the wished-for effect on him, she sent away for another bottle, of which he drank also. This effectually answered their expectations; and Mr. Hayes became thereby intoxicated, and deprived of his understanding.

He, however, made shift to get into the other room, and, throwing himself upon the bed, fell asleep; upon which Mrs. Hayes reminded them of the affair in hand, and told them that was the most proper juncture to finish the business. [*]

* The description of the murder and the execution of the culprits, which here follows in the original, was taken from the newspapers of the day. Coming from such a source they have, as may be imagined, no literary merit whatever. The details of the crime are simply horrible, without one touch of even that sort of romance which sometimes gives a little dignity to murder. As such they precisely suited Mr. Thackeray's purpose at the time—which was to show the real manners and customs of the Sheppards and Turpins who were then the popular heroes of fiction. But nowadays there is no such purpose to serve, and therefore these too literal details are omitted.

Ring, ding, ding! the gloomy green curtain drops, the dramatis personae are duly disposed of, the nimble candle snuffers put out the lights, and the audience goeth pondering home. If the critic take the pains to ask why the author, who hath been so diffuse in describing the early and fabulous acts of Mrs. Catherine's existence, should so hurry off the catastrophe where a deal of the very finest writing might have been employed, Solomons replies that the "ordinary" narrative is far more emphatic than any composition of his own could be, with all the rhetorical graces which he might employ. Mr. Aram's trial, as taken by the penny-a-liners of those days, had always interested him more than the lengthened and poetical report which an eminent novelist has given of the same. Mr. Turpin's adventures are more instructive and agreeable to him in the account of the Newgate Plutarch, than in the learned Ainsworth's Biographical Dictionary. And as he believes that the professional gentlemen who are employed to invest such heroes with the rewards that their great actions merit, will go through the ceremony of the grand cordon with much more accuracy and despatch than can be shown by the most distinguished amateur; in like manner he thinks that the history of such investitures should be written by people directly concerned, and not by admiring persons without, who must be ignorant of many of the secrets of Ketchcraft. We very much doubt if Milton himself could make a description of an execution half so horrible as the simple lines in the Daily Post of a hundred and ten years since, that now lies before us—"herrlich wie am ersten Tag,"—as bright and clean as on the day of publication. Think of it! it has been read by Belinda at her toilet, scanned at "Button's" and "Will's," sneered at by wits, talked of in palaces and cottages, by a busy race in wigs, red heels, hoops, patches, and rags of all variety—a busy race that hath long since plunged and vanished in the unfathomable gulf towards which we march so briskly.

Where are they? "Afflavit Deus"—and they are gone! Hark! is not the same wind roaring still that shall sweep us down? and yonder stands the compositor at his types who shall put up a pretty paragraph some day to say how, "Yesterday, at his house in Grosvenor Square," or "At Botany Bay, universally regretted," died So-and-So. Into what profound moralities is the paragraph concerning Mrs. Catherine's burning leading us!

Ay, truly, and to that very point have we wished to come; for, having finished our delectable meal, it behoves us to say a word or two by way of grace at its conclusion, and be heartily thankful that it is over. It has been the writer's object carefully to exclude from his drama (except in two very insignificant instances—mere walking-gentlemen parts), any characters but those of scoundrels of the very highest degree. That he has not altogether failed in the object he had in view, is evident from some newspaper critiques which he has had the good fortune to see; and which abuse the tale of "Catherine" as one of the dullest, most vulgar, and immoral works extant. It is highly gratifying to the author to find that such opinions are abroad, as they convince him that the taste for Newgate literature is on the wane, and that when the public critic has right down undisguised immorality set before him, the honest creature is shocked at it, as he should be, and can declare his indignation in good round terms of abuse. The characters of the tale ARE immoral, and no doubt of it; but the writer humbly hopes the end is not so. The public was, in our notion, dosed and poisoned by the prevailing style of literary practice, and it was necessary to administer some medicine that would produce a wholesome nausea, and afterwards bring about a more healthy habit.

And, thank Heaven, this effect HAS been produced in very many instances, and that the "Catherine" cathartic has acted most efficaciously. The author has been pleased at the disgust which his work has excited, and has watched with benevolent carefulness the wry faces that have been made by many of the patients who have swallowed the dose. Solomons remembers, at the establishment in Birchin Lane where he had the honour of receiving his education, there used to be administered to the boys a certain cough-medicine, which was so excessively agreeable that all the lads longed to have colds in order to partake of the remedy. Some of our popular novelists have compounded their drugs in a similar way, and made them so palatable that a public, once healthy and honest, has been well-nigh poisoned by their wares. Solomons defies anyone to say the like of himself—that his doses have been as pleasant as champagne, and his pills as sweet as barley-sugar;—it has been his attempt to make vice to appear entirely vicious; and in those instances where he hath occasionally introduced something like virtue, to make the sham as evident as possible, and not allow the meanest capacity a single chance to mistake it.

And what has been the consequence? That wholesome nausea which it has been his good fortune to create wherever he has been allowed to practise in his humble circle.

Has anyone thrown away a halfpennyworth of sympathy upon any person mentioned in this history? Surely no. But abler and more famous men than Solomons have taken a different plan; and it becomes every man in his vocation to cry out against such, and expose their errors as best he may.

Labouring under such ideas, Mr. Isaac Solomons, junior, produced the romance of Mrs. Cat, and confesses himself completely happy to have brought it to a conclusion. His poem may be dull—ay, and probably is. The great Blackmore, the great Dennis, the great Sprat, the great Pomfret, not to mention great men of our own time—have they not also been dull, and had pretty reputations too? Be it granted Solomons IS dull; but don't attack his morality; he humbly submits that, in his poem, no man shall mistake virtue for vice, no man shall allow a single sentiment of pity or admiration to enter his bosom for any character of the piece: it being, from beginning to end, a scene of unmixed rascality performed by persons who never deviate into good feeling. And although he doth not pretend to equal the great modern authors, whom he hath mentioned, in wit or descriptive power; yet, in the point of moral, he meekly believes that he has been their superior; feeling the greatest disgust for the characters he describes, and using his humble endeavour to cause the public also to hate them.

Horsemonger Lane: January 1840.

William Makepeace Thackeray – A Short Biography

William Makepeace Thackeray, was born on July 18th, 1811 in Calcutta, then British India, where his father, Richmond Thackeray was the secretary to the Board of Revenue in the British East India Company. His mother, Anne Becher also worked for the British East India Company.

His father died in 1815, and his mother sent Thackeray to England the following year while she remained in India and would, sometime later, marry her childhood sweetheart. En-route to England the ship stopped for provisions on St. Helena. The Imprisoned Napoleon was pointed out to him by a servant with the words that he "eats three sheep every day, and all the little children he can lay hands on!"

Finally, back in England the young Thackeray was sent to school, initially in Southampton and Chiswick, before being moved to Charterhouse School. Charterhouse and Thackeray did not take to each other but the time became a valuable source for his later work "Slaughterhouse". Despite his less than respectful recalling of his time with them Charterhouse placed a monument in the chapel after his death.

In his final year at Charterhouse a troubling illness delayed his departure to attend Cambridge University. Over the course of his life Thackeray would suffer from ill health, much of it brought about for his fondness for "gluttling and gorging". Excess was something he could enjoy and for a man who stood some 6' 3" it would appear to the eye that, initially at least, his large frame could absorb much of that excess.

However, Thackeray's lazy attitude to completely mastering anything he set his mind too, especially where ambition for academia was involved, meant he departed Cambridge little more than a year after joining. He had however published two short works in University periodicals. As an author, he would have quite some impact on English literature in the years to come, so it seems difficult to reconcile that he felt no urgency to pursue writing at that time.

He now spent some time travelling across Europe stopping at both Paris, to study art, and to winter in Weimar. Back in London a final attempt was made on a professional career. This time studying law at Middle Temple. It lasted no more than a few months.

Now, having reached 21, he received his father's inheritance. It was a very substantial estate of 17,000 pounds, an enormous sum of money at the time. However, although Thackeray had youth he lacked a little in energy and certainly much financial experience. He funded not one but two newspapers, and neither was to prove successful. Gambling seemed enjoyable and certainly he had money to lose, which he did on a regular basis. Further investments in two soon-to-fail Indian banks quickly ensured little of his good fortune remained.

He now had to consider taking up yet another profession. Thackeray turned to art hoping that his studies in Paris would prove of benefit. Unfortunately, they did not. His ambivalent attitude continued until on August 20th, 1836 he married the 20-year-old, Isabella Gethin Shawe. It seemed to prove a turning point in many ways.

The marriage would produce three daughters; Anne Isabella in 1837, Jane, in 1838, who tragically died in infancy and Harriet Marian in 1840.

Now, as a husband and father, Thackeray seemed at last to understand his responsibilities to nurture and provide.

His early efforts at "writing for his life" were to establish his career as a foremost author. His main employment was with Fraser's Magazine, a sharp-witted and sharp-tongued conservative publication for which he produced art criticism, short fictional sketches, and who would also serialise two of his novels. He also found time, between 1837 and 1840 to review books for The Times and to make regular contributions to The Morning Chronicle and The Foreign Quarterly Review.

In his earliest works, which he wrote under various pseudonyms including; Charles James Yellowplush, Michael Angelo Titmarsh and George Savage Fitz-Boodle, he tended towards savagery in his attacks on high society, military prowess, the institution of marriage and hypocrisy.

Between May 1839 and February 1840 Fraser's published Catherine. Originally intended as a satire of the Newgate school of crime fiction, it ended up being more of a picaresque tale. Thackeray also began work on what would eventually become A Shabby Genteel Story.

However, Thackeray, having successfully found a career that he cared about and had the talent for, found that his personal life was about to descend into chaos. After the birth of her third child in 1840, Isabella, sank into depression. At first Thackeray, didn't think too much of it. He needed to work to earn an income to support his family and finding that Isabella was distracting both herself and him he realised he could get no work done at home and so spent more and more time away until finally, in September 1840, it dawned upon him how serious his wife's condition had become. Struck by guilt, he set out with his wife to Ireland. During the boat crossing she threw herself into the sea, but was thankfully pulled from the waters. Her mother who had little understanding of her daughter's illness was of little help and perhaps a hinderance. After four-weeks they returned to England. From November 1840 to February 1842 Isabella was in and out of professional care, as her condition waxed and waned.

Isabella eventually deteriorated into a permanent state of detachment. Thackeray desperately sought cures for her, but nothing worked, and she ended up in two different asylums in or near Paris until 1845, after which Thackeray took her back to England, where he installed her with a Mrs Bakewell at Camberwell. Despite her condition Isabella would outlive her husband by 3 decades.

After his wife's illness Thackeray became a de facto widower, never able to establish another permanent relationship.

In 1843, through his connection to the illustrator John Leech, whom he had met at Charterhouse, he began writing for the newly created magazine Punch, in which he published The Snob Papers, later collected as The Book of Snobs. Thackeray was a regular contributor to Punch until 1854.

Thackeray had earlier received some success with two travel books, The Paris Sketch Book and The Irish Sketch Book, the latter marked by hostility to Irish Catholics. The book appealed to British prejudices, and on that basis Thackeray now became Punch's Irish expert, often under the pseudonym Hibernis Hibernior. It was Thackeray's writings that were the basis for Punch's notoriously harsh, hostile and condescending depictions of the Irish during the devastating Irish Famine (1845–51).

As well as his regular columns and contributions Thackeray worked on his novels. In The Luck of Barry Lyndon, which was serialised in Fraser's in 1844, he explored the situation of an outsider trying to achieve status in high society, a theme he developed more successfully a few years later with Vanity Fair.

Thackeray achieved more recognition with his Snob Papers (serialised 1846/7, and published as a book in 1848), but the work that really established his fame was the novel Vanity Fair, which first appeared in serialised instalments beginning in January 1847.

Published as a book the novel had a slow start but eventually sales rose to 7,000 copies a month. Just as importantly, it was the book that everybody was talking about. Thackeray finally had a name that gained notice and was reviewed in journals such as the famed, and much sought after, Edinburgh Review.

The accolades and success also gave him a respite from writing everything in a manner that would help ensure income rather than literary respect. Even before Vanity Fair completed its serial run Thackeray had become a celebrity, sought after by the very lords and ladies whom he satirised. with the character of Becky Sharp, the artist's daughter who rises high by manipulating all around her.

Pendennis followed in 1849-50, but it was interrupted halfway through writing for 3 months by a severe illness. Some accounts say it was cholera. Pendennis is a semi-autobiographical bildungsroman that draws on, among other things, Thackeray's disappointments in college, his ambivalent relationship with his mother, and his insider's knowledge of the London publishing world.

This novel ran at the same time as Charles Dicken's David Copperfield, and their dual appearance brought about the first of many comparisons with Dickens. Thackeray, for his part, felt that he and Dickens were battling for supremacy, though he would never equal Dickens's popularity, except with the critics.

Interestingly the two were involved in a spat which became known as the "Garrick Club affair". Thackeray and Dickens had skirmished over the "Dignity of Literature" and had other slight disagreements but this literary quarrel caused a rift in their friendship that lasted almost until the end of Thackeray's life. The relationship was healed only in Thackeray's last months, through a surprise meeting and handshake on the steps of a London club. Thackeray had taken offense at some personal remarks in a column by Edmund Yates and demanded an apology, eventually taking the affair to the Garrick Club committee. Already upset with Thackeray for an indiscreet remark about his affair with Ellen Ternan, Dickens championed Yates, helping him to write letters both to Thackeray and, in his defense, to the club's committee. Despite the intervention of Dickens, Yates eventually lost the vote of the Club's members, but the quarrel was laid out for the public in journal articles and pamphlets. "What pains me most," Thackeray said at the time, "is that Dickens should have been his adviser, and next that I should have had to lay a heavy hand on a young man who, I take it, has been cruelly punished by the issue of the affair, and I believe is hardly aware of the nature of his own offence, and doesn't even now understand that a gentleman should resent the monstrous insult which he volunteered".

Aside from these quarrelsome, distracting literary disagreements and Isabella's on-going illness life was good for Thackeray. He was to remain as he put it "at the top of the tree," for the rest of his life. The works for which he is so well remembered; Vanity Fair and Barry Lyndon had established that but he continued to write and produce novels, stories, sketches and works profusely.

To remain at such a high level in both quality and quantity is somewhat surprising given the continuation and escalation of various illnesses which continued to haunt him.

With Isabella still unwell Thackeray did seek out other women, in particular Mrs Jane Brookfield. Despite his hopes, it always felt that he was pursuing her as she battled the problems of her own marriage and turned to Thackeray for comfort and support. A source for these relationships often came on the lecture tours of Great Britain and the United States which he now entertained. These tours gave the public a chance to see and hear their hero's and provided another valuable source of income for those invited to tour. Whilst in in New York he met the Baxter family. Sally, the eldest daughter, enchanted the novelist—as a number of vibrant, intelligent, beautiful young women had done before her—and she became the model for Ethel Newcome. He visited her on his second tour of the States when she was married to a South Carolina gentleman. His choosing of married women in the shape of both Jane and Sally was ill-advised and both relationships led nowhere but did take quite some time to disassemble and for reason to set in.

In 1852, The History of Henry Esmond was published as a 3-volume novel without first being serialised and in a special type meant to imitate the appearance of an eighteenth-century book. This was the most carefully planned of Thackeray's novels. The book was celebrated for its brilliance, and Thackeray recognized it as "the very best I can do". At the time, it caused a sensation thanks to its controversial ending, wherein the hero marries a woman who early in the novel seemed more like a "mother" to him.

The eighteenth-century held a great attraction for Thackeray and he had previously set both Barry Lyndon and Catherine there as well as the sequel to Esmond, The Virginians, which takes place in North America and includes George Washington as a character.

Thackeray had twice visited the United States on lecture tours during this period as well as given lectures in London on the English humorists of the eighteenth century, and on the first four Hanoverian monarchs. The latter were published in a book as The Four Georges.

Interestingly Thackeray also decided that Politics was something he could more than dabble in. In Oxford he stood as an independent for Parliament. He was narrowly beaten by Cardwell, a politician who was substituted for the man Thackeray thought he was going to run against, although Thackeray's advocacy of entertainment on the Sabbath would have done little to help his campaign. Even so the margin of his defeat was only 1,070 votes, to Thackeray's 1,005.

In 1860 Thackeray became editor of the newly established Cornhill Magazine, a role he never felt truly comfortable in, preferring to contribute as a columnist on the Roundabout Papers. However, the financial compensation was by all accounts quite extraordinary. The Cornhill began its history with a record circulation and a number of distinguished contributors swayed onboard by Thackeray's reputation. It was in the Cornhill that he serialised his last complete novel, The Adventures of Philip in 1861-62. (After his death, the incomplete Denis Duval would also appear there in 1864).

After two years as editor he stepped down, primarily to concentrate on writing novels again. A piece he wrote for the Cornhill at this time "Thorns in the Cushion," one of The Roundabout Papers, fondly assembles the pains he felt in rejecting manuscripts on the one hand and receiving criticism of the magazine on the other. It seemed a good time to move on.

Thackeray's health had worsened during the 1850s and he was plagued by a recurring stricture of the urethra that laid him up for days at a time. He also felt that he had lost much of his creative impetus. He worsened matters by excessively eating and drinking, and avoiding exercise, though he enjoyed horseback-riding. He has been described as "the greatest literary glutton who ever lived". Indeed, his main activity apart from writing was eating and drinking and many of his stories include elaborate scenes and themes on his fondness for them.

On December 23rd, 1863, William Makepeace Thackeray, after returning from dining out and before dressing for bed, suffered a massive stroke. He was found dead on his bed the following morning. He was only fifty-two.

His death was entirely unexpected, and shocked family, friends and indeed the entire Nation.

It is said that at his funeral service thousands of mourners turned out to witness his passing. He was buried on December 29th at Kensal Green Cemetery, London.

The Yellowplush Papers (1837)
Catherine (1839–40)
A Shabby Genteel Story (1840)
Second Funeral of Napoleon (1841)
The Irish Sketchbook (1843)
The Luck of Barry Lyndon (1844)
Notes of a Journey from Cornhill to Grand Cairo (1846)
Mrs. Perkins's Ball (1846), under the name M. A. Titmarsh
Stray Papers: Being Stories, Reviews, Verses, and Sketches (1821-1847)
The Book of Snobs (1848)
Vanity Fair (1848)
Pendennis (1848–1850)
Rebecca and Rowena (1850)
The Paris Sketchbook (1840)
Men's Wives (1852)
The History of Henry Esmond (1852)
The English Humorists of the Eighteenth Century (1853)
The Newcomes (1855)
The Rose and the Ring (1855)
The Virginians (1857–1859)
Lovel the Widower (1860)
Four Georges (1860-1861)
The Adventures of Philip (1862)
Roundabout Papers (1863)
Denis Duval (1864)
The English Humorists of the eighteenth century: A Series of Six Lectures (1867)
Ballads (1869)
Burlesques (1869)
The Orphan of Pimlico (1876)

Thackeray wrote a numerous number of articles for magazines and the like as well as contributing many picture sketches to articles and his own books. Many were then collected and published together. We have listed his major works only for this bibliography.